Summit Road

Tim —

With gratitude for
your support!

Dawn

Dawn Hogue

WATER'S EDGE PRESS
SHEBOYGAN, WI

ISBN: 978-0-9992194-9-2
Library of Congress Control Number: 2021953093

Water's Edge Press LLC
Sheboygan, WI

watersedgepress.com

Credits:

Cover images licensed through Getty Images
Composite graphics by Monique Brickham
Interior image by the author
Quotations and excerpts from John Muir,
Walt Whitman, and William Carlos Williams
are in the Public Domain.

for Candy

"When we try to pick out anything by itself, we find it hitched to everything else in the Universe."

— John Muir, *My First Summer in the Sierra*

Part One

Part Two

Part Three

Part Four

Part Five

Epilogue

Part One

Intruder

WISCONSIN 1968

Marion Goodman squinted through the rifle sight, unable in the hazy moonlight to clearly see the shadow prowling in her vegetable garden. Her hands trembled. Aiming a rifle had never been as easy for her as it was for some. Her father had taken her hunting when she was a girl and though he beamed with pride at her first kill, Marion had never forgotten the shock of death, the vacancy in the doe's eyes, the knowledge she had taken a life. This was different. An old coyote had taken three of her best laying hens, and if that was him out there, she was determined to get him.

A warning would send the animal into the open where, she hoped, she would have clear aim. Marion pressed the trigger and the shot echoed across her garden and the meadow beyond. Nothing moved.

"Don't shoot me," cried a female voice.

Marion felt a chill on the back of her neck. "Who's out there?" she called from the porch. A bank of clouds edged past the half moon, allowing Marion to see a stringy figure now standing by the wrought-iron gate. "What do you want here?" Marion said, feeling her heart pound. She tried to quiet her fear and listen. From a distance, an owl's scream pierced the silence.

"Don't shoot," the girl repeated.

Marion lowered the weapon. The owl's murderous scream still rang

1

in her ears. "Come closer," she said. Her shoulders rose in a chill. It was nearly ten p.m., and the warmth of the sunny June day had evaporated. Moths and mosquitoes swarmed the yellow glow of the porch light, its hobnail glass dirty with frass. Only minutes earlier, Marion had stood in her nightgown and robe at the screen door, ready to go up to bed for the night, when she heard rustling in the garden. Now she watched the girl shuffle towards her.

"You don't need to be afraid of me," Marion said. "Do I need to be afraid of you? Is there someone else out there, someone waiting by the road?" Marion craned her neck to survey the driveway.

"No," the girl said, now at the edge of the porch steps. "I'm alone," she said, then dropped her chin. Her hair fell across her chest in two long braids, frizzed from neglect. She wore a long skirt and held a large knapsack at her side.

"Who are you?" Marion said. "What are you doing here?"

"I—." The girl began to tremble. She choked back her sobs.

The owl screamed again, drawing the attention of both Marion and the intruder.

"You're hungry?" Marion said. "Out there looking for food?"

The girl nodded.

Marion looked again at the driveway but saw only the porch light flooding out onto the gravel.

"Well, you better come in," Marion said. "I suppose I can't send you away unfed."

Marion opened the door and motioned for the girl to go first. Once inside, Marion placed the rifle in the gun rack near the door. She flipped the switch for the light over the kitchen table and motioned for the girl to sit.

"Or do you need the toilet first?"

"Yes," the girl said. "Please."

Marion led her down the hall to the half bath and turned on the light. The girl went in and clicked the door shut behind her.

Marion knew she ought to call her friend Roger, the county Sheriff, but held off going to the phone for the time being. She hated to bother him, especially not yet knowing if there was reason for concern.

When the girl emerged from the bathroom, her face looked cleaner. She would need more than a splash of water, Marion thought. The girl was filthy.

"Go ahead. Sit."

The girl pulled out a chair and sat on the edge, her knapsack on the floor by her feet.

Marion creaked on the kitchen faucet and filled a tall green glass, then set it on the table in front of the girl.

Marion imagined Roger's barrage of questions. *Who is she? How'd she end up at your place? Your farm isn't exactly on the main road. Did you check to see if she had friends? A boyfriend? Why did you let her in the house, Marion? You should have made her stay on the porch.*

"Are you gonna call the cops?" the girl asked.

Marion's eyes widened in surprise. Was this vagabond a mind reader? "Do I need to?" Marion glanced toward the porch door. "You said you were alone? Or is there a boyfriend out there yet?" A lunatic that might make this girl do anything. It had happened before, Marion knew. Just the memory of that young couple from Nebraska brought a lump into Marion's throat. Starkweather, his name was. With his girlfriend Caril, they had murdered ten people before they were finally caught.

"Why don't you answer my question?" she said.

"Ma'am?"

"What are you doing all the way out here? I'm the only house for at least a mile. It's very late and—. You are alone?" Marion asked again. The situation was beyond making sense.

The girl put the glass on the table and wiped the corner of her mouth. She opened her mouth to speak, but a loud belch emerged instead. Her hand flew to cover her mouth, her freckled cheeks red.

Marion erupted in laughter. This girl, wayward and lost, Marion decided, was no murderer. She was just a child. And right now, she needed to be cared for. "All right," Marion said. "I'll get the whole story out of you soon enough, but for now you can at least tell me your name."

"Bridget," the girl said, smiling for the first time.

Marion pulled a covered dish from the refrigerator. "It's ham salad leftover from lunch. I hope that'll be okay."

"Yes. Thank you," Bridget said.

"Glass of milk?" Marion asked after she was done making the sandwich.

Bridge nodded and took her plate to the table.

While the girl ate, Marion made additions to her shopping list and listened to the ticking clock. It seemed to mimic her own heartbeat, and she was glad for the rhythmic sound. At this time of night, her house out on Summit Road sat in stillness. On nights when she went to bed with her windows open, about all Marion was likely to hear outside were leaves chattering in the breeze or now and then a critter at the edge of her lawn. Raccoons or opossums foraging for food. At this time of night, most folks were home watching television or in bed. If someone had given Bridget a ride, she should have heard the car pass, but she hadn't, and that worried her. And if the girl had walked to her place from farther away? In the dark? That also worried her.

"Where are you from, Bridget?" Marion asked. "And how on earth did you end up here?"

Bridget looked at her but said nothing.

"The most logical answer is you've run away from home. You can't be older than—."

"I'm sixteen."

Marion peered over her reading glasses at Bridget, not sure what to believe. "Aren't your parents sick with worry over you?"

Bridget gave a scornful grunt and shook her head.

"Oh, they must be," Marion said. "How long have you been gone?"

"A while. But it's fine. I'm doing okay."

Marion's eyebrows narrowed in doubt. "Fine? Yet here you are in my kitchen, starving, dirty. Had I not heard you out there? Goodness knows. You'd have slept in a ditch somewhere?"

"I might have slept on your porch."

"You might have. And you would have left, still hungry, before I came out in the morning to feed the chickens, and I would be none the wiser."

"Yeah. I guess so," Bridget said.

Marion had a hard time with the truth that life beyond her reckoning existed, that people lived in ways foreign to her, foreign to the way she thought things ought to be. But maybe such life had always existed. She remembered one Saturday, the year her father died. She'd gone to her mother's for the day. Marion Goodman was Miss Schwarten then, a recent graduate of Milwaukee Teachers College and the new fourth grade teacher at the grade school in Plymouth. She felt lucky to get the job so close to home, only six miles from Elkhart Lake, where she grew up and where her mother still lived.

That afternoon a thunderstorm had formed without warning. With the black clouds closing in, Marion and her mother were outside frantically pulling the morning's wash off the line. Marion remembered how her mother had frozen, one hand poised over the next clothespin, her eyes wide with alarm.

Standing at the edge of their yard, an unshaven, gray-haired hobo held his hat against his chest. Marion choked down her initial fear to squeak out a hello.

"Good afternoon," Marion said.

"Shhhh," her mother had hissed, dropping her hands into her apron pockets. "You go on, now," she said to the man. "We don't want any trouble."

Maybe it was the man's poverty or his humility—Marion never quite understood where her courage had come from—but in that moment she calmly approached the stranger and asked, "What can we do for you?"

Despite Marion's mother's misgivings, the two women fed the

stranger and kept him dry until the storm passed. He thanked them for the food and for the sandwiches they wrapped in waxed paper for him and for the coins they insisted he take. As they watched him walk out of their yard on the same path he'd first come by, Marion's mother implored her daughter to never, ever do something like that again.

And yet, here she was, faced with another hobo, so to speak, one who likely needed a lot more than food and temporary respite from a storm.

"Aren't you afraid?" Marion asked.

Bridget shrugged, then got up and took her plate to the sink.

I was a tough kid, Marion thought, but I would be afraid.

The back stairway to the second floor started in the kitchen. At the top of the stairs was the bathroom to the left and a bedroom straight ahead. Marion flipped on the ceiling light in the bedroom.

"I thought you could sleep in here tonight," Marion said. "Unless you would rather sleep on the porch?"

Bridget laughed, and Marion was glad. There was something likable about this girl.

"It's nice," Bridget said.

Down the hall toward the front of the house were four more bedrooms, two at the front of the house, one with a door to the upstairs porch. Bridget admired the front staircase that opened into the front foyer.

"I hardly use it," Marion said. "I mostly go to and from the kitchen."

One of the two middle bedrooms overlooked the driveway and barn and was set up as Marion's sewing room. Across the hall was Marion's bedroom, the largest of the five bedrooms. It mirrored the floor plan of the living room directly below, with the same big bay window to the east. Her room even had a fireplace, a smaller version of the one in the living room.

"Wow," Bridget said. "I've never heard of a fireplace in a bedroom."

"I don't really use it either," Marion said. "Though at Christmas, I put pine boughs on the mantel."

When Marion and her late husband Harve first bought the house, they would build fires on cold winter evenings, lie in bed in each other's arms, and listen to the crackling wood. In those moments, they felt there was nothing else they needed. In each other, they had everything.

"I'd use it all the time," Bridget said, pulling Marion out of her thoughts. "I love to watch fires."

"They're mesmerizing all right," Marion said, then she led Bridget back to the bathroom.

"This is larger than my bedroom at home," Bridget said as they stood in the bathroom.

While Marion lowered the stopper and turned the two faucets, Bridget stood against the wall, close to the white and yellow checked curtains on the window. She could see the garden from there, the back porch light spilling out onto the neat rows where she had hidden in the dark. Water rushed from the spout and began filling the tub. Marion went into the hallway to the linen closet and grabbed two white towels and a jar of rose petal bath salts, which she gave to Bridget.

Bridget took the salts but looked at Marion as if she had handed her a live toad.

"It's bath salt. You can sprinkle some in the water if you like. Smells awfully nice. I forget to use it most of the time myself, but when I do, I don't ever want to get out of the tub."

Bridget unscrewed the jar and brought it to her nose. She breathed in the scent and closed her eyes.

"Go ahead," Marion said.

Bridget pinched a few crystals and let them fall into the tub.

"That piddly amount isn't going to be worth the trouble," Marion said. She took the jar and poured a generous amount into the roiling water under the tap. "There. That'll do." She screwed the lid back on the jar.

"Smells nice," Bridget said.

Marion turned the water off. "You can go ahead and get in the tub.

I'll be right back. Just going to find you some pajamas."

When she returned moments later with the nightgown, Bridget stood, still fully clothed where Marion had left her. I'd be shy, too, Marion thought.

"All right. I'll leave you alone now. When you're done, you can come back downstairs. And toss your dirty clothes down the laundry chute." Marion pointed to a handle-pull near the floor set into the bead-board wall between the door and the pedestal sink. Eyeing the girl's knapsack, Marion asked, "Any other clothes in there I could wash? The bag, too. It could use a scrub, don't you think?"

"I," Bridget hesitated. "It's got clean underwear. My brush."

"Well, of course," Marion said. "I didn't mean to pry."

Bridget opened the bag. She took out a wadded up cornflower blue cardigan, several pairs of underwear, and a dingy bra and sent them down the laundry chute. She set her brush on the edge of the sink. Then she stood and waited.

"You take as long as you like. No hurry." Marion closed the bathroom door tightly behind her. She went into the back bedroom where Bridget would sleep. She clicked on the nightstand lamp and felt glad she had dusted the furniture a few days earlier. The sheets were clean, so there was little else to do except turn down the bed and open the window for fresh air.

Marion loved this room. She had hoped a child would occupy it in her long-ago years. But that desire dimmed once and for all, when the doctor, who could find nothing apparently wrong, concluded she and Harve were simply one of those unlucky couples. Not long after, she'd decided to please herself and create a room she would have liked to sleep in as a child. She had chosen tiny pink roses on soft willow green stems for the wallpaper. The antique bed frame had belonged to Harve's grandmother, as had the painted pine sink stand where Marion now kept several small pots of African violets. They did well near the room's east window. Marion felt satisfied, seeing them now full of pink and purple blooms.

Before going downstairs, Marion went down the hall to her own room and searched her bookshelf for something the girl might enjoy, in case she wanted to read. Marion decided on a collection of poems by Robert Frost. She laid the book on the nightstand. "Though if I were in her shoes," Marion said out loud, "I'd be asleep the moment my head hit the pillow."

Once Marion had left her alone, Bridget stood still and felt a tightness in her chest. When she understood the feeling, she let out a long-held breath. She was safe here. The room was silent except for a few reticent drips from the spout. Before getting undressed, she scavenged her bag for the blood-stained underpants. Days earlier, she had run out of sanitary napkins and had been using rolled toilet paper instead. Bridget filled the sink with water and shampoo and swished the garment under the suds as she had done many times in gas station sinks.

Bridget stripped off her clothes and pushed them down the chute. She undid her braids and removed the tortoise shell comb from above her left ear. When she reached for the one on the right, she discovered it was missing. Puzzled, she wondered where she might have lost it. She could not recall when she'd last brushed the loose hairs and reset the combs. Maybe she had lost it in the garden.

Bridget stepped into the gleaming white tub and breathed in the fragrant water. Warmth penetrated her bones. She breathed slowly, purposefully. She drew up her knees and slid forward in the tub, then plunged her head under the surface.

Sitting up again, Bridget poured shampoo into her palm and rubbed her hands together. She lathered her hair and scrubbed her scalp which itched fiercely. She plunged her head back under the surface and moved it side to side to rinse the foam from her hair. Bridget lifted her face out of the water but remained submerged enough so that water filled her ears and magnified the sound of her own heartbeat. She rubbed shampoo foam over her breasts, under her arms, and across her belly and thought of the baby she had lost.

She had not told her parents when she first realized she was pregnant. But her mother had figured it out. "Women always know," her mother had said with both pity and compassion. "Your lustful nature will be the ruin of you one day" was all her father said, but for weeks afterwards, he refused to acknowledge her at all.

Bridget loved the baby from the moment she realized she was pregnant, so when Samuel, her boyfriend, first uttered the word—*abortion*—she thought he was just desperate and they'd figure out a different way.

"We could run away," she had argued.

But Samuel said no. His words struck her ears as if she were under water. *Finish high school. Go to college. Live the lives we are supposed to live.*

Then one day after school, instead of driving her to school, he drove her to a clinic. "It's better this way," he said, opening the door for her. He stood at her side and made sure she signed her name. Afterwards, he led her, weak and pale, to the car, where they drove out of the city to a cliff overlooking the Mississippi River and watched the afternoon sun sparkle on the water. He held her and told her it would all be better soon. At that moment, still great in the loss of what could have been, she felt she at least had Samuel.

But that very weekend, he came to tell her things between them were over.

"You know I'm right," he said, as if she had come to the same conclusion he had. "It's better this way."

Bridget slipped his ring off her finger, and scoffed as she handed it to him. Later she imagined him at home, unwinding the baby blue mohair yarn she'd used to make the ring fit. He had unwound everything, and he had left her alone with nothing left to love. That night, she packed in anger, tossing her things in an old knapsack she'd found in the attic. There was nothing for her at home. She felt like a ghost. Leaving all the emptiness behind her seemed like the only thing she could do.

While she waited for Bridget, Marion stood at the back door. A cool breeze blew through the screen. She thought again about the improbability of circumstances that had occurred that evening. She glanced at the sky hoping for another glimpse of the moon. *The man in the moon.* An old song her father sang to her when she was a child played in her memory. But dark clouds kept the moon hidden. Maybe it would rain. Her garden needed a good soak.

The round-faced clock on the wall near the door to the laundry room ticked off the seconds. On a crocheted doily in the middle of the table sat a vase bursting with the daisies Marion had gone out to snip minutes earlier. She fussed over the arrangement, but as she did so, she felt the gesture was foolish. And yet, after she'd turned down the bed upstairs for Bridget, a bed that hadn't been slept in for many years, she had mulled over that odd pronouncement from Hebrews: *Be not forgetful to entertain strangers: for thereby some have entertained angels unawares.* She mused on whether the wandering teen was an angel sent for some important reason that would later be revealed. Marion shook her head. "She's a runaway, not a guest," Marion said out loud. She pulled one less-than-perfect blossom out of the vase and tossed it off the porch before closing the back door.

Bridget padded quietly into the kitchen, the scent of roses and shampoo preceding her.

"You smell wonderful," Marion said, turning to the girl. "God knows it must have felt good to wash your hair. That's a Teutonic masterpiece you're carrying around there."

Bridget's blue eyes narrowed, her forehead creased in confusion.

Marion laughed. "What I meant is you've got great thick hair. Mine's always been thin and never really looked good any way but short," Marion said. "Are you still hungry?"

"No. Thank you," Bridget said, covering a yawn behind her hand. "I'd like to go to bed, if it's okay?"

"Well, of course. That's exactly what we both need to do."

Marion led the way up the stairs. Once Bridget was inside her room,

Marion said, "shout out if you need anything."

"I will, but I'll be fine," Bridget said, and then "Thank you."

Padding down the hall to her own room, Marion looked back when she heard Bridget's door close. Roger would absolutely have a fit about this, she thought. She decided right then and there not to tell him about Bridget. She'd be on her way the next day anyway. What would be the point?

Escape

"Come on, Terry," Maria said, her soft hand caressing his angular jaw. "Get high with me."

The two stood in the midst of a crowd of people trying to get in to see a band at a popular nightclub. Minutes earlier Terry had merged with the crowd to get away from a car that had been tailing him. A couple of blocks west of the club, the car had nearly run him up the curb.

"Hey faggot," a thin, black-haired teen had taunted from behind the wheel. "I like your pretty skirt."

The passenger, another young male, laughed at that remark. He had leaned over and called out, "Get that at Macy's? I think I should get one just like it."

While his harassers laughed, Terry ran into a nearby alley and hid for a moment behind a high bank of boxes and trash cans. The car's headlights lit the long alley as it turned his way. Soon the driver must have realized the congested alley was too narrow, so he backed out into the street. Terry took off down the alley, and when he turned the corner, he saw the crowd and forced his way in.

Almost immediately Maria spotted him, Terry was still flushed and sweaty. She threw her arms around his neck. "Haven't seen you in so long," she said, tugging at his boa, pulling off his wig. "There. Like you better as you," she said.

Terry smiled and took his wig from her. He looked for the car in the street but saw only a string of yellow taxis. He had escaped one threat, but with Maria, he faced a different kind of danger. Donette, the woman Terry lived with, the woman who knew more than he'd ever know about staying safe on New York's streets, also knew about Maria. She was a well-known junkie. "Surprised that tiny thing is still alive. She's a reckless kid," Donette had said.

Maria pulled Terry away from doors of the club. "Don't care about going in anymore," she said. Maria chattered about the band. "I saw them twice last week. The singer and I—." She slipped her arms around Terry's waist. "Well that's over, and now you're here." She smiled and stood on her toes to kiss him. She smelled of wine.

"I should get going," Terry said. "Donnie's probably expecting me."

"She's not your mom, you know."

"Yeah, I know, but—." In his head he heard Donette's voice: *That girl's bad news.*

"I really—." Terry tried pulling away from Maria, but she wouldn't let him go.

"Oh, come on, Terry. Can't you see it's gonna rain?" she whined. "Let's go up to your room."

He should have said no. He wanted to say no. But she had a way of drawing him to her. And her voice, the way it lured him like a siren's song, was a drug of its own. Those sick jerks had frightened him, and all he could do was run away like the seventeen-year-old weakling he was. At least Maria made him feel wanted.

Moments after the syringe fell from his hand, Terry Abbott was blissful but completely unable to move. He could do nothing but lie against the pillows and feel his heart slowly beating, hear his blood flowing through him. Later, a burst of thunder shook the room and nudged Terry from milky oblivion. His eyes fluttered open. The rain, louder, pelted against the window. Maria's slim, warm form beside him curved inside his own. Her body jerked in a brief spasm. She moaned. Terry reached for her hand. It felt cool. His forehead began to sweat, his mouth so dry he could barely swallow. Terry stared at the spider-webbed edges of a small hole in his bedroom window. The cracks trapped shards of light and glowed yellow. He watched raindrops suspended on the glass and waited for them to fatten and fall.

The only light in Terry's small room at the rear of Donette's second-floor flat came from outside, from the security lamp over the door to the garden below. It was enough to illuminate the room's pink and gold wallpaper and the brown water stain the size of a dinner plate around a large fleur de lis near the ceiling above his bed. Near the small closet facing the bed stood a white wicker folding screen festooned with long silk scarves and the boa he'd worn that night. On one side of his bed, near the window to the small balcony that overlooked the garden, sat a wobbly wooden bistro chair he had rescued from the street the year before.

On the near side of the bed stood an orange crate Donette had salvaged for him from the little bodega next door. He'd covered it with a red and orange paisley bedcover. On top sat a small brass lamp and a Baby Ben wind-up alarm clock. Inside the crate Terry's books were stacked: *Leaves of Grass*, which he bought last year at a little bookstore in Greenwich Village, and *The Hobbit* and *Huck Finn* the two books he had brought with him when he left his mother's home in Milwaukee, over two years ago—the day after his stepfather had trapped him in the basement, pushed him against the concrete wall, and forced his urgent hand down Terry's pants. It had not been the first time his stepfather had assaulted him, but it would be the last.

There were still moments Terry felt proud of his fifteen-year-old self, who had not let fear or uncertainty keep him from escaping his abuser. "He was braver than I am," Terry said quietly in the dark. Terry listened for any sound beyond his door, any indication that Donette was home. Fear that she'd kick him out of the place he felt safest and most loved twisted his gut. Behind closed eyes, sparks of bright light dizzied him, and he felt himself lift from the bed in a nauseating chill. Only hard, deep breaths brought him back. From then on, he focused on staying awake. He had to get Maria out of there soon.

Refugee

Donette Brown stood nearly six and a half feet tall in her black high-heeled boots. She stretched her muscular calves to ease their ache. She was dead tired, and the damp night air had seeped deep into her bones. She had already turned three quick tricks, the last one an overly pale man who wore a toupee the uneven color of some sickly rodent. All the man had wanted was to bury his face in her breasts. It was the easiest money of the night, but he had made her so sad she couldn't stand it. Ten minutes into nestling, that's what she called it, the old guy's toupee slid sideways, and in the streetlight glare through his windshield, she saw his eyes, rimmed red, tears ready to spill. That had been enough for her to call it quits for the night. Now she looked forward to getting home, soaking in her old, claw-foot tub and climbing into bed. She planned to sleep good and long.

She was still angry about finding Maria in Terry's room that morning, and losing herself in the city hadn't taken away the sting of betrayal she felt. Terry had come to mean too much to her. While she was calmer now, that morning she had been so close to kicking Terry out, she had grabbed some of his things and started stuffing them into his duffle. But she didn't want him to leave—not then, not now. She only wanted him to be safe. At least Maria ran out of the apartment terrified. It was unlikely she'd be back.

After her tirade, Donette lay for a while on her unmade bed, angry, her chest heaving. Through the window screen, she heard Mr. Sanchez, who ran the bodega next door. His voice was gruff and impatient. "I told you a hundred times. You gotta wipe that glass good or it gets streaky." Taking calmer breaths, Donette pictured the new kid Sanchez had hired shrinking into himself, already deciding he wouldn't come back to work the next day. Something about the way Sanchez berated the boy eased her own anger. Being mad did nobody any good.

Terry had come into her life two years earlier. Donette had been working her usual corner with her friend Maureen, who had said it smelled like rain.

"Rain?" Donette said. "You can't smell no rain."

When a few drops of water hit Donette on the cheek, Maureen said, "You smell that?"

They laughed and decided to head home early before they were both drenched. They hugged and said their see-you-tomorrows and sleep-tights. Donette turned toward her apartment building, heels click-clacking on the sidewalk as she hurried home.

When she turned one corner, she knocked into a stocky, dark-haired man who held a frightened blonde child by the shoulders. His unshaven face was only inches from the girl's. "You better—," he was shouting.

"What you doin' to that child?" Donette barked.

"Mind your own fuckin' business," said the man, tightening his grip on the girl. Had the man studied things more, he would have seen that even without heels, Donette towered over him. He also had no way of knowing she had fought her way out of similar situations, not just because she was stronger than most men, but because men never expected a woman to fight back.

She did not move.

"I told you," the man said, "back off."

Donette shoved herself between the man and the girl, freeing the child, who rocked unsteadily on her feet before finding support against the brick wall of an out-of-business furniture store.

"Just stay there, honey," Donette said.

The man realized it wasn't worth it. "Fuckin' crazy," he said. He spit onto the pavement, then walked across the street to his car. Once inside, he revved up the engine in a show of false power before squealing away.

Turning to the girl, Donette opened her arms. "Come on with me, honey. I'll get you home safe. What on earth you're doing out here all alone is beyond—."

"I'm okay," came the voice, but not of a young girl. "I guess I can—."

Donette looked closer. The blonde hair was a wig. It had shifted in the scuffle. Underneath was dark hair pinned flat with bobby pins. Flat chest, too. How had she missed this before? This was no little girl accosted on her way home from wherever. This was a working boy.

"Haven't seen you before," Donette said, suspiciously. "Where you from?"

At first the boy said nothing. He looked up at Donette, his young jaw tight and resolute, maybe choking back the urge to cry.

The rain began to fall in huge drops, darkening the sidewalk one blotch at a time. "You wanna stand out here and get soaked or are you gonna give me some answers?" Donette said.

He told her his name was Terry. He was fifteen, from Long Island. His father had kicked him out of the house after a big fight.

"You don't sound New York to me. But I suppose you better come along. I won't get no sleep if I have to worry all night about you."

When they got to her apartment, they were drenched. That eye is starting to darken," she said, reaching toward Terry's cheek.

"He hit you?"

Terry didn't answer. Donette let Terry stand, dripping on the throw rug just inside the door, while she went to her bedroom to put on a pair of slacks and a sweater. She emerged from her room with her hair wrapped in a towel and her arms loaded with folded clothes, a sweatshirt and pair of pajama pants. She pointed to the bathroom and told him to toss his wet things in the tub. While he changed, Donette put the kettle on and added an extra tea bag to the pot. Then she made up a bed on the sofa.

"Now you look like somebody," she said when he stepped out of the bathroom, his dark hair toweled, but still damp, his face clean, the pajama pants rolled twice at the hem.

He smiled, a real and honest smile that she would come to love seeing. They sat together quietly, cups of tea on her little oak table. Terry, her refugee, didn't speak much that night, but he had been an easy one to love from the start. His story—like others she had heard—broke her heart. Young girls, boys too, lost in their own lives found their way to New York because of novels or magazines they had read. Somehow, they expected the city would save them. Yeah, thought Donette, I been there, too. I been you.

While Donette lay on her bed listening to Sanchez, Terry left the apartment. When she realized he was gone, she couldn't help but feel she was mostly to blame. She was glad to see his duffle still on the floor in his room right where she had thrown it. She picked it up and set it on his bed. She hoped it meant he would be back soon, after he had time to think things through.

After breakfast, she sat at the kitchen table and counted her cash from the past week. She rolled the nicest bills, secured them with a rubber band, and tossed them in an old pillowcase she kept in her closet. Most of her earnings went into brown envelopes labeled *groceries*, *rent*, and *beauty parlor*. She kept the envelopes in a box on top the refrigerator. Terry kept his money in his room, but always gave her his fair share for rent and groceries each week. After sorting her money, she got dressed, tied a scarf over her head, loaded her wire laundry cart with an overstuffed canvas bag and a box of detergent, and headed two blocks west to the Sudsy Duds laundromat.

"I suppose he could have—." She stopped in mid-thought, as she watched towels tumble in the dryer. There was no surmising where Terry might have gone.

She waited for him the rest of the day, but he had still not returned when Donette left the apartment at nine. She met Maureen by Jake's Lounge and caught up on the gossip. Donette had already decided Maureen didn't need to know about the incident with Maria. Maureen pulled out a cigarette and tried to tempt her friend.

"You know I quit that habit," Donette said, though she almost accepted one, just to settle her nerves.

Maureen took a john down the block to the old hotel they often worked out of. The owner got a twenty percent cut, but he kept the sheets clean and the rooms swept. It was an arrangement that suited them all and kept the pimps away. Donette waited for Maureen to return. It was a slow night and she hated standing alone. That cigarette sounded better and better.

A stale breeze blew loose pages of a newspaper down the street toward the East River. There was more than garbage in that cesspool, Donette thought. There were so many stories. Sometimes you didn't know what to believe. New York was a hard city and sometimes people, even kids like Terry, just disappeared.

Donette got home just after one a.m., slid off her boots, and kicked them under the hall tree. Her heels burned. She had to pee so bad she was afraid she wouldn't make it to the toilet. Sitting there now, she let out a deep sigh, and realized she smelled lemon oil and something else. Cake? She smeared cold cream over her face, wiped red and black smears off with tissues, then lathered her skin with soap. In the mirror she saw only weariness.

Out of the bathroom, she looked around. The living room had been cleared of clutter. The *Life* magazines she had left strewn across the coffee table were stacked neatly to one side and the table gleamed from polishing. Couch pillows had been fluffed and placed neatly, one on each end. Even the crocheted afghan she had tossed over her while she had napped that afternoon was neatly folded over the back of the chair.

Down the narrow hall, Donette saw that Terry's bedroom door was closed and no light seeped out from under it. She went to the kitchen. The day's dishes, which she had left in the sink, had been washed, dried, and put away. On the table lay a plate of oatmeal cookies wrapped in a napkin. Folded like a tent, a note read "I'm sorry." Donette sat and ate a cookie, read the note again, folded it in her hand, then went to bed.

At 1:30, Donette clicked off her bedside lamp and lay on her back, staring at the ceiling, watching streetlight shadows. Terry was on her mind, of course. But so was whole the grimy world.

In 1949, when Donette was twelve, her daddy ripped the family from their Alabama tenant farm in the middle of the night, shoving her and her little sister into the back of the car, her mother silent in the front seat. The rusting sedan bounced over every rut in the road along the way. She asked her father only once why they had to leave. "Why Daddy?" He answered her with the back of his hand across her face. She never asked again, but from that moment Donette knew her father was no one she could depend on.

She had heard her mother mutter one time, "can't pay no bills." Was money the problem? Was it something else? To Donette's way of thinking, her mother seemed more likely to run away, if that's what they were doing. Her mother was the one who suffered on the farm, working harder than all of them put together. Cooking and housework didn't keep her out of the fields. What's more, her mother was a frail woman who seemed always to be bruising herself. "Clumsy, I guess" she told her girls when they asked about a new scrape or bruise.

Donette had worked in the fields, too, and she could not remember a time when she hadn't been responsible for her little sister, Cissy. But being children, they were also sometimes shooed off to play. She remembered the old live oak past the field near a grassy-shored creek. With Cissy staring up at her from the ground, Donette would climb the tree as far as she could go, even daring to creep out to the end of a long, moss-draped limb, where she could reach out her hand to touch the sky, its clouds giant versions of the white cotton tufts she pulled out of pods and stuffed into her sack.

Years later Donette learned they had left Alabama because her father owed money to a white man, and he couldn't pay. When Donette's mother revealed this truth, she added bitterly, "Wish they'd a killed him, sometimes."

In Pittsburgh they moved in with Uncle Joe, who was not her uncle, but her father's friend, who had moved north years earlier for a steel mill job. Uncle Joe sometimes looked at Donette in way that made her feel she ought to hide from him. While she and Cissy and her mother slept in a small bedroom at the rear of the upper flat, her father and Uncle Joe went out each night to "raise hell," or at least that's what her mother called it. Cissy seemed to have no trouble sleeping on the thin floor-mattress, but Donette often found herself awake during the night, her body cold and aching.

That summer, eight-year-old Cissy ran out into the street and was struck by a car. She lay in the hospital for two days before she died, never once opening her beautiful black eyes. If she had, Cissy would have known that her mother and her sister had sat at her bedside day and night, praying. Her father, who had abandoned his family in spirit when they left Alabama, chose to abandon them for real when Cissy died. Donette never saw him again.

Because Joe treated her mother with kindness and because her mother had no idea how else she would feed or care for Donette, Caroline Murray married Joe Williams. Things were nice for a while, but not long after, Donette's new father trapped her beneath him on her bed, unzipped his pants, and made a mess on top of her dress. The second time, she later understood, he raped her. But at fourteen, Donette did not know that word. She knew only the pain and the shame—a shame so deep she couldn't speak of it, not even to her mother.

Donette's mother did not leave her second husband because he was late with the rent or short on grocery money. She left because one morning she found coral lipstick on his jacket collar, a color she did not wear. On the bus to Montgomery, where her aunt Bernice lived,

Donette drew butterflies in a notebook. Caroline Williams imagined her husband at work, blissfully whistling juke joint tunes, as he often did, completely unaware that his secret cigar box full of poker money was empty.

For a time, Donette believed she would never marry, but when she was eighteen, only two months after graduating high school, she met Ronnie Brown. When he pulled her to him and held her in his arms, the heat from his body radiating into hers, she understood why women lose their fortitude. Helpless to do otherwise, she said yes when he knelt before her and proposed, his face gleaming proudly, his skin newly barbershop-shaved. Donette heard a voice warning her, but she refused to listen and swore her marriage would be different.

Ronnie was a good husband, at first. One evening as Donette counted out her tips on the coffee table—$1.35—mostly dimes and nickels—not even close to balancing out the pain in her throbbing feet, Ronnie had watched sympathetically as she rubbed her ankles.

"You just go on in there tomorrow and tell that old man if he don't hire another waitress tomorrow, you goin' to quit," he said. He came to her side, lifted her feet onto his lap, and massaged the ache out of her arches.

At first Ronnie invited her to go with him to the clubs on Friday and Saturday nights. Eventually he stopped suggesting they "go blow off steam" together. Instead, he readied himself, as if to impress a date, and left her alone, saying things like "it's just me and the boys tonight." Later he stopped even trying to give her a reason.

Soon it became clear to her that Donette could not rely on Ronnie either. Now when she spread her tips on the kitchen table before her husband's greedy eyes, she held back a few nickels and dimes and kept them in a coin purse her mother had given her. When the purse got full, she took the coins to the bank to turn them into bills, which she hid in the laundry hamper, a place she was sure Ronnie would never look. An uncertain future was never far from the edges of her life. She had to be ready for it.

Two years after their wedding, Ronnie called her from the police station. He and two other men had been arrested for armed robbery. "It wasn't me, Donnie," he explained on the phone. "I was just driving. They told me they were just going in to buy whiskey." Even if Ronnie was telling the truth, there was no way of turning things around. Donette visited Ronnie in prison just once. "Can't you do something, baby," he pleaded. What could she do? And since she couldn't bear to witness his failure, she left him.

She also left her mother who was happy living with her sister Bernice, cleaning houses for rich white women. Donette was only 22. A new decade was about to begin. The 1960s would be good for black people, she thought. The country was starting to change. Leaders like Dr. King were speaking of fairness and freedom. In 1959, Donette Brown chose her own freedom. She chose New York, a city that allowed her to disappear and find herself all at once.

When she had first come to New York, Donette had looked for a good job. She had learned to type in high school and was fast and accurate. She saw herself as a secretary. Or she could learn bookkeeping. She was quick with figures and understood how to manage money. But no office manager gave her a second look. She had no resume, no references.

While living with her Aunt Bernice, Donette sometimes helped her and her mother clean houses. She realized she might have to clean houses, like she'd done at times in Montgomery, to earn money to pay for night classes.

Jobs like that were easy to get, but she had a hard time hanging on to them. One after another, she was fired. Soon Donette understood it was because she refused to adopt the submissive language and docile postures she had seen in her mother and aunt. As a child, seeing her mother demeaned by harsh or unfair treatment had been hard for Donette. She vowed she would never let another person treat her the way her mother and aunt had sometimes been treated.

One day Donette overheard her employer complaining to another maid that the new girl was "awfully sure of herself." When Donette peered around the corner, she saw the maid lower her posture in acknowledgement that such an attitude would not be tolerated.

Before long, Donette found her body was the only commodity worth anything. She still wanted more, but most days, she was not unhappy. The life she had come to live gave her certain freedoms, but it demanded things of her, too, not least of which was relinquishing any hope, for the time being at least, that she could live like other people did. People secure the routines of normal life—careers, children, church on Sundays, summer vacations—all things the women she had briefly worked for took for granted. All the things that insulated her and those like her from other, vastly different realities in life.

Donette rolled to her side and looked into the sliver of sky visible through her window. A cluster of stars stood against the blue-black night. I would have liked to have gone on to school to learn about such things, she thought. NASA had sent men into space, and it astonished her to read in the paper that they were planning now to send them to the moon. The world was huge and so much was possible and yet impossible all at once.

The slamming of a delivery truck door on the street below startled Donette awake. A quick look at her alarm clock showed 7:00 a.m. "Damn," she muttered. She had been dreaming, running under freshly washed sheets hanging on the line, her grandfather laughing, the sun bright on her young face. When she opened her eyes, she was sorry to let the dream go. She wished she could close her eyes and go back to her grandfather's house, a one-bedroom cabin at the edge of Mr. Andrey's land bordered by a shady woods.

An hour later, still unable to get back to sleep, Donette swung her feet to the floor, tucking them into her slippers. It was then she remembered the note, the cookies, the house tidied in penance. She tightly tied the belt of her yellow chenille robe about her waist and headed down the hall, past the living room, to the dark kitchen, where she flipped on the ceiling light and clanked about making coffee.

Minutes later, Terry emerged, his head hanging in shame. She wanted to reach for him, pull him close to her, hug him for all he was worth, as her mother used to say, but instead she just gave him a pretend pout, at first slight, then exaggerated.

He rolled his eyes, then smiled.

"Go ahead. Sit down, and I'll make you an egg," she said.

He pulled out a chair and slumped into it, resting his elbows on the table. She set his coffee before him.

"Thanks," he said.

Donette laid the plates on the table. She took a spoonful of apricot jam and smeared it on a piece of toast. While they ate, she rolled her words around in her head. Then, because she knew no other way, she blurted out, "Why'd you do it? Why'd you let her pull you back down that road?"

"I don't know."

Donette looked into his lie. Just kept looking at him until he bowed his head. She said nothing, just let the silence speak for her. *I want an answer.*

"It had been a shitty day," he said finally. "When I ran into Maria—I guess I just wanted to feel good."

Donette got up and brought the coffee pot to the table, filling his cup, then hers, before setting it on a trivet.

Terry sponged the last of his egg yolk with the corner of his toast. "I'm tired of feeling bad all the time, tired of all the—. Just tired," he said.

"Sounds like you want to go home," Donette said.

Terry said that wasn't true, that there was nothing for him back there.

"The way I see it, you woke up," she said. "Right? That shit didn't kill you, but it could've." She emphasized the last line as if to say, *you hear me?* "My grandma always said, when you wake up, it's God telling you he ain't finished with you yet."

27

Terry nodded. He finished his coffee, then scooted his chair away from the table. He reached for Donette's plate and set it in the sink with his. As sudsy water filled the dishpan, Terry got a clean dishrag out of the drawer and handed a flour sack towel to Donette.

"Terry honey, your life—all this—it's just a bump you tripped over. You'll figure it out. You'll find your way."

Nineteen Candles

MINNEAPOLIS 1968

Nineteen candles on a two-layer birthday cake were melting into wax pools on top of green frosting. The tablecloth Rob Lang's mother had bought for the occasion—thin paper printed with pink-frosted cakes, glowing candles, and colorful balloons—seemed to him the perfect detail for furthering his mother's delusion that he was still her little boy.

"Come on," his mother said. "Make a wish."

A wish? I wish I had never been born. No. That's not right. I wish I had not been born to you.

"I wish for a happy year ahead," he said, "for all of us," then he blew out the candles. A cloud of smoke blurred his mother's clueless smile. What Rob had actually wished for, if wishes had the power to make anything happen, was that both his parents would die. Lately he'd been fantasizing about a car accident.

"You're so sweet, Robby," Arlene Lang said. She plucked the candles out of the cake and laid them on a napkin.

"Yeah. Sweet," Robert Lang senior said with a scoff. "I still think it's ridiculous to make a birthday cake for a nineteen-year-old. He should be out on his own by now and not living off his parents."

"Just stop," Arlene said. "Why wish him away?" With a long knife, she cut into the cake. She laid a generous slice on a plate and handed it to her son. A second, larger piece, went to her husband. She laid a small piece on her own plate. "There," she said, putting her napkin in her lap. "I hope you like it."

Rob scraped off the thick frosting and left it in a mound on the edge of his plate.

"Would have been better with ice cream, Arlene," Rob's father said.

"Yes, dear. I know. I told you how sorry I am that I forgot to buy some."

Rob gobbled his caked, then pushed his chair away from the table.

"Just a minute," Arlene said to her son. She then looked intently at her husband, who had just shoveled another big bite of cake into his mouth.

"Oh, right," he said, chewing as he spoke. Robert reached into his lap for an envelope and handed it to his son.

"It's not much," Arlene said, "but it's just so hard to get you what you need, now that you're almost a man."

Rob read the card. On the outside was a caricature of a chubby fisherman holding a fishing pole with a huge, green fish dangling from its end. "Hoping your day is your best catch yet," it said inside. A twenty-dollar bill fell onto the mound of frosting.

"Uhm. Thanks," Rob said. He sat there for a moment longer, thinking there might be something else, one of his father's speeches about how great life was when he was a boy. But Robert had turned his attention back to the last chocolate crumbs on his plate.

"Okay," Rob said, as he got up to leave. He picked up the twenty and folded it in half. He left the card on the table next to his plate. As Rob walked towards his room, he thought about the car crash he had wished for. It should be something so awful it would make the news. There should be other people killed, too. There should be bodies thrown from cars. Even the cops would feel sick over what they were witnessing. They'd go home and tell their wives they had never seen anything so gruesome.

Diversion

Minneapolis 1968

Rob sat on the edge of Steve's bed. Steve, his sixteen-year-old pot dealer had just asked him if he was going to Sparrow's party. Sparrow's parents were on a trip and would be gone the entire weekend. Everyone was going, Steve said.

"I'm not sure that's my scene," Rob said as he watched Steve weigh his purchase on a scale that looked like standard high school science equipment.

"I heard the house is like a mansion or something," Steve said. "I can't even believe Sparrow invited me, to be honest with you. I mean, we were in a play together, but she's a year ahead of me."

"That looks light," Rob said, gesturing to the pot.

Steve laid the baggie on the scale again, dropped in a pinch more, then sealed the bag and handed it to Rob. "I always thought Sparrow was pretty stuck up, you know? But she's the best-looking girl in school, right? You don't turn down an invitation from a girl like that."

"I suppose not," Rob said, handing Steve a ten-dollar bill.

"Everybody's going. I'm surprised you weren't already invited," Steve said.

"My invitation must be lost in the mail," Rob said with a sardonic laugh.

Rob had met Steve that spring, when he'd introduced himself to a group of boys smoking cigarettes outside a local high school. Rob told the boys he was a new transfer student, a senior.

Steve had expressed envy. "Lucky you, man. I've got two more years at this hell hole."

While the boys smoked, they talked about cars and complained about teachers. Before long, Rob inquired if any of them knew where he could score some pot. The others nodded towards Steve, who smiled. That afternoon Rob met Steve in the parking lot of a nearby bowling alley.

"So how come I've never seen you around school?" Steve said. "I mean, like not at all?"

"You're a sophomore. We don't have classes together," Rob said, as if that was all that needed to be said on the subject.

The truth was Rob had graduated from another school the previous year. If Steve continued to doubt Rob, he never brought it up again, and over time, whenever Steve talked about school events, Rob played along as if he understood. Eventually Rob learned enough from Steve's incessant school stories to protect his lie.

Rob rolled a joint, stuck it between his lips, then neatly folded the baggie and put it in the inside pocket of his jean jacket, where his hand grazed the fabric of his shirt and the memory of that morning. His fucking draft notice had come in the mail that morning. He immediately knew what it was, so before his mother could get her eyes on it, Rob slipped the envelope between the buttons of his shirt, then tossed the rest of the mail on the kitchen table.

Later in his room, he ripped open the envelope and stared at the letter inside. "June 8, 1968. ORDER TO REPORT FOR INDUCTION." A letter from the president. That made him laugh—as if Lyndon B. Johnson himself had personally sat down at his desk to order Robert W. Lang, Jr. to join the armed forces—a call to some great adventure. He had one month to report, barely enough time to think.

Before he left the house, he slid the envelope under the old chemistry and history notebooks his mother insisted he keep for college. Rob never saw himself in college—he hated sitting in classrooms, listening to teachers talk about stuff that didn't matter in real life, but college men got deferments. It was all too much. The noise of the future is what had made him anxious for a joint in the first place. And now, there was a party to go to, a way to take his mind off all of it, and even better, the best-looking girl in school would be there. Why not, Rob thought.

Rob flicked his lighter and held the flame to the joint.

"Hey. You can't smoke that in here, man," Steve said, looking at his bedroom door as if it would burst open any second. "My mom might be out there, carrying a laundry basket or something."

"Some drug dealer you are," Rob said.

Steve reddened. "Yeah? You don't got parents?"

Rob slid his lighter into his pocket, put the joint in his wallet. "Yeah. All right," Rob said. "We can light it up on the way to your party. You driving?"

Chicken Feed

WISCONSIN 1968

Marion was folding a load of laundry when Bridget entered the kitchen. "There you are," she said. "Didn't know if you were ever going to get up. It's nearly nine thirty. I've about run out of quiet things to occupy myself with."

Bridget hung her head like a scolded child.

"My goodness," Marion said. "I was just teasing. You could have slept all day if that's what you needed to do."

Thank you, Bridget wanted to say. She stood stiffly, not quite sure what she should do next. As kind as Marion had been yesterday, Bridget still felt intimidated by the woman who'd drawn her out of hiding with a rifle.

"You want coffee?" Marion asked. "Or juice?"

"Coffee," Bridget said.

"The cups are in the cupboard to the left of the stove. Sugar's in the yellow Tupperware thingy there on the counter, and if you like cream, it's in the refrigerator."

Bridget poured coffee and sat at the table.

"Sleep well, though?" Marion said.

"Yes. But some noisy birds woke me up early."

Marion got up and poured herself another cup. She unwrapped a package of cinnamon rolls and set them it on the table in front of

Bridget.

"I heard them, too. There's a robin's nest somewhere close and those babies are a raucous bunch. They'll be gone in a few weeks, but for now they're an early alarm clock, aren't they?"

Bridget slathered her roll with butter,

"I washed your clothes," Marion said.

Bridget stopped chewing for a moment and looked apologetically at Marion. It had been a while since her clothes had been washed properly. "Thank you," she said. "I really appreciate it."

"Later I'll get my sewing basket," Marion said. "You can find a button you like to replace the one that's missing on the waistband of your skirt. And there's a small rip near the hem that should be fixed."

Sewing was an art Bridget's mother had declined to teach her after one failed attempt to learn when she was ten. Trying to make the tiny stitches, Bridget had pricked her finger and bled into the white poplin baptismal gown her mother had her working on. Her mother had reacted viciously. *Are you too stupid to learn such a simple thing?*

"I don't know how to sew," she said.

"I can do it for you," Marion said. "Or I can show you. A girl should know how to sew. Boys too. Just a handy thing to be able to do."

"Okay," Bridget said.

Marion got up, washed out her cup, and unplugged the percolator. She glanced out the window overlooking the back yard.

"I don't know what you're planning, but if you don't need to leave right away, do you think you could help me out today? I need to go to town for chicken feed. After that I should pick up a few things at the grocery store."

Bridget was surprised at how pleased she felt. "Sure. I can go with you."

"I was hoping you'd say that. I scrounged up a pair of Levi's for you to wear."

Marion took Bridget into the laundry room and handed Bridget the blue jeans and one of her sleeveless shirts from where they lay on top the dryer.

"These should fit," she said. "Jeans might be a bit long, but you can roll the hems."

Bridget thanked her and closed the door. She held the jeans up to her waist. Her mother never let her wear pants, much less jeans, which she said were "low class." Bridget folded the nightgown and laid it on the on the counter next to two cardboard containers of various colored eggs and her own clothes, which Marion had washed and were now neatly folded. She put on a clean bra, then the blue jeans and blouse Marion had given her. The laundry room was a bright, sunlit yellow. The open window looked out onto the driveway and the barn. Outside a cardinal called from a distance. The western sky was a bright, cloudless blue.

At the co-op, Marion bought three bags of chicken feed, a scuffle hoe, and a hundred-foot garden hose. Bridget helped Marion hoist the fifty-pound bags into the bed of the pickup. After that, they gassed up the truck, mailed two letters at the post office, then went to the grocery store. In addition to Marion's regular groceries, they bought a carton of ice cream, strawberry, because Bridget said it was her favorite flavor.

On the drive home, Marion fiddled with the radio searching for news, but every station crackled with static. It had been only two weeks since Robert Kennedy's assassination, and she still felt anxious when she thought of it. Such a senseless act and coming only a month after Martin Luther King Jr.'s assassination, Marion feared for the future of the country. She had lived through tough times, but neighbors turning on neighbors? Race riots? Killing political leaders? When would all the madness stop?

The day Bobby Kennedy was killed, Marion's sister had called to see if Marion had heard the news. "I suppose there will always be evil and violence in the world," Vivian had said. "And we can't do a thing to stop it, except try to be good people and do right, each and every day." While Marion was not accustomed to philosophical wisdom from her sister, Vivian had made a good point. Marion found comfort in thinking that if everyone she knew, at least, was just trying to do right, then her own little part of the world might not be in as much trouble as the rest of the world seemed to be.

And yet, here was Bridget. She had not run away from home for no reason. After the weather report, Marion switched off the radio. Bridget, whose elbow jutted out the open window, faced the passing countryside and gazed at the miles of cattle fencing and occasional Holstein herds grazing on the rolling fields.

"You know," Marion said, keeping her eyes on the road, "I'm still curious how you ended up at my stuck-in-the-middle-of-nowhere house?"

"I saw your post about fresh eggs on a bulletin board at a diner," Bridget said.

Marion nodded. "And I suppose the sign by my mailbox is just the same as a welcome mat?"

"My grandma sold eggs, too," Bridget said. "Before she died. And she had a big garden, so I thought you might have one. I hoped there might still be peas and maybe a few early beans. I was only going to pick some, then leave. I waited at the road by your mailbox until your lights went out. I thought you'd never even know I was there."

"But you had no idea I have eagle ears, did you?" Marion said, pleased with her pun.

"Or that you had a rifle," Bridget added. "Nobody's ever shot at me before."

Marion lifted her right hand from the steering wheel and waved it loosely. "To set the record straight, I did not shoot at you. I shot over you." Her hand back on the wheel, Marion said, "Scared you though, didn't it?"

Bridget said that it had. "Can I ask you something?"

"Well, sure. Are you not allowed to ask questions where you're from?"

Bridget's eyes widened. She closed her fingers into a fist, then relaxed them in her lap.

Marion saw she might have struck a sore spot.

"Why do you live in such a big house, all by yourself?" Bridget asked. "Didn't you ever get married?"

Marion said, "I was married, but he died. Now, I'm alone, except for vagrants who see my egg signs." Marion grinned.

"I'm sorry."

"Wasn't your fault."

"I mean, I'm sorry for you," Bridget said.

"Oh, that's all right. I knew what you meant," Marion said, pulling into her driveway. "Let's get these groceries in the house, then get this feed unloaded."

Bridget helped Marion empty the feedbags into the steel hopper that dispensed the feed. After that, Marion showed Bridget how to release a lever to drop a measured amount of feed into the flat metal pan below the hopper. Then she directed Bridget to carry the pan of feed into to coop and set it on the floor near the self-filling water pan. Two red hens squawked at the intrusion but settled down once the feed was set before them.

"We're a bit late feeding them today," Marion said. "They'll survive, the little complainers. Can't believe I let the hopper get so empty. That's not like me." Marion picked up one of the hens and brought her to Bridget, who eyed the bird warily. "Go ahead and pet her if you like. She won't peck at you."

Bridget stroked the silky feathers.

"Soft," she said.

"They are, but don't get mushy over them. They're not kittens. Once they stop laying, they are headed for my Dutch oven." She set the hen back on the ground. "I'll come out later with a basket. You can help if you like. Probably won't get too many eggs today. I had quite a few yesterday."

Before heading into the house, Bridget looked over the garden, which buzzed with honeybees. A white trellis of pole beans sprouted dozens of blossoms. One of six young tomato plants had come loose from its stake. She would fix it for Marion later. Bridget closed her eyes, lifted her face to the sky, and breathed deeply. The air was sharp with the smell of fresh mown hay. It was a beautiful day. Bridget wanted to freeze this moment so that her life would always be sun-filled and peaceful. But she knew she did not belong here. Beautiful days like this were meant for someone else.

After lunch, Marion showed Bridget how to sew the rip in her skirt and how to anchor a button so it wouldn't come loose in the future. Afterwards, Marion said she needed to rest.

While Marion napped on the couch, Bridget headed back to the garden, this time not to raid but to work. She may not have known how to gather eggs or to sew on a button, but Bridget knew how to weed a garden.

First, she needed to take care of the little tomato. Bridget wound the twine around the stake, then gently looped it around the stem of the plant and tied a knot. Before long it would wind itself up and over any attempt to contain it. She laid her hand over her nose and drew in the tomato's crisp scent. If she were ever asked what she thought the sun smelled like, this is what she would say. Even in the dark, a garden smelled bright and alive.

Next, she set herself to weeding. When she was five, Bridget had learned the difference between a useful plant and a weed. Her father had shown her how to use a hand trowel to loosen and remove a weed. At first, the job was fun. Then, she pulled a baby carrot by mistake. When her father saw what she had done, he slapped the carrot from her hand.

"You've ruined it," he scolded. "I told you," he said, pointing to wide leafed plantains and the clover-like oxalis, "those are the weeds."

Over the years Bridget learned about garden weeds, lawn weeds, and even people weeds that grew up to become people who "ought to be ashamed of themselves."

Bridget was determined to weed Marion's entire garden before she woke. She wanted to surprise Marion. Bridget imagined the next day, long after she had disappeared into the night, that Marion would come out to cut lettuce or pick berries and see all the neat paths, all her plants upright and strong. It would be her way of saying thank you.

After the dinner dishes had been washed, Marion and Bridget sat back at the table, bowls of strawberry ice cream in front of them.

"I was a teacher," Marion said. "For 35 years, mostly middle school— 7th grade. I just retired a year ago, and right after, my husband, Harve, and I drove out east to New England. Have you ever been out there?" Marion asked.

Bridget shook her head.

"I hope you go some day. It's a beautiful place. Mountains and the ocean. Harve and I had lobster for the first time. That was worth the trip alone."

"I haven't had that either," Bridget said.

"Then after we got home, while we were planning our next trip, the man had a heart attack and died." She sighed. "I still miss him every day. It's hard, after doing nearly everything with someone else for so long, to get used to being alone, making decisions alone." Marion laughed. "There were days after he died that I felt like joining him. But I'd hear his voice telling me I was too young for that." She nodded. "He'd be right, of course. I no longer have my whole life ahead of my like you do, but I guess 62 is too young to give up."

Bridget scraped the last of her ice cream from the little glass bowl and brought the spoon to her mouth, releasing it with regret. Bridget slid the bowl towards the middle of the table and crossed her arms, elbows on the table.

"I left a while ago. Things were bad, at home."

Marion let the girl speak.

"My dad. He's really strict. I had this boyfriend and—." Bridget hesitated. She couldn't find the words to say the rest.

"Do you ever call them and let them know you're well?"

Bridget nodded. "I did call a few months ago. My mom was crying and begging me to come home. Then I heard my dad in the background. "Is it her?" he said. He must have ripped the phone away. He didn't say hello or anything. Just hung up the phone."

"How do you manage? My goodness. In winter? It must be so hard."

"You meet nice people. And there are hostels, you know, where you can stay cheap. And churches, too. But ministers sometimes call the police."

"Are there many out there, like you?" Marion said. "Runaways?"

"Not everyone is a runaway. Some people are just out traveling. I mean, that's what they say. At first I was alone. Then I fell in with a group, but if you're a girl, eventually someone wants something from you."

Marion expressed alarm.

"It's really not as bad as it sounds," Bridget said.

"No. I'm sure it's worse than it sounds."

Bridget shrugged.

"Well," Marion said, pushing her chair away from the table. "I guess we're not going to solve the world's problems tonight are we?"

She rose and took Bridget's empty bowl. Outside, the last remnants of light glowed gold and pink. A noisy June bug beat its wings against the screen, and after an hour of mindless TV, Marion said it was time for bed.

"You go on up," she told Bridget. "I'll be along shortly."

It was four a.m. when Bridget slipped out of bed and dressed in her own clothes. She was grateful the old floor did not squeak as she moved silently about the room. Before she'd gone to sleep, Bridget had repacked her knapsack, folding things neatly, organizing instead of shoving. She laid the nightgown on the bed along with the other things Marion had given her, not knowing if she was meant to keep them, not wanting to presume she should.

41

Bridget crept carefully down to the kitchen, where she filled her small canteen with water. She hoped Marion would not mind if she took some food. When she opened the refrigerator, she saw a plate of leftover chicken, each piece wrapped in waxed paper. Near the chicken was a mason jar filled with pickles. Beside that, a paper lunch bag labeled: cookies. Bridget took it all, chicken, pickles, cookies. She was sure Marion had meant for her to take them. Someday, Bridget said to herself, I will pay her back. It was still dark as death when she stepped off the back porch and disappeared into the night.

Courage

MILWAUKEE 1966

Terry Abbott would always say that he was twelve years old when his childhood ended, the year his parents got divorced. While Terry's father was at work, his mother had packed the car, pulled him and his fourteen-year-old sister, Linda, out of school, and shoved them like bags of laundry into the back seat. Then, as if being chased by the police, she drove north to Milwaukee, hours away from Elmwood Park, Illinois, the only home Terry had ever known, and thrust herself into her sister's sympathetic arms.

"I couldn't take it anymore," Connie Abbott told her sister. "The man has no backbone. A goddamn thunder crack scares him. A grown man should be able to face a day without drowning his fears in a bottle."

For two months, until his mother could earn enough rent money for a place of their own, the three of them had slept in one bedroom, Linda in the double bed with their mother, Terry in a sleeping bag on the carpeted floor.

A week after they left home, the phone rang, and Terry answered it. It was his dad.

"Come get us, Dad," Terry pleaded. Aunt Peggy doesn't even want us here."

"I would," his father said. "You know I would. But your mother—."

His mother came into the room. "Who are you talking to?" she

43

said, taking the receiver from his hands, listening a moment. "Stanley. I told you to leave us alone. We're through with you. If you call here again—." She didn't finish her threat but slammed the receiver down.

"But why, Mom?" Terry said.

"Because he's no good. That's why."

Terry cried that night, slipped down in his sleeping bag. Terry loved his father and knew his father loved him. It wasn't fair, he thought. It wasn't fair.

Things really fell apart nine months later when Terry's mother married Richard Petrovich, the man, Connie told her children, who would make everything right. From the start, Terry realized Richard was a threat, from Terry's inability to please his stepfather, always seeming to do everything wrong, to Richard's irrational outbursts, anger directed at only Terry. "He's just under stress," Connie said, excusing her husband's flare ups.

Then the abuse started. At first, it was physical threats. Richard would trap Terry against the wall, sometimes not even speaking, and just hold him there for a few moments before releasing him. "Gotta build up your strength, if you're going to hold your own against me," Richard said once, laughing. All the ugliness happened in the dark or away from his mother's view. Dick's quiet, but threat-filled words kept it secret: "Don't tell your mother. She will only be angry with you."

Terry's teachers began to express concern, telling his mother that Terry was a loner, didn't interact much with the other children, was often distracted, stared out the window. Reading is good, they'd say, but that's all he does.

In the car after one parent-teacher conference, Connie lifted the glowing end of the car's cigarette lighter to her Pall Mall. "Teachers think it's wrong for a kid to read?" she said out the side of her mouth as the cigarette ignited. "That's ridiculous. There's nothing wrong with you. I didn't have a lot of friends when I was your age, either. I turned out fine."

In the back seat, Terry's eyes burned with smoke. He felt a choke in his throat.

After that, Terry's mother no longer went to school to talk with his teachers. As long as he didn't bring home failing grades, she assumed all was well. She even stopped asking "how was school," when he got home. She just shouted hello from the living room and went back to watching her television program. In Connie's mind, she worked hard—morning receptionist at a dentist's office, then housework in the afternoon—she didn't need any aggravation from her son.

It was true that he read a lot. Terry could escape in a book. He was safe in books. He read everything the school librarian recommended. He read *A Wrinkle in Time* twice before returning it. His favorite books were those where young heroes showed inner strength despite their fears.

When Terry turned fifteen, he gave up childish books and childish notions. Life was not a fairy tale. Life did not have happy endings. That spring, Terry's English teacher assigned his class *The Adventures of Huckleberry Finn*. While his classmates groaned, Terry paged through the book, anxious to get home and start reading. Before long, Terry realized that in Huck, he had found a compatriot.

Terry pictured himself with Huck and Jim on the raft, especially at night, stars in the sky, steamboats coughing sparks into the dark. But it was Huck's elaborate scheme to escape his Pap that intrigued Terry the most. More and more he felt he had to escape, too. He could not tell his mother about the horrible things his stepfather did to him. He was sure she would not believe him. He had to get away, and Huck Finn gave him courage.

On his final night at home, when Terry wriggled out of Dick's rigid grip for the last time, he ran up the stairs to his room to plan his escape. He would stay in the house one more night. In the morning his mother would rouse him awake, thinking everything was fine. She would tell him, as usual, to get ready for school. She would watch him head down the street as he always did, toward the bus stop. Around the corner, though, he would cut across a yard, head north instead of south. He would wait until his mother and Dick had gone to work. Then he would return to the house, take what he needed, and be gone for good.

With Huck Finn in mind, Terry fantasized about what his life could be like after leaving his mother's house. Without a raft or a river, he would be on foot. Instead of Jim, maybe a dog at his side—a stray he'd meet up with and befriend. Terry decided would write about the places he passed through and the interesting people he met. He would draw maps, like Tolkien's, of real locales and imaginary ones.

When the sun went down and he huddled in alleys for the night, Terry conjured a new town. Writers and dreamers would live there. When he arrived, they'd open their arms and take him in. They'd show him to a small house set in a willow wood. A yellow desk would sit under a south-facing window. "We pretty much keep to ourselves here," they would say, "but are ready to help whenever you need us." But this fiction only warmed his soul. It did not warm his body.

Terry learned quickly that real small-town hospitality was a myth, that the world was not filled with people eager to help you. And real towns were alive with vagrants of their own. Two nights earlier, Terry had found a covered alcove adjacent to a band shell in the town square. He'd fallen asleep, safely out of the rain. Hours later he was startled awake by a gruff drunk who accused Terry of stealing his spot. Afterwards, Terry had walked for an hour looking a place to keep dry.

The next morning, he entered a small cafe, a green striped canopy over the window, where a sign advertising endless refills was hand lettered on the glass. Terry slumped into a booth and looked at the menu. When the waitress arrived, she did not greet him, but instead stood at his table, her back arched. She sucked her teeth.

"You better show me your money first," she said.

Terry laughed. Was she kidding?

"Show me," she said. "I don't plan to get stiffed by your like again."

He laid a five-dollar bill on the table. Once she was satisfied, she took his order, but without the jovial manner he saw from her with other customers.

After Terry finished eating, he paid his bill at the table and asked where the restroom was. When he emerged, the waitress kept her eye on him. She followed him out the door and watched as he walked down the street. Terry was certain that moments later he would be in handcuffs.

That night, standing on the shoulder of another highway, Terry thought of the story he had begun writing. In it, the protagonist was lost, alone, sometimes afraid. But one foot in front of another, he refused to give up.

Sparrow

When they got to Sparrow's house, Rob and Steve had to park halfway around the block.

"This party is going to be huge," Steve said, brushing his long bangs away from his eyes.

Rob shook his head. Steve had been right about the house. It wasn't the mansion Rob had expected to see, but it was big. The Greek Revival home sat on an expansive lawn that sloped down to a shady boulevard. The boys headed up the stone path to the front door. Two columns supported the two-story portico that protected the front entrance. A black wrought iron porch light hung underneath, illuminating the double wide door, gleaming side lights giving the boys a glimpse of the throng of teenagers within.

The boys stepped into the foyer. A heavy oak bench was littered with jackets. A mound of shoes covered the floor. Steve kicked off his shoes. Rob kept his on.

"You're supposed to take off your shoes," Steve said.

"If anyone has a problem with my shoes," Rob said, leaning into Steve's face, "they can let me know."

Steve turned quickly away.

The living room, three times as big as Rob's parents' modest counterpart, was filled with young people, their heads bobbing close together, laughing, some with eyes closed, moving to the beat of the music.

"Where's the beer?" Steve said.

"What's your hurry?" Rob said. He elbowed Steve in the ribs. "Who's that?" he said.

Steve gave Rob a puzzled look. "You need glasses? That's Sparrow."

Rob realized he had slipped up. Even in a large school, a girl like this would be so popular, everyone would know her. "Ha ha," he laughed. "Her hair looks different."

Sparrow was singularly beautiful. Long Nordic blonde hair reached past her shoulders. Her icy blue eyes fringed in heavily blackened lashes. She stood near a highly polished ebony grand piano next to a dark-haired girl of unremarkable features. The girls were surrounded by four boys who had still not outgrown their adolescent pudge. Boys who had no idea how to talk to girls like Sparrow. She seemed to soak up their obsequious attention. As Rob and Steve passed by on their way to the kitchen, Rob could not help but notice her braless breasts under a gauzy, white peasant top.

Rob and Steve pushed through the swinging doors into the kitchen, where they found boys in letter jackets around the burlap-wrapped beer keg. Compared to the subdued lamplight in the living room, the kitchen lights were blinding. Glass doors in the ceiling-height cabinets reflected the light, making it even harsher.

Rob had seen a kitchen like this before. When he was seven and home from school with a fever, his mother had taken him to where she worked as a housekeeper. He remembered the cold feel of the marble countertop against his hot skin. "I just polished that," his mother had said, "Don't get it smudged with your fingerprints." Later, she had bundled him in blankets and put him to sleep on the floor in the living room. She said she dared not let him lie on the couch.

Beers in hand, the boys wandered back to the living room. Rob and Steve found an empty space beside a set of bookcases. From this location, Rob could see the piano perfectly.

"Sparrow's parents have a lot of books," Steve said.

"People like this always have a lot of books to show how educated they are, but they're just jerks like everybody else," Rob said.

Steve gave Rob a perplexed look, then shrugged him off. "I'm gonna grab another beer," Steve said. "You want one?"

"I'm good," Rob said. "Whatever brand this is, it smells skunky."

Steve's expression showed he did not understand. "Well, my cup was mostly foam," he said, "so I'm gettin' another one."

"Knock yourself out," Rob said.

Steve's absence was Rob's opportunity to seek out Sparrow. She was still at the piano. Her hair caught the light from a brass lamp centered above a large ornately framed painting of a nude woman reclining on a gold brocade chaise. The deep red drapes behind the woman provided a backdrop for Sparrow and her entourage. When Rob moved in, the other boys, as if compelled by some supernatural force, moved away. The shortest of the boys laughed off the intrusion and said, "Guess we oughta mingle. We'll catch ya later, Sparrow."

She smiled, but immediately turned her attention to the newcomer. "This is Betsy," Sparrow said, extending her arm to introduce the girl standing next to her. Sparrow did not introduce herself.

Rob nodded, but didn't say anything. He stood there, pretending to sip the now warm beer.

"Do I know you," Betsy said. "You don't go to our school, do you?"

Rob ignored her. He wasn't there to make small talk with Betsy.

"You're weird," Betsy said. She shook her head. "I'm gonna get some pretzels, Sparrow. I can bring you some if you want." Sparrow said she didn't want any. Before Betsy left, she gave Sparrow a "be careful" look.

Sparrow shook her hair and rolled her shoulders. She turned her attention back to Rob who was now alone with her.

"I don't know you, do I?" she said, insinuating that there was no reason she should. She leaned back against the piano and moved her head side to side in time with the music.

"Probably not," he said. "I graduated a couple of years ago. I'll be a junior at Winona State in the fall. I'm here with my little brother. He's around somewhere." Rob craned his neck as if to look for him. "Gotta try and keep him sober. Sometimes he's got a problem. He really does."

"That's nice of you," she said.

"Nice," Rob said, "that's me." He dipped his chin slightly, looking first at the floor, then into her blue eyes so intently she dropped her own, as if uneasy.

Rob's taut muscles were evident under the blue chambray shirt he wore. "I like your shirt," Sparrow said. She raised her hand, as if to touch his thick, almost black hair, but caught herself in time. She drew her hand to her mouth, smoothing her laugh lines then pulling her lower lip into a pout.

Rob leaned in to be heard over the music, which someone had turned up even louder. "You a senior?" he asked. "You seem more mature than—."

"I don't even want to think about school," she said, then closed her eyes and hummed along with the song. Her body swayed and she combed her fingers through her thick, white-blonde hair before freeing her hands to seek out the space above her head. She moved like a belly dancer.

This girl is high. She has to be, Rob thought. "You got records in your room?" he asked.

Sparrow stopped moving and opened her eyes. She looked into Rob's face. An auburn-haired girl fell against Sparrow, sending her into Rob's arms.

"Sorry," the girl said and moved on.

Rob set Sparrow straight but did not hold onto her.

"It's kinda crowded in here," she said. Then she took Rob's hand and led him single file through the crowded room and up the stairs.

Upstairs was cooler and the noise subdued. The carpeted hallway smelled like furniture wax and cut flowers, not like sweaty teenagers and beer.

"So, this is where the magic happens," Rob said, suggestively.

He could tell she did not catch his meaning. She smiled and asked him if he wanted the grand tour. Before he could decline, she led him from one room to the next. Her innocence had been cute, at first, but after he had seen bedroom after bedroom—and god knows how many bathrooms, Rob was becoming impatient.

"Where's your room?" he said.

Sparrow brushed his shoulder with her fist in a coy punch. Taking her lead, he acted as if the blow had hurt him. He winced and said, "Owww," in an overly dramatic way that made her laugh. He could see this chick liked all that Romeo stuff.

In her room finally, Sparrow pointed out photos of her with her horse that she no longer rode. Rob was not the least bit interested in why she gave up riding, but he slid his arm around her waist and leaned in to whisper, "that's too bad." He was even less interested in the small, seashell-encrusted jewelry box she held out before him, gleaming as if she were presenting some royal crown, until she opened it and he saw a perfectly rolled joint nestled in blue velvet.

Now this was more like it, he thought. She held her fingertips to her lips as if to say, now don't tell anyone about this. She handed him the joint, and he pulled out his lighter from his jacket pocket. Sparrow put her favorite Doors album on the turntable, then danced her way to her door and clicked the lock. After that she cracked open one of the windows, festooned with pink priscilla curtains.

Rob held out the joint and Sparrow took a long hit. While they smoked the joint, she explained about each of the ribbons displayed in a large frame on the wall: some white, some red, mostly blue. She pointed out the little ballerina trophy that she and her dance troupe had been awarded when they were seven years old.

"I'm not into all that childish stuff anymore," she said.

She might not have felt like a child, Rob thought, but she kind of still lived like one. Either that or this was just what high school girls liked. He really had no idea.

Then she turned off all the lights but one, a dim, beaded lamp near her bed. Sitting on the edge of the bed, she held out her hand to Rob and led him to join her there, where he pulled her close to kiss her.

"Mmm. You're a good kisser," she said.

But Rob wasn't there to talk. He stopped only to look at her, brush a wisp of hair off her cheek, then kiss her neck, her throat, teasing as if he'd bite. She giggled and told him to be careful. He laid her down onto the bed. She slid over on the mattress and made room for him. Up on his elbow, he leaned over, kissed her long on the mouth, while Morrison sang. Rob slipped his hand under Sparrow's waistband.

"No," she whimpered. "Not that. Just—you know."

He didn't know, but he slowed down, let his hand move back to her hair. Moments later he made his move again.

"I mean it. I don't want to—," she said.

"Oh, come on, baby," he countered. "Light *my* fire."

While she strained against him, he managed to unbutton her pants and slide her zipper, almost as one fluid motion. Sparrow grabbed his hand and tried to force it away, but she was not strong enough. He easily wrenched out of her grasp. Rob had never had to force it before. Girls had always given in. He couldn't understand why she was putting up a fuss. It was she who had lured him upstairs, led him to her bed. He stopped a moment, with her trapped beneath him.

"You know you want it," he said. Without another word, he finished what he had come there for.

Suspicion

Roger Armistead's patrol car pulled into Marion's driveway. As always, he drove slowly, taking care not to injure one of the hens that sometimes roamed freely outside their coop. He noticed Marion had driven her old tractor out of the barn. The green John Deere was parked in front of the big sliding door, gleaming in the sun as if it had just been washed. And sure enough, the garden hose was coiled nearby, and the gravel drive in front of the barn was dark and wet.

He turned off the engine but left the key in the ignition. He stepped out and stretched. His back had been bothering him lately, and sometimes sitting in the car, even for short periods, worked on a nerve that sent tingling pain down his left leg. He set his hands on his hips and leaned back, then turned to the side, trying to loosen his old muscles. Roger Armistead did not like to think that he was getting older, though he would turn 63 this year. Margie, who had come to work for him back in 1940, when he had first been elected, was two years younger than he. She pestered him now and then about both of them retiring.

The truth was Roger had no idea what he would do with himself if he wasn't sheriff. The public agreed with him, as he had never faced an opponent. Roger was also hesitant to retire because he still had not adapted to being a widower. Grace had been dead for three years, and each night when Roger came home, he still expected to see her in her apron, setting the table or checking on a roast. He missed lying next to her each night, that more than anything else. He missed how she smelled of lavender soap, and how soft she felt in his arms. They had never been an adventurous couple, though they spoke of one day traveling across the country or even to Europe. Gracie had thought it would be wonderful to see the Eiffel Tower or the Vatican. But now that she was gone, Roger rarely thought about the future, even about the day when he and Margie would be forced to retire. He did not let himself think beyond the present. Work was all he had.

Roger left his hat in the car, but otherwise wore his full sheriff's uniform. He had not come to Marion's farm to buy eggs. He was here on business.

"Well, look what the cat dragged in," Marion said, stepping out onto her back porch. She wiped her hands on a dishtowel.

Roger walked toward his old friend. He and Marion had known each other their entire lives. They had lived only four houses apart when they were kids. Along with Marion's older sister, Vivian, the three controlled the neighborhood gang, though it was Marion who was willing to join Roger in a bit of mischief. In high school, Roger had felt more and more that Marion was the girl he would marry, but she had not returned those feelings, and life set them on divergent paths that would not cross again until Roger moved home after his time in the army.

"Planning on plowing?" Roger asked, stepping onto the porch.

Marion looked confused for the moment, then remembered the tractor, which she'd washed earlier. She laughed. "I think my plowing days are over. I was in the barn a couple of weeks ago, saw that old thing, and thought I probably ought to sell it before no one wants it. I got a call yesterday. A guy from Campbellsport saw my ad and is headed up to take a look."

Roger nodded. "Probably a good idea, but don't you go selling it for less than it's worth. If he looks destitute, I wouldn't put it past you to just give it to him."

She motioned for him to follow her into the house. "Oh, don't you worry about that," Marion said. She laid the dishtowel on the counter and went to the refrigerator. She took out a blue glass pitcher. "Iced tea, Roger?"

"That would be fine."

She ran warm water over the aluminum ice tray to loosen the ice, drew back the lever to dislodge the cubes. She dropped several cubes into each glass, then filled them with tea.

"You hungry? I could put together—."

"Tea's fine. Thanks."

"Sorry. I don't have a lemon."

"That's okay. Lemon grates my teeth," he said.

They sat for a few minutes, sipping tea, talking about the weather and Roger's newest deputy, Arnie Johnson.

"You remember Arnie?" Roger asked.

Marion said she did. Arnie had been one of her students and she'd been sure he would never amount to much. Fractions and decimals confused him in the worst way.

"How's Arnie doing?" she asked.

"Oh, I suppose he'll work out all right in the end. He's a hard worker and he means well, but sometimes I think he's not got the good sense God gave him. I think he's watched too many police shows on television. We don't run into many hardened criminals around here, and Arnie might be looking for more excitement, so sometimes he makes things out to be something they just aren't."

Roger's tea was gone, so Marion slid the pitcher over to him. He refilled his glass.

"Speaking of excitement," Roger said, easing his way into the point of his visit. "Fond du Lac sheriff reported some break ins. They haven't caught anyone yet, but a store owner thought he saw two boys loitering downtown a couple of days before his shop was burglarized."

"I hope no one was hurt," Marion said.

"Have you seen anything suspicious? Anyone hitchhiking? Or out on your road who looks like a delinquent. You know, a hippie type? We've heard reports from other counties that runaways are sleeping in parks and waysides, stealing from grocery stores."

"Nothing suspicious. No." Marion looked away quickly.

Roger nodded. He looked around the kitchen. It would be nice, he thought, to take more time now and sit and talk with his old friend. But he needed to get to the next farmhouse. He wanted more than one person's report. He looked directly at Marion now, noticed an unruly wisp of her silver hair. As a girl she'd been a freckled-face brunette. In high school, she'd grown tall and lean and carried herself with such confidence that she drew people to her, even if she had been somewhat aloof and solitary. She was prettier than ever now, Roger thought, then shook that notion out of his head.

"I would be grateful if you'd let me know if you see anyone. And if you do, don't you try to handle things yourself. Call me right away."

"Of course, Roger. I will let you know."

Roger stood up, rubbed his hand under his nose, nodded, then said, "Good luck with that tractor. Don't be a sucker, Marion. Drive a hard bargain."

The rain was fierce that night. At one thirty, Marion leapt out of bed to close windows. The storm had driven the rain nearly sideways and left a puddle on the floor under the bathroom window, so she mopped it up with a towel before going down to shut the window over the kitchen sink.

Back in bed, Marion endured only a few more minutes of house-shaking thunder before giving up hope of sleep. She sat up, turned on the light, and read Frost's poetry, the collection she'd put on the nightstand for Bridget. But even her favorite "Mending Wall" could not hold her attention.

"What on earth do runaways do when it storms?" she wondered.

Bridget had been gone for two days and Marion could not stop thinking about her. There was something about that girl that Marion sympathized with, even pitied. She knew the girl had not told her everything. Her story about the boyfriend didn't hold together. A teenage girl might rage at her parents, tell them she hates them, and slam doors when they insult a boy she likes or forbid her to see. She does not run away from home. Teenage infatuations faded like morning glories. Even so, the girl had been such a sweet thing. Weeding the garden for one thing. Marion hated thinking of Bridget out there, alone in the world now. She would be easy prey for— . Oh, she couldn't think that way. Bridget was strong. Determined, that was for sure. She would be all right. She had to be.

Hitchhiker

INDIANA 1966

A semi-trailer truck slowed and pulled over just west of Angola, Indiana.

"Hop aboard," the driver said, like a train conductor, when Terry opened the door. The driver apologized that he couldn't take Terry all the way to New York. "I gotta get this load of tubs and toilets to Pittsburgh by midnight or my company'll dock my pay."

Though it had been a sunny day, now, at 6:30 p.m., dark clouds filled the sky.

"What's a kid like you going to New York for, anyway," the man asked.

"I've got friends there," Terry said. He almost blurted out the hoped-for scenario—a group of poets and writers, like souls who would band together. But the dream belonged only to him.

The driver looked at Terry as if inspecting a payload. "If you say so," he said.

"When I was your age—what're you? Sixteen? I was working for my old man. He was a sorry son of a bitch, too. But believe you me, I never got out of line with him, and if I did, my backside heard about it."

Terry made his own appraisal of the driver. He wasn't a young man. His unkempt hair was steel gray, like his two-day beard. His pouch of a stomach hung over his belt and jiggled against the steering wheel as he drove. But most of all, unlike most men who offered Terry rides, this one couldn't stop talking.

Terry learned about the man's first truck, about the tough times on the road, about what jerks highway patrolmen were, about which truck stops had the best food, about which truck stops had back-room poker games. He was especially bitter about how "a man could hardly get ahead anymore, cuz the office types were always tryin' to cut wages and taking away the perks."

Driving a truck couldn't be easy work, Terry thought, and it probably got lonely, so Terry listened politely. More than once he heard echoes of Huck's Pap railing against the "govment" or Dick's tirades about how it "just wasn't the same at the office since they started letting women do men's jobs."

After dark, the driver turned on the radio. "I suppose I've about talked your ear off, huh kid?"

"It's fine," Terry said. The weatherman warned of torrential downpours in eastern Ohio, where they were now. So far, they had only driven through light rain, barely needing the windshield wipers.

At 8:45 p.m., the driver pulled into a truck stop, saying he was in the mood for a cheeseburger. Terry said he'd have one, too, and he wriggled in his pocket for some coins.

"That's okay," the driver said. "I got you covered."

Terry followed the driver into the building to use the toilet and wash his hands. When he emerged from the men's room, the driver thrust the bag of burgers and two bottles of Coke towards Terry.

"Hold this, will ya? I gotta drain the pipe, too."

When he came out, wiping his hands on his grimy pants, he told Terry he preferred to eat in the truck. It had begun to rain harder now. The two sat in the cab, a Country-Western station on the radio, the singer plaintively wondering why her man could not be true. They ate the burgers and washed the satisfying but greasy taste down with the Cokes. Terry smiled in the dark when the driver let out a loud belch.

"Now, it's time to pay," the driver said, in a voice that put a choke in Terry's throat. The driver wiped his mouth, tossed his napkin on the floor. His pale face looked almost dead in the parking lot lights. He smiled a sick smile and pulled a knife from his shirt pocket. As he eyed the blade, turning it side to side, it glinted in the yellow-green light. "Gotta carry it," the driver said. "You never know what types you might meet on the road. He slid his tongue over his teeth, tsking loudly.

Terry edged to the door, the burger wrapper wadded in his fist.

"No, son. You ain't going nowhere."

The driver grabbed Terry by the back of his collar and pulled his head down.

When it was over, the driver clicked the knife closed and told Terry to get out. The truck's taillights glowed red in the dark as Terry stood immobile on the wet, black pavement. His knees weak, he smelled rain on asphalt, cheese and stale urine, and a smell he had, until that night, only associated with his own shame.

The Morning After

At ten Sunday morning, the day after Sparrow's party, Rob's mom came into his room to tell him he had a phone call, someone named Steve. Rob lay under his crumpled blanket, motionless. She stooped to pick up a dirty shirt to toss in the hamper.

"Do I know him?" she asked.

"What?" Rob said, in a fog.

"Robbie," she said, louder this time. "You have a phone call."

"Jesus. Can't anybody get any sleep around here?"

"That's no way to talk. No way to talk to me," she said.

His head hurt. He had smoked another joint after leaving Sparrow's house. Then he'd bought a pint of bourbon and had ambled around in a park to let the night dissipate before climbing on the city bus home. Now he needed water, not a phone call from a moron, but his impatient mother stood at his doorway with her hands on her hips.

"Shit," he shouted into his pillow. Then Rob plodded into the living room, where the black receiver lay on his father's desk. His father was in his robe reading the paper, his hairy legs up on the ottoman. He looked up at his son but said nothing, then he dissolved back into the business section.

"Hello," Rob said, mumbling into the phone.

On the other end Steve said, "What took so long, man?"

"What do you want?" Rob said impatiently.

"I thought I should call you to tell you Sparrow is spreading a rumor about you," Steve said. "She's saying you forced yourself on her."

"What are you talking about?" Rob said.

"She's saying you kinda forced her to have sex with you."

"I was there, Steve." Rob said. "She was begging for it."

"Well, that's not what she says."

"Did she tell her parents?" Rob asked.

"How the hell do I know," Steve said.

"You're just full of information aren't you Steve, old boy."

"Hey whattaya want? I'm telling you, aren't I? I called at least."

"Yeah, you're right, and I appreciate it. I really do."

Rob shook his head, held the receiver against his chest while he considered the situation.

"Everything all right, son?" asked his mother, who lurked nearby.

"Peachy," he said.

"Got it," Rob said, now speaking with Steve. "You have a nice day, too." Rob hung up.

"Who was that dear?"

"Just a guy," Rob said.

In the kitchen, Rob turned on the tap, stuck his head into the sink, and gulped at the cold stream. Then he clomped back down the hall, slammed his bedroom door, and got back into bed.

A little after one o'clock, Rob awoke, more clear-headed than before, and Steve's phone call started to sink in. *"You kinda forced her or something."* Rob wondered if he might actually be in trouble. After all, Sparrow's old man probably had some connections—lawyer types, or worse. His stomach burned with worry.

Arlene Lang had covered her son's lunch plate with foil. Rob pulled it from the refrigerator and gobbled the tuna sandwich. He poured a glass of milk, then another. The note on the kitchen table said his parents had decided to drive to the river for lunch at that place they liked so well. "Maybe next time," his mother had scrawled, "you'll be up to coming along?" Rob had to give it to her. She was persistent.

Rob sat on the floor in his room and stared at the crumpled draft notice in his hand. Vietnam might be interesting, he thought. He might become something there, rise in the ranks, become a leader of men, earn some medals. As a lieutenant, he'd be the guy who'd shoot the shit with those under his command. His men would admire and respect him. But such illusions about army life did not last long. No matter how he looked at it, in the end, Rob could not imagine himself humping through the jungle with an M-16 over his shoulder. All of that hero shit might have lured in those ROTC guys, but Rob had never been good at taking orders, and that's what being in the army would mean.

He had to figure a way out, and he had to act, soon. He didn't know exactly how the army worked, but he was pretty sure you couldn't just ignore a special invitation from the President. He smirked at the thought.

Robert Lang, Sr. was one of those men who could never catch a break. When he met Arlene, they were seniors in high school. Bob's family had moved to Greenfield, Oklahoma, a small town in the eastern panhandle so his father could take a job as the new postmaster.

Arlene's family had lived in Greenfield for generations, and she loved it there except when she got older and realized her town had a limited selection of interesting boys. So, at the beginning of her senior year when handsome Bob Lang was introduced to the class by their home room teacher, Arlene Rogan's world view brightened considerably.

The new boy never had a chance. Not that he had fought her off, for Bobby, as she called him then, found Arlene equally attractive. Eventually school dances and soda dates at the Rexall turned into country drives in the evening. On one such evening, Arlene told Bobby he could "go all the way." She had heard that you couldn't get pregnant if you did it only once. Before long she understood the clear signs to the contrary.

Only a week after graduating high school, Robert and Arlene Lang were a married couple with a child on the way. Shelley Lang was born the next November. By the time Shelley was toddling around the house, Bob was working as an accountant and Arlene longed for another child. With life in order, she thought it wouldn't hurt to hide her diaphragm now and then. In August of 1948 Robert Winston Lang, Jr. was born, and Arlene could not have been happier.

A month later, Bob came home from work and told his wife he had been let go, saying the firm felt they had one too many accountants. What Arlene Lang never learned was that her husband had been embezzling money from his company. Bob had denied it, of course, when his boss confronted him, and had indignantly asked what proof they had. It was true their evidence was circumstantial, but by process of elimination, they were certain it was Bob who had taken hundreds from their clients. Not only did they want him gone, but they also sought to bar him from working as an accountant anywhere else in Oklahoma or most of northwest Texas.

The Langs managed to get by on their savings and the generosity of Arlene's parents, but before long what had really happened got through to Bob's father-in-law. He told Bob one night as they stood on the front porch smoking, that if he ever did anything to disgrace his daughter again, he'd be staring into the business end of a shotgun. While Bob had faced Arlene's father undaunted, inwardly, he had trembled with anger and fear. Afterwards, and despite Arlene's ardent objections, the young family crammed as much as they could in their 1946 Ford Super DeLuxe station wagon and drove east to Kansas City, then north to Sioux Falls, South Dakota, where Bob imagined he would find not only a lucrative new job, but also the remnants of the Wild West he had loved reading about as a boy.

A job in Sioux Falls lasted four years, then they were off again, this time to Yankton, where Jack McCall, the man who had shot Wild Bill Hickok in a Deadwood saloon, had been hanged. Such stories appealed to Bob's sense of adventure, and he began his habit of telling tales of the old west at dinner, with details so vivid it was as if he were reliving his own pioneer days. After Yankton, it was Chamberlain. After that, they fled further north to Fargo.

With each upheaval, Arlene missed her home in Oklahoma more than ever. So, finally, after an unusually brutal winter in Fargo, Arlene gave her husband an ultimatum—find them a more convivial place to live or she would leave him and take the kids back to Oklahoma. Many years after that moment, Bob Lang wished he had called her bluff and let her go. Instead, the Langs moved to Minneapolis, where he accepted a lower paying job beneath what he considered to be his superior skills. It was May 1965.

Rob was sixteen when his parents dragged him to Minnesota. His nineteen-year-old sister Shelley refused to go along. He remembered thinking, as his mother begged his sister to be reasonable, how envious he was that Shelley could make her own life now.

It was a long drive to Minnesota. Arlene and Bob blamed each other for their daughter's rebelliousness. When they weren't arguing, Rob's parents quietly stewed in their own bitterness. When they reached the city, Rob's mother pointed out buildings, signs, places that looked interesting, places she thought they might want to visit, but he had no interest in any of that. Minneapolis was just one more place his father had dragged them to, one more place to feel trapped in a life he hated.

In Fargo his father had rented a moving truck, telling his son he didn't see any reason the two of them couldn't manage the job. The truth was, Rob did most of the work himself. Whenever his mother carried out even the lightest of boxes, her husband told her not to be ridiculous, and took the box away from her, thrusting it instead into Rob's arms. When Rob dared to complain, his father told him to keep that noise to himself.

"You're a man now," his dad had said.

In mid-July, after Arlene had told her husband she was having trouble making ends meet, Bob Lang told his son it was time he did his part for the family's finances. In fact, Rob's dad had the perfect job picked out for him. The accounting office where his father worked needed a clean-up man. The manager agreed Rob could work a few evenings a week.

"You must see this as a great opportunity," his dad said. "May as well start to prove to the world that you're a true Lang. Not afraid of a little work or starting at the bottom to work your way up."

Reluctantly, Rob started work that July at Atlas Accounting. After four weeks of emptying wastepaper baskets and cleaning toilets, one of the secretaries reported several dollars missing from her desk, and she accused Rob. Who else had access to the office when no one else was there, she claimed. When he was called in to the manager's office, Rob's red-faced father was sitting there. Rob denied having taken the money, even though of course he had. The company couldn't prove anything, but Rob was fired. His father, who paid the secretary four dollars out of his own wallet, told her how sorry he was. Jesus, Rob thought. It wasn't like it was four hundred dollars.

Besides not having to scrub another urinal at Atlas, another upside for Rob was that his father did not speak to him for weeks afterward, except to say that the moment Rob finished high school, he would find another job or move the hell out of his house.

Rob had no desire to start cooking and cleaning for himself. He had no idea how a washing machine worked. He could figure it out of course, but why would he do all of that when his mother still took care of him as if he were ten. A week after graduation, Rob took a job at a nearby diner, where he sliced tomatoes and onions or whatever else they wanted him to do. He also bussed tables and washed dishes, all of which he could do while high. He liked mindless work. It was also fun to flirt with the waitresses, which paid off as they sometimes shared their tips with him.

His mother urged him to enroll in college, so he could get a respectable job—maybe become an accountant like his father. What a laugh, he thought. But she had a point. Swanky office jobs did not go to high school graduates. The few times Rob thought of quitting and putting his efforts into school, he held off, because he had gotten close to one of the waitresses, Beth, a single mom with a two-year-old kid. She had invited Rob to hang out at her place one night and it had grown into a regular thing. After her kid was in bed, they'd get high, listen to music, and talk about how much they hated Minneapolis. Sometimes Rob talked about the two of them—and the kid, too—taking off for some place warm, like Florida. She liked that idea and said it would be nice to see palm trees and the ocean.

Rob lit a cigarette and scoffed. He looked at the draft notice crumpled on the floor. He could still go to Florida, or somewhere else, but he would go alone. After the incident with Sparrow, Rob knew he had to put Beth out of his mind. It wouldn't be hard. She was just a waitress, and she'd get over him sooner or later.

Ships at Sea

NEW YORK 1966

On Terry's first night in New York, he had felt the rumble of the city in his chest. The city was a painting in motion. Steam rising from sewer grates bleeding into the night air, the buzz of neon signs jutting over sidewalks, lights coloring the crowds who moved and talked around him.

Guitar sounds drew him down five steps into a nightclub in the Village, and, as if it was something he did every weekend, Terry mingled with the late-night patrons. He bought himself a rum and Coke and was surprised that no one questioned his age. He imagined himself living Holden's life. In his mind the nightclub became the Wicker Bar, where he impatiently waited for Carl Luce. Terry could lose himself, he realized, in such fantasies. It helped him cope, but there were times he wondered if he would ever find his own life, one that he was not afraid to live.

Fueled by the camaraderie of those who had had too much to drink, Terry fell in with Marc, a nineteen-year-old folk singer, and a girl named Elise, who shared a one-bedroom in the East Village. For a few days Terry slept on their couch until one morning he woke up, hungover from too much red wine, to find himself abandoned, his wallet empty.

Soon Terry could see that being homeless in the Midwest wasn't like being homeless in New York. On nearly every street corner, Terry imagined someone waiting to beat him up, even if he hadn't done anything. With no money, no place to stay, and no job, Terry tried again, smoothing the wrinkles in his jacket, and politely inquired at a corner diner about a job as a dishwasher or bus boy. A short, gray haired man, heavy black glasses underlining wiry, wayward eyebrows, repeated what Terry had heard before.

"We just ain't hirin', kid."

"Go back home to Indiana," they'd say. "Go back to your Ma." It seemed Terry had "Midwestern Teen" printed in big letters all over him. The night after he left Marc and Elise's place, or whoever's place it really was, Terry roamed the streets. Every restaurant—all the savory aromas wafting out into the street—only intensified his hunger. In an alley behind a spaghetti joint, Terry searched the trash for bread, but when he took the lid off one of the cans, he just couldn't bring himself to sift through garbage in the hopes of finding something clean to eat. He needed to make money.

It was the echo of the truck driver's last statement to him, "a pretty boy like you should have no trouble making a living in a city like New York," that pushed him toward a life he would never have believed he would live.

His first days turning tricks had been an exercise in doublethink—and the more he exercised that ability, the more he was able to maintain in his mind two contradictory ideas and believe in them both. He was a Midwestern teen searching for a way to dream, but he was also a New York prostitute working to survive. As long as Terry could separate what he had to do to survive from who he really was, he had no trouble looking at his own face in the mirror.

Like a lost puppy, Terry seemed to elicit sympathy from about everyone he met, and not all of them ended up taking from him in the end. For a few weeks, he paid for an alcove—not really a bedroom—in an overcrowded flat with other "working girls." There were, it seemed to Terry, prostitutes on every corner of the city.

One of the girls in the flat suggested Terry would make more money if he dressed as a female, saying some men were looking for that kind of experience. She showed him in the bathroom mirror how he could sweep his hair down over his eyes, do his make up to accentuate his narrow face. And she showed him other things, too, like how to cultivate the body language which would complement the effect. She gave him one of her older wigs, a blonde pageboy. She helped pin his hair and then arrange the wig so it looked natural. "You're a proper transvestite now, aren't you love?" she said. She took him to the mirror. Those were his eyes that looked back at him, but he recognized nothing else. She had given him, he realized, a way to again become the invisible boy. This life would be one layer of his life, nothing more, and as Terry would learn, life had many such layers, all under the outer edge that people called normal, an outer edge so many picked at, worried over, that was ready to be peeled back at any time.

On the street, while they worked, Terry studied the girls. He saw how they spoke with deference, glances aside or to the ground, putting themselves in submission to gain the upper hand. Powerful men liked to control. The girls seemed to know that and how to exploit it.

So it wasn't that he didn't appreciate the irony of his current situation. It was convoluted, all right. Just like Holden Caulfield, Terry felt he was the most terrific liar you ever saw in your life. An actor. A phoney, even. And none of the degenerates who sought him out night after night would ever know him, not really. He found just knowing that made all the difference.

Even so, he kept searching for a regular job. He washed dishes at a Chinese restaurant until he found he couldn't keep up. The owner's wife who saw dishes piling up waved her hands and screamed at him in Chinese. Terry could not understand her words, but her anger was clear enough, and at the end of his shift, the owner, a sweet man, showed him the door, his measly pay for two days hardly worth his itchy, red hands. At night in his tiny space, after a lukewarm bath, after he had turned himself back into Terry, he wrote, wandering off in escape fantasies, inventing, on paper, a life he still dreamed of.

Then, even that safety net ripped wide open. One of the girls accused him of stealing from her. His protests were useless. Walking the streets that night, he knew the real thief had cooked up the story against him. Two nights later, cold, hungry, and facing a beating, Donette found him. At that moment, Terry had never felt more helpless or more grateful.

To show his appreciation, Terry did his best to be a good roommate. He paid his share of the rent, always on time. He took care never to be one of those people who left trails of themselves wherever they walked, expecting others to pick up after them. He kept his room neat, his shared space in the bathroom clean. He insisted on washing the dishes. He even cooked for her, made something his mother had called "Hot Dish," a concoction of browned hamburger, rice, onions, green beans, and mushroom soup, which Donette had never had before. While she first eyed the casserole with suspicion, she found it to be tasty enough that she asked him to make it every Sunday night. Sunday Hot Dish, they called it.

What Donette liked him to do most of all was read to her. One Sunday after they had washed dinner dishes, they sat in the living room, he reading *Leaves of Grass*, she paging through a month-old hand-me-down copy of *Vogue*.

"Read me something from that poetry book," she said.

He turned the page to, "In Cabin'd Ships at Sea," and read.

"The boundless blue on every side expanding,
With whistling winds and music of the waves,
the large imperious waves,
Or some lone bark buoy'd on the dense marine,
Where joyous full of faith, spreading white sails,
She cleaves the ether mid the sparkle and the foam of day,
or under many a star at night. . ."

Donette remarked she had never been on the sea—though she laughed and said she guessed the Staten Island Ferry counted as a boat and the East River was sort of like a sea. After that first time, she often asked Terry read to her. "Cabin'd Ships" became one of her favorites, because she said the words made her feel like she was moving up and down with the waves, her eyes fixed on the white sails that climbed into an infinite blue sky.

It was hard not to like someone who could get that much out of a poem, Terry thought.

Secrets and Lies

SUMMIT ROAD, WISCONSIN 1968

When the sun flooded into her bedroom, Marion woke, her dream still so vivid that when she opened her eyes, she was surprised to find herself in her own bed. In the dream, she had been with Roger in a new red sedan. They were driving on a long, straight highway toward snowcapped mountains. Marion remembered what Freud had said about dreams then laughed. "Oh, what did he know anyway," she said out loud, then glided her feet into slippers and shuffled down to the bathroom, where she looked out the window onto the garden and the area north of the hen house, surveying for obvious signs of damage from the storm. Seeing only a few downed branches with their ruffled bouquets of leaves, she felt relieved. In '57 a raucous gust had uprooted a fifty-foot spruce that just missed the barn as it crashed to the ground.

It looked to be a mild and sunny Sunday morning, yesterday's humidity replaced by lighter air, and Marion was glad she had not overslept. She splashed cold water on her face, patted it dry, pouted momentarily at the widening freckles that had begun to mark her age, more so than the wrinkles at the corners of her eyes. Her sister Vivian told her about a cream that was supposed to fade dark spots. But Marion felt that fretting about beauty was a waste of time. She believed women only worried about their looks if there was a man to please. She ran a brush through her short, silvery hair and approved of how it brightened her summery tanned face and deep blue eyes.

At the kitchen counter, Marion used an old dishrag to wipe the few eggs that looked dirty. Keeping fresh straw in the coop meant that most of the time her eggs didn't need cleaning. It was Marion's practice not to wash them, as water removed the protective bloom from the shell that kept out bacteria and allowed her to store them longer, without refrigeration. Once buyers had them home, they could wash the eggs and store them in the refrigerator. For now, the eggs were ready for sale and stacked out of the sun on the pantry shelf in their cardboard containers, in full and half dozen lots. She had gathered seventeen eggs this morning. A good amount.

"Ding dong," rang out her sister's voice at the back door. "Anybody home?"

Marion had not been expecting Vivian, but her appearance wasn't a complete surprise as Viv thought nothing of dropping by out of the blue. There goes my peaceful morning, Marion thought, then plastered a smile on her face and called out, "In here. Come on in," although Vivian was already halfway inside, holding the screen door with her hip so she could bend to retrieve a large tote bag she had set by the door.

"Brought cookies," Vivian said in her high-pitched, warbling voice.

Drying her hands, Marion watched Vivian unload the bag. "I see," Marion said, not sure who was going to eat what looked to be at least four dozen cookies.

"I brought you raspberries, too," she said, setting out two pint-sized containers. Marion grew raspberries of her own, a fact she had pointed out to her sister in the past. But Marion said nothing. It wasn't worth it. Arguing with Vivian accomplished nothing. And Vivian always meant well.

Vivian helped herself to a blue and white transferware dinner plate from the cupboard and arranged some of the oatmeal raisin cookies she'd baked the day before. The last one in her hand wouldn't quite fit on the plate, so she lifted it to her mouth. "Delicious, if I do say so myself," she said. "I brought enough for you to freeze."

The kettle she'd put on when Vivian arrived whistled sharply. "Want tea, Viv?"

"You know I do." Vivian plopped herself down at the long end of the table and ate her cookie. She reached out for the plate.

"I kick myself that I didn't fight you harder for this Blue Willow set," Vivian said, "after Mom passed. They were her favorite, you know?"

It grated on her nerves the way Vivian spoke sometimes as if Marion had not also been her mother's daughter, as if she was not also aware of the things her mother cherished. This was not the first time Vivian had hinted about wanting the set of china. If Marion didn't enjoy the dishes so much herself, she thought she might just give in and let Vivian have them, just to put an end to it. But honestly, Vivian could afford to buy her own if she really wanted a set.

Marion poured hot water into the teapot, then set it and the sugar bowl near her sister before getting coffee for herself.

"Don't know how you can drink coffee. Tastes like bark to me," Vivian said, stirring her cup, clinking the spoon against the china.

Marion decided it would be best if she refrained from asking her sister if she had ever eaten bark. Instead, she said only that she prefers coffee in the morning.

"To each his own, I guess," Vivian replied.

"Good cookies," Marion said. With Vivian, a compliment went a long way. She needed to be told that she did things well.

"Did you hear about Pastor Simonich?" Vivian asked, her voice suggesting scandal. "He's getting remarried. Isn't that a shocker? At his age?"

Marion smiled. "I suppose he can do as he pleases, Viv."

"Well of course he can. And it's been, what, ten years now since Mary died. I'm sure he's been lonely, but, well the man's sixty-four, at least, maybe older. Not the marrying age, certainly."

"I hope he'll be very happy," said Marion, who refused to be pulled into Viv's gossip.

"That's not what I meant," Vivian said. "I only meant that you don't hear about folks our age getting married again. I've been a widow for six years and never once did I imagine trying to find myself another man."

"But if one showed up and swept you off your feet," Marion said, "you'd sing a different tune."

"Oh hush."

"Not sure if it's the coffee or a hot flash, Viv," Marion said, "but I've got to get out into the breeze. Sun's off the back porch now. Let's sit out there awhile before you have to go." It was Marion's way of nudging her sister towards her car.

"But we were so comfortable right here," Vivian said.

"I can bring the plate out if you want," offered Marion, who was now at the sink rinsing her cup.

"Oh, I'd better not," Vivian said patting her hips. "I will take more tea though."

The sisters moved to the back porch where Marion's two white ladder back rockers faced the garden. Before settling in her rocker, Marion dragged a scraggly potted geranium into a triangle of light.

"That thing's seen better days," Vivian said.

"I know. I hate to lose it, but it might be better off in the compost heap. It did beautifully in the house all winter, but I got greedy and set it outside too early this spring. I think it got a bit of frostbite."

Vivian nodded but offered hope. "You never know. Remember Dad said nothing would kill a geranium."

"Yes, well he took better care of them than I do," Marion said.

Marion and Vivian's father had understood plants. But like Marion, he was not romantic about them. He understood that all life has cycles, a beginning, and an end.

Vivian lived in a cedar-shingled Cape Cod that blended beautifully into a gentle hill on the shore of Lake Michigan south of Sheboygan. The white-balustered front porch that spanned the width of the slate gray house faced the lake. On clear mornings the sunrise painted rosy color over the house and gardens, no matter what time of year. From the house, a worn path sloped to the shore through wispy reeds and rolling dunes. The sound of water was always nearby, at times furiously beating the sand, other times moving gently in and out in a quiet cadence.

Marion loved Vivian's house, even though she never felt warm there. Even in summer, sometimes lake breezes were so cool she'd get the shivers. Marion wished she could spend time there alone. The silence at the lakeshore was different from her rolling hill and meadow silence. Each place spoke something the soul needed to hear. But you could only hear it if you sat still perfectly still and listened, which was nearly impossible for Vivian.

"This breeze is lovely," Vivian said. "What's more, I've got to admit something else about this countryside of yours."

"And what's that?" Marion asked.

"The air is fresh. Awfully sweet today. I've had to put up with those damn alewives dying all over. If the breeze blows west, I can barely breathe. One of my neighbors goes down and rakes them up and burns them in a barrel he's hauled down to the beach, but that stinks, too. God awful. If they don't figure it out pretty soon, I might have to think about moving in with you for a while. The lake view is pretty, but goodness gracious, if you've got to hold your nose to look at it, what good is that?"

The notion that her older sister might move in with her gave Marion a chill in her spine. "I saw Eugene Marquardt's hay mower out this morning," she said, not taking Vivian's bait. "Nothing is sweeter than fresh cut hay, that's for sure," Marion said. "Of course," she continued, "when the manure spreaders are out, our diary air is something else entirely." Marion laughed.

Vivian tipped her cup and sipped the last of her tea. She leaned down to set her cup on the floor when a tortoise shell hair comb caught her eye. She picked it up and held it up for Marion to see.

"I know this isn't yours, not with your sheep-shorn head," Vivian said. "Who does it belong to?"

Of course, it was Bridget's. How had she not seen it before now? "Who knows," Marion said. "Could belong to anyone. Your tea's gone,

Viv. Can I get you a bit more?"

Vivian held up the comb as if inspecting it for clues. "What're you hiding?"

"I'm not hiding anything. People stop by all the time to buy eggs. It probably belongs to one of them."

"Why are you acting so odd about it? I know people come by for eggs. But is egg buying such a vigorous proposition that someone would lose a comb?"

"I don't know."

"What're you not telling me?"

"Nothing."

"All right then," Vivian said, focusing her gaze squarely on her sister. "Tell me about that young girl who was with you at the grocery store."

Marion gasped. How did Vivian know? Some local gossip must have told her.

"Is that why you came here? To ambush me?"

"I suppose I thought you might add what seems to be pretty interesting information to the conversation," Vivian said. "But I guess not. So, who was she?"

"Just a girl."

"What girl? A girl you took to the grocery store?"

Marion's chest tightened. "Oh, very well. A young girl showed up a few days ago. She'd run away from home. She was so hungry. If you'd seen the poor thing, you'd have done just what I did."

"I'm not sure that's true," Vivian said. "Have you told Roger? He ought to know if there are runaways about."

"I haven't told anyone," Marion said. "But it appears my business is the talk of the town."

Vivian laughed. "Well did you think you could show up in town with a strange young girl without people taking notice?"

"She's not a criminal for goodness sake," though as she said it, Marion realized she had no idea if Bridget had ever committed a crime. She simply felt that the girl could not have done anything truly illegal.

"I still think Roger should know."

Marion nodded. "I planned on telling him," she said.

"I worry about you out here all alone. You bet Harve would have sent that girl on her way. You can't just be opening your door to strangers. What if something had happened to you?"

"I can take care of myself. You don't have to worry. Besides, you're all alone, too. What difference is there?"

"I do worry. And my neighbors are much, much closer. I can walk across the road to borrow sugar if I need to. We all look out for each other. I've told you, you ought to sell this place and move in with me, or at least into town where you would have close neighbors. If you're a target for vagrants, which apparently you are, I think you ought to seriously reconsider."

"Oh, nonsense. Target for vagrants. Don't let your imagination run away with you. I was never in any danger while she was here, and I'm in no danger now. You do not need to be concerned."

Marion stood up, held out her hand, implicitly asking for the comb, which Vivian surrendered.

"All right. I'll drop it for now," Vivian said. "But that doesn't mean I'm not still concerned."

Vivian took her teacup inside. When she returned to the porch, she laid her hand on her sister's arm. "If you're not too miffed at me, maybe you could drive to Sheboygan next week for a visit. If the lake stink isn't too bad, we could walk along the shore, maybe even pack a picnic."

Marion did not visit her sister as often as Vivian wished she would, so to make peace, Marion agreed. "That would be nice, Viv. Thanks. And don't worry. I'll be careful. Besides, what are the chances that another runaway is going to show up at my door?"

Vivian, who had taken her car keys out of her purse before slipping it over her arm, agreed. "I suppose that's right. You live out here in the sticks, after all. Sometimes *I* can barely find your driveway. And I'll see you next week?"

"Yes. I won't forget," Marion said, as she escorted her sister to the driveway where her big blue Lincoln Continental was parked.

Vivian waved, then drove away.

Marion walked back to the porch. She recalled Vivian's comment about Harve. "He would too have taken her in," she said out loud. "Harve always was a bigger softie than me. He would have wanted to adopt that girl, Harve would have." To purge her agitation, Marion pulled on her straw hat and garden gloves. She picked up the spindly geranium and headed to the compost bin and then set to work on the flowerbed along the front porch. She scraped at the ground with a garden fork and tossed the weeds into the empty flower pot. "You always think you know everything, Vivian," Marion said. "Well, you don't."

That afternoon, Marion was running the vacuum when she saw Roger Armistead's squad car pull into her driveway. She turned the machine off and took a quick look at herself in the mirror. She was pretty sure she knew why he was here. Her visit with Vivian. But she wouldn't confess right away. She could be wrong.

"You need more eggs already?" she said at the back door.

"I'm set with what I've got, but Margie said if I drove out this way to stop and pick up a dozen for her."

Roger took off his hat and wiped his forehead with the sleeve of his forearm. After a cool morning, the day hat turned hot and humid again. This seesaw weather—mild one week, tropical the next—wore on a person. You couldn't get used to it. Even though many would disagree with him, Roger was starting to prefer winter to summer.

Got time for something to drink?" Marion offered.

"I suppose a glass of water would be good, but I can't stay long."

Inside, Marion got ice from the bowl in the freezer and plunked a couple of cubes in two glasses, then filled them with water. She handed one to Roger, who nearly emptied his glass right away. Marion smiled, held out her hand for the glass to refill it, but he shook his head.

"No. Thanks. This did the trick." Roger pulled a chair out and sat.

He laid his hat on the table.

"Listen, Marion. I didn't come for eggs. This is official business."

The skin on the back of Marion's neck prickled in apprehension. She wondered what he knew. Marion set her glass on the table, held her wrists out for handcuffs. "Going to arrest me, Sheriff?" she asked, smiling. When she saw that her friend did not return the playful gesture, she realized how serious he was. "Is there a problem?"

"I heard you had some company last week."

I knew I shouldn't have told Vivian, she thought, then pulled out the chair opposite Roger and sat down. "It was nothing, Roger. Just a girl."

"Your sister is worried about you. You should have told me. When I came by the other day, you said you hadn't seen anyone suspicious."

"I would hardly call the girl suspicious."

"What would you call her?"

Marion said nothing.

"She's a runaway," Roger said, "and you caught her stealing."

"When you and I were kids we snuck into old lady Brunner's yard and 'stole' apples. Were we thieves?"

"Not the same and you know it. We were just kids."

"That girl wouldn't have hurt me for anything. She is just a lost soul. I gave her food and shelter. Isn't that what we're called to do in this life, Roger?"

"You should have called me," Roger said, rubbing his forehead. "We have agencies for kids who need help." He asked Marion for a couple of aspirin.

She took his glass to refill it, then got the pills.

"Maybe you're right, Roger," she said handing him the aspirin and water. "But I was in no danger. That girl was just a puddle of helplessness."

"Helpless? She was sneaking into gardens, breaking into stores, stealing from cash registers."

"You can't know she did those other things," Marion said, agitated.

Roger asked her if she had searched her house to see if anything was missing. "Most people don't realize things are gone until much later."

She said no.

"A thing might be missing," he said, "and just you think you forgot where you put it."

"Oh Roger, I'm not senile. I know where my things are, and everything is where it is supposed to be."

Roger's tone turned harsh. "Where did that girl come from? Where did she go?" he said.

Marion said she didn't know where the girl had gone and wondered if maybe Roger and Vivian were right. She might have been in more danger than she realized. Bridget did not seem capable of harm, but what might a desperate person do to survive? The characters in the murder mysteries she was fond of reading had often seemed normal, especially at first. The actual murderer was always the person she least expected. The one whose neighbors counted as a quiet, keeps-to-himself kind of person.

"I hear what you're saying Roger, but my instinct says differently."

Roger sighed. "I see I can't protect you from your instinct, but your good sense ought to tell you that if anyone else like that girl shows up, you need to lock your doors and call me right away. I insist on it, Marion."

Marion assured Roger she would do that. Anyway, she thought, no one else would be rummaging through her garden any time soon.

Planning Ahead

MINNEAPOLIS 1968

It was Monday evening, two days since Sparrow's party, and after Steve's phone call, Rob had heard no more about all that ridiculous "rape" trouble. Still, it was not easy letting go of the notion that somewhere in a dimly lit office lawyers might be discussing their strategies to ensnare him. It seemed to Rob that everyone, from Sparrow's rich parents to the United States government, was converging to bury him.

After dinner while his parents watched *Here's Lucy*—yukking it up over her dumb antics—Rob re-packed his duffle bag, shoving the draft notice in first, a roll of emergency cash, then just enough clothes to get by on. That morning he'd gone to the barbershop and told Dean to make him look like he'd just got out of basic training. "Planning ahead, eh, kid?" Dean had said, which made Rob smile. Not the kind of planning you think, Dean old boy.

With all the pieces in place, Rob couldn't wait to get away. One more night, he thought, as he lay on his bed, imagining the days and weeks ahead, mentally walking through different scenarios, including what he'd do if he got pulled over by the cops, how he'd weasel out of things. He'd have to remember to drive like an old lady so he wouldn't be stopped for speeding. At one point Rob considered driving over to Beth's, thinking it would be fun to have her along after all—to keep him company. But her kid, that little bastard, would ruin it.

Later, he tried to fall asleep, but the TV was so fucking loud. Even with his pillow over his head, he could hear every word. His parents didn't turn it off until after Johnny Carson, who was funny and all, but Jesus, his dad was seriously deaf. Even then, Rob couldn't relax, so he opened his window and lit a joint, smoking just enough to calm his nerves.

The next day was Arlene's bridge day, and she kept herself busy all morning tidying the house. She knocked on Rob's bedroom door around 9:00 a.m. to see if he wanted her to make him some breakfast. He yelled that he just wanted to sleep.

"You don't have to be so nasty," she yelled into her hands. She steadied herself against the kitchen counter trying not to cry. Moments later, she pulled on her oven mitts and took the last batch of sugar cookies out of the oven.

When Rob plodded into the kitchen about a half hour later and helped himself to a bowl of Rice Krispies, she tried again at pleasant conversation. This time, he did not give her a hard time. She told him she thought his new haircut looked nice, and he thanked her. Mothers needed so little to make them happy, Rob thought. After he ate, he took a shower, shaved, then wrapped his razor and extra blades in a towel and took them to his room, where he organized his things one last time.

For the role he would soon play, Rob had taken one of his dad's casual shirts—the beige one with a red pin stripe along the collar edge. Over the shirt Rob wore the blue and green plaid sports jacket his mother had made him get for his high school graduation. Without her badgering, he never would have picked out such an old-man jacket, but now Rob was glad he hadn't tossed it in trash. Paired with the polyester shirt, the jacket made him look like a real nerd—one of those guys still living in the fifties who hadn't noticed times had changed. Old guys loved you when you looked like that. You weren't a threat to them, like long-haired hippies were.

Rob waited until 12:30, when his mother and the neighborhood biddies had their butts in their chairs, nibbling egg salad sandwiches. He waited until their first hand of bridge had been dealt to make his move. Rob found his mother's purse in her room and took $8 from her wallet. He left her two singles—just so she wouldn't remember him as completely heartless—then slipped her car key off her key ring, grabbed his jean jacket and duffle bag from his room, and walked quietly through the kitchen, out the back door to the carport where his mother's car was parked. The women paid no attention to him, and he hoped with all their laughter, they wouldn't hear the motor start.

Twenty minutes later, Rob arrived at Lucky Lou's Used Cars in his mother's mist-blue Chevy Bel Air. He pulled up to the bright yellow office hut in the middle of the lot. The salesman, an older guy with sparse graying hair combed over his shiny bald head, leapt out of the office.

"Great day to buy a car," the man said, his hand extended to Rob.

Rob shook the man's hand and took care not to appear too eager to see the salesman.

"I'm Glen Johnson," the salesman said.

"Bob Lang," Rob said, then told the tale he had rehearsed. "This car," he said, patting the fender, "is a beauty and I wouldn't part with it, except, well, we bought it for our fifth anniversary. My wife—. That is, my late wife, chose it. But since she died, I can barely stand to drive it, so I guess I'd like to trade it in, if you've got anything I'd be interested in."

Glen let his chin drop and gave Rob a moment.

"It was cancer," Rob said. "We never saw it coming."

"My deepest condolences," Glen said. "I'll sure do my best to help you out. Christ. That's a tough break."

Glen showed Rob several newer models, but Rob said he was looking for something more economical. Then Glen took him over to a dark blue '64 Ford Falcon. Glen explained that some minor rear end damage had been "fixed up good" by their body shop.

On his test drive, Rob had noticed the gas tank almost on empty, so when Glen was talking up the practicality of the car, Rob said "I don't know. Maybe I oughta wait."

"Listen," Glen said, "if you pull in at the station around the corner, I'll fill 'er up for ya. Will that do it?"

Rob told Glen he was a gentleman for that. "Yes," Rob said. "That would do it."

Back in the office, Glen offered Rob a seat while he put the paperwork together.

"Still seems like I'm getting the better end of the stick," Glen said as Rob signed over the car title to complete the sale. At least his signature, Robert W. Lang, was not a lie. Not technically, anyway. Then Glen counted $250 into Rob's outstretched palm, nearly the entirety of the till. It was the amount they had agreed on to even out the deal.

"No. You did me a favor. This car has too many memories."

Glen reached out and touched Rob on the shoulder. Rob almost recoiled from the gesture, but he remained steady and stayed in character.

"More of her things," Rob said, as he took his duffle bag from his mother's car. "Thrift store next."

Glen nodded his understanding. "You take care now," he said, "and best of luck to you Mr. Lang."

"I won't forget your kindness," Rob said, then he started the engine and drove slowly out of the lot.

Once he was out of Glen's sight, Rob exhaled a deep breath and revved up the engine. This car at least looked like something he might buy on his own. It would do, he thought, for now. He had one more stop before he made his way out of the city for good. At the U.S. Army Surplus and Supply store, Rob bought a new fatigue jacket and two army issue t-shirts. The store clerk, a guy in his fifties, said he was sad to have read in the paper that some of these new boys had been burning all their uniforms when they got home. "If I could, I'd tell 'em that someday they will regret it."

Rob said he had kept all of his stuff. In fact, he was here today because he wanted to get a bit more, because he knew one day his kids would want to see it all and hear his Vietnam stories.

"What was it like?" the man said. "I fought in Okinawa, and that was rough.

Rob said he imagined it was the same.

Outside the store Rob bought a bottle of Coca Cola and drank it in one long gulp. He wiped the sweat from his forehead, then chunked the bottle into the return slot.

Back on the road, Rob drove south towards Iowa. It was 4:30. The air buffeted his open window, but he didn't mind the noise. It sounded like hopeful energy to him. Rob imagined his father coming home from work now, taking a gin and tonic from his wife and asking her where her car was. His mother would look surprised. She'd say Robbie must have taken it. And old Bob would say, "Did he ask you if he could take the car?" Later, when their son had still not returned after dinner, Bob Lang would consider calling the police. But Arlene would argue, he'll be back soon. Despite the scene he imagined, Rob knew it was far more plausible that his father had already phoned the police, so he sped up toward the exit for Albert Lea.

Guard Dog

Roger Armistead quietly led the dog up Marion's porch steps, sure he was overstepping his bounds. The nine-month-old yellow lab had belonged to his deputy Arnie Johnson, whose three-year-old son could not get over his fear of the animal.

"I don't understand it," Arnie had said a week earlier. "Sarge is just the sweetest dog, wouldn't hurt a flea. But he barks at the mailman. Guess that's what scares my boy."

"What you going to do with him," Roger had asked, a plan already simmering in his head.

"I dunno. I guess I could put an ad in the paper. See if anybody wants him. I couldn't put him down." The last word had caught in Arnie's throat and Roger could tell Arnie loved the dog.

Sarge would be a good companion for Marion, not to mention a good guard dog, which she needed even if she would never admit it. Harve and Marion's old golden retriever died about a year before Harve passed. Roger remembered Marion saying something about being too old to break in a new puppy when he had asked if they would get another dog. With Sarge, she wouldn't have that worry.

Roger knocked.

Marion appeared at the screen door, wiping her hands on the red gingham apron tied around her waist. "Afternoon, Roger. Who's your friend?"

"This is Sarge. How're you doing today?"

Marion came out on the porch and bent down to pet the dog.

"You're a pretty boy, aren't you?"

Marion stood tall, every inch of her five-foot nine stature. She inhaled deeply. She knew exactly what Roger was up to. Sarge took a step toward Marion and licked her hand.

"I suppose you're going to make me fall in love with you instantly, aren't you, boy?" She petted Sarge on his head. "Is that the plan Roger?"

Roger's face contorted in a sheepish acknowledgment of the truth. Nothing got past this woman.

"He was—is—Arnie's dog, but it seems he's found himself suddenly homeless."

"Why? What's the problem?"

"Oh, nothing with the dog. It's their kid. Scared to death of him."

Marion rubbed the dog under the chin. "Scared of you, beautiful boy?" Marion said in baby talk.

Sarge barked, not a threatening sound, but as if to say, "I like you."

"His name is Sarge?"

At the mention of his name, Sarge barked again.

"That's right."

Marion laughed. "Of course. A deputy's dog would be called Sarge."

"It's no secret I am worried about your safety, Marion, out here all alone. You think Sarge could help in that regard? Arnie says he's got a strong protective nature."

Marion looked into the dog's luminous chocolate eyes. She had to admit, she often missed having a dog following her around. Marion looked into Roger's eyes.

"I bet you think you're pretty clever, Roger."

"Just saw an opportunity to solve two problems at once."

Marion moved to her rocker and sat down. "Come, Sarge. Come."

Roger let go of the leash and Sarge headed to Marion and sat in front of her. She took his head in her hands and scratched under his floppy ears. "Oh, you like that, don't you, boy?" Sarge laid his head on her lap. "I swear this dog understands everything that's going on here. Spose you didn't bring any food for him?"

"In the car."

"Figures."

Part Two

Fear

At 11 p.m., Terry stood under the pinging spray of a barely warm shower. Afraid he would never come clean, Terry soaped up one more time and rubbed hard, scrubbing away the blood from his hands and the lingering smell of the man himself—aftershave, cigar smoke, sweat.

Terry stepped out of the tub and dried quickly, then put on his kimono. He breathed to calm his pulse that raced, not just from fear, but from uncertainty, not knowing of what he should do next. In the mirror, Terry saw a welt on his cheek he had not noticed earlier. He examined his neck, which had begun to hurt.

In his room now, Terry sat in the dark on his bistro chair by the window and smoked a cigarette. Each wailing siren quickened his pulse. *I need to concentrate. I need to figure this out*, he screamed in his head, but the harder Terry tried to push from his mind what had happened earlier that night, the more it forced itself to the present.

So vivid was the impression of that alley, the pink flickering glow of the neon sign over the liquor store's back door, the dark edges of the alley, a bank of overflowing trash cans, a bulwark of cardboard boxes. More than once Terry had led tricks to this alley because it had provided cover and safety.

The only thing that he could not recall was the man's face. Terry didn't know if that was good or bad. The man had been well dressed, had worn expensive shoes. He was probably used to stepping into board rooms not over garbage. And yet, he'd known to drive to this neighborhood. He'd known exactly what he was seeking, something dangerous, something on the edge. Surely it had thrilled him to step into the shadows. Terry knew about men who found escape by such means. These men were prostitutes' bread and butter, as Donette would say.

Before it all went wrong, Terry had leaned into the man's car window and asked the innocent starter: "You lost?"

"Just looking for my date," came the reply, the appropriate signal.

At first glance, Terry thought this man could easily have engaged a Fifth Avenue hooker, one of those pretty girls dressed as real dates who came to your room. Those girls didn't even look like prostitutes. The hotel managers or concierges who got a cut of the profits always looked the other way.

"What kind of girl do you like?" Terry said. He brushed the bangs of his blonde wig out of his eyes, lashes caked with black mascara, his lids lined heavily, his lips deep red. He wore his purple feather boa to hide his prominent Adam's apple. He wrapped it once around his neck and let it trail below his white patent leather belt. It swayed against his hip bones as he moved.

As Terry worked his angle, the man breathed deeply, not nervously as so many did, but deliberately, as if this moment was part of the adventure and he wanted it to unfold slowly.

"I can be whatever you want," Terry said.

"I want. That is, I need—."

The man took in Terry's modest chest, his face, pretty, feminine, but also the rough evidence of a shaved chin, no matter how carefully covered in makeup. Terry loosened his boa, stood tall in his heels, and stretched his long neck.

"Yes," the man said. "You're exactly my type."

"Ten bucks," Terry said.

The man reached into his jacket and removed a gold money clip. He took out a ten and returned the clip to his inside pocket. He handed the bill to Terry, who took it quickly. The bill was crisp and new, unlike most he accepted, and it refused to lay flat against his skin when he tucked it into his bra.

"Where do we go?" the man asked, urgency now in his voice.

Terry jerked his head toward the alley. "In the alley. I'll be there waiting." Then under the greenish light cast by his windshield, the man's lips curled in a sick smile, his teeth white and perfect. Terry sensed something wasn't right and should have walked away then. He felt a slight prick of apprehension but dismissed it. He had felt worse warnings that turned out to be nothing.

Moments later in the alley, the ten spot still rough against his chest, his backside pressed to the man's hips, Terry did what he always did. He imagined himself on a train, sitting in one of those private compartments like he had seen in movies, just him, traveling alone, out the window a vast, golden prairie. Snowflakes the size of half dollars floated to the ground, his face so close to the window that his breath steamed it over, sometimes so much he had to clear it with the sleeve of his jacket, and when the window was clear again, he watched the sky over distant mountains turn pink and then slowly darken into night. It would be cold outside in his dream, not muggy and sticky like tonight, but a clean kind of cold. Inside the train car, nestled in the velvet seat, Terry was always warm and safe, headed away from everything he had never wanted.

Sometimes after it was over there would be an awkward "thanks," but most of the time shame sent the johns out of the alley ahead of Terry without a word said. At the sound of the man's zipper, Terry stood upright and adjusted his skirt. The boa had fallen from his neck and lay on the ground. He turned to retrieve it, and when he stood up, he was facing the man. Before Terry could react, the man had reached out and had grabbed him by the throat.

"You've been a bad little whore, haven't you?" the man said.

Terry's heart pounded in his ears. The boa fell from his fingers to the ground. With both hands, Terry tried to pry himself free, but the man squeezed tighter. Terry sent his slender arms into flailing punches. He hit and hit, but the world was going black. Terry felt himself go cold just as the man released him and pushed him to the ground, followed by a kick to the ribs. Terry lay, knees curled, struggling to catch his breath. He felt like vomiting, but knew he had to keep his head and find a way to run. Squinting, Terry looked toward the edge of the alley, where the streetlight fell on the empty sidewalk. If only someone would walk by. But even if that happened, Terry wondered if he would be able to scream for help.

The man looked down at Terry, who lay helpless, and laughed. "You going to let that little kick stop you? Oh, come on. It wasn't that bad. I could have done worse."

Terry coughed. His tongue tasted like metal.

"Aren't you going to fight me like a man?" his attacker taunted.

Terry remained mute.

"Answer me," the man growled. Then he reached down and wrenched Terry up by the arm. "Or maybe you really are a little girl after all." The man's grasp tightened on Terry's arm. Then, laughing, he let go.

Terry could barely breathe. He wobbled on one of his high-heeled pumps. The other had slipped off when the man had knocked him down. Then Terry saw the blade gleaming in the dark. Even before he realized what he was doing, Terry took a step back, aimed the pointed toe of his shoe at the man's groin and kicked.

In a glinting arc, the knife fell to the asphalt. Terry saw the blade lying at his feet. He kicked it to the wall and backed away from the man who was grasping at his groin.

"You useless piece of shit," the man said, laboring to breathe. He rose and staggered towards Terry, still clutching his groin.

Terry quickly retrieved the knife. It was a pocketknife, like the one his father used to cut hemp rope to bundle old newspapers, with a large blade that sliced through the thick rope as if it were yarn. Terry held the knife out in front of him now, his hand quivering. Finding his raspy voice, Terry said, "You get out of here."

"What? You gonna kill me?" The man took a deep breath, straightened to his full height, and pulled his unfastened belt from its loops. He stepped closer to Terry and swung the thick leather belt like a whip. The heavy buckle whirred against Terry's cheek.

The stinging sound of the belt was the last sound Terry recalled. After that, the alley became silent. No cars on the street. No voices. No sirens waxing or waning. During those next moments in the damp shadows, neither Terry nor the man seemed even to be breathing.

The man probably never expected Terry to maintain his hold on the knife. He expected to overpower the boy, as he had already done. But as the knife plunged into him, the man fell forward, taking Terry to the ground with him, their bodies collapsing as one.

Once Terry regained his breath, he understood what he had done. At the same time, stillness faded. Voices sounded on the street. The neon light buzzed. A far-off siren blared.

Terry grunted and pushed the man onto his back. Terry rose to his feet, the knife gripped tightly in his hand. A deep red stain saturating the man's white shirt widened near the base of his ribs. Terry wiped the blade on his sweater, already sticky with blood. He closed the knife and slipped it into his skirt pocket. Terry looked around, fearful someone had seen it all, expecting the police to arrive in seconds.

Terry's hands were cold, like winter, and his heart pounded in his ears, telling him urgently to get out of there. He stumbled back a step and gasped. He had brought his heel down on something sharp. A rusty latch. Not glass. No cut. The pain focused his brain and he remembered something. Terry reached into the man's jacket and found the gold money clip. He quickly searched the man's other pockets, but found no wallet, nothing but the man's keys. Taking them but not the car seemed like trouble. And yet he had touched them, so he slipped the keys with the money clip into the pocket of his skirt. Police would think it had been a robbery.

Terry found one of his shoes at the base of the brick wall. The other was under the man's leg. He slipped them on and stood, unsure of what to do next. Terry knew he couldn't leave the alley looking like he did. He pulled his sweater off, thinking he would wear it inside out, but the blood had soaked through the flimsy knit. His boa would cover it, he thought, but where was his boa? He saw it lying beyond the man's body and he walked around the man to retrieve it. As he shook the feathers free of alley grit, Terry heard a subdued grunt, then a moan. He wasn't dead. What if the man survived and identified him? Terry thought about the knife. Finish him off. But no. Terry was not a killer.

Another siren squealed, this one closer. Fear rose in Terry's throat, tasting of bile. He had to hurry. He walked through the alley, away from the street where it had all begun such an endless short time ago.

Blocks later, Terry threw his shoes, sweater, bra, boa, and wig in a sparking trash barrel and watched them burn. Even though he wore a skirt, anyone who happened to see him emerge from the alley would remember a dark-haired, shirtless young man. As he passed the river, Terry threw the keys and the knife over the railing. He watched the ripples in the water expand until they disappeared into the river's surface. Then he turned toward home.

Terry finished his cigarette, his nerves only slightly calmer. With each passing hour, he felt removed from the possibility someone had seen him escort the man into the alley. Terry worked different corners because he did not want to be a regular face anywhere, but people knew him. People knew he was Donette's boy. He stared at the money clip, fat with bills, new bills. He would use it to get away. By the time anyone did connect him with the man in the alley, if they did, he'd be far away from New York.

Terry heard Donette come in. He hid the money clip under his bedspread and turned off the lamp. He lay down and drew up his knees. She sometimes checked on him before she went to bed, just to make sure he was home safe. She said she had a hard time getting to sleep if she knew he was still out there on the streets. Terry heard her footsteps approaching, his door creaked open, then softly closed. Moments later, she closed her own door.

He had nothing to fear from Donette, but Terry dreaded facing her. He would write her a note explaining why he had gone. He didn't think she would, but she might tell him it would be best to go to the police on his own. It was an accident, she'd say. Self-defense. Both true, but Terry had no intention of giving her a chance to make that argument. He planned to be gone before daylight.

Terry turned the lamp back on, retrieved the money clip and counted the bills: $324. It was a fortune. With his own savings, he had enough to leave Donette his share of next month's rent, and still have plenty to get him wherever he wanted to go.

Terry lay on his bed, dressed in jeans and a t-shirt, foundation smeared over his cheek and neck to camouflage the worsening purple. The Baby Ben on the orange crate said 1:45 a.m. By 4:30, he would be out the door and on his way. Willing himself not to fall asleep, Terry watched moonlit clouds out his window and listened to the sounds of the night.

Donette's knock and her standard "yoo hoo" woke Terry, who had been struggling in a dream to loosen himself from a chokehold. His faceless attacker wore a black hooded cloak, and Terry could discern only the sickening sweet smell of aftershave and cigar smoke. Eyes open now, Terry stared at the ceiling and breathed slowly, trying to shake off the nightmare. When it finally registered it was morning and he was still home, Terry leapt out of bed, sorry instantly that he had done so, for he had never been more sore. Twelve thirty? "Shit," he said. "Shit!"

When Terry emerged from his room, Donette greeted him.

"Morning, Sunshine. You hear the ruckus this morning? Maybe not. You been dead to the world, it seems. I was getting worried. Anyway, Super figured our hot water problem had to be a clogged shower head.

Who ever heard of that? You should've seen him tapping on it a couple of times with his big ole wrench. When he turned the water on to see the miracle—." She laughed. "Nothing, of course. I swear, I could do his job better. So, he finally hooked up a new water heater I bet he's had down there for a week. Cheap bastard. Not like it's his money was spent on the thing. Anyway, we got hot water, finally. Hooray!"

Terry smiled and saw the coffee pot was empty. He'd just have juice.

Donette's head was still wrapped in her towel turban. She was at the kitchen table filing her nails. "You slept a long time, honey. Bad night?"

Terry's chest prickled in fearful recollection. He glugged the orange juice and poured more. "Normal, I guess."

"You sure?"

"Yeah."

"Maureen called this morning. Since it's such a nice day, she thought we should blend in with the tourists and go see the Statue of Liberty. Or take the Staten Island Ferry for a ride. You wanna come?" she said, in a coaxing tone.

Terry knew how much Donette loved to observe tourists and try to figure out where they came from. She'd look at what they wore and listen to how they spoke. If she felt like having fun with them, she'd role play characters. Once she and her friend Maureen pretended they were sisters whose father had just died and they were on their way to the funeral home on Long Island. They had a group of women from Michigan in tears over their story. When they told it to Terry later, after a few whiskey sours, they nearly fell on the floor laughing.

"It'll be fun."

"No."

"Suit yourself."

The flat was empty by 1:30. Terry paced the floor. Flashes of what had happened the night before tormented him and turned his stomach into a knot. He expected any minute the police to break down the door and wrestle him to the ground. They'd manhandle him, twist his wrists into handcuffs, and tell him he was despicable. How could he have attacked such a great man? A tremendous supporter of the police. In the jail cell, his wrists turning purple, Terry would shiver and shake and curl into a ball.

Terry climbed into the shower, this time as hot as he could stand it, and let the water rush over him. After, he stood with his head against the tile and let the water drip from his body. After, he sat in his kimono on the balcony outside his bedroom window and smoked a cigarette. Then another. In the garden below, two gray squirrels scampered around the roots of a spindly Japanese Maple the super had planted last summer. Terry loved that tree. He felt it was like him, in a way, struggling and out of place.

He had to get out of New York. There was no questioning that, but if he left now, Sanchez would see him, other girls he knew might wonder about his bag. The cops might be on the streets, questioning people. Had anyone seen anything suspicious? Terry wondered if the man had survived. Given a description of him. No. He couldn't leave in the bright glare of daylight. He would have to wait until the next morning, and he would set his alarm this time, tucking it under his pillow so it wouldn't wake Donette when it went off.

That afternoon, Terry kept busy dusting the furniture and running the carpet sweeper over the rugs. He made himself a peanut butter sandwich, the first thing he'd had in his stomach since the orange juice. He found he could only choke down a few bites. He wasn't hungry, and it hurt to swallow.

To pass time after the cleaning was done, he tried to read. His books were packed in his duffle, so he looked through Donette's magazines. But everything he tried to distract him from his obsessive thoughts failed. Eventually, he stretched out on the couch and stared at the ceiling. He played a mental game, the same one he had played as a child. The ceiling became his home, the white expanse the floor of his alternate universe. Arranging and rearranging fictional furniture quieted him and he fell asleep. When Donette arrived home at six, Terry didn't hear her.

"Terry, honey," Donette said, touching his shoulder.

His eyes opened, dry and sore. When he swallowed, it hurt. He hoisted himself and sat on the edge of the couch, his head in his hands. Then, he sat back, looked at her, and forced a smile.

"How were the tourists?" he said.

"Tourists were fine. How about you tell me about your neck? How about you tell me what the hell happened to you?"

Terry reached up, put his hands to his throat, realized he'd forgotten to reapply the makeup. Donette's eyes were full of concern and worry. She sat next to him.

"Tell me," she said.

Bus Ticket

New York 1968

Donette knew the alley near the liquor store where Terry had been attacked, so she had no trouble imagining every detail as he told her what had happened. Her shoulders shook in an empathetic shiver. "Men like that," she said, "good riddance."

They sat in the kitchen. Terry finished his sandwich. Donette poured the rest of a bottle of Pepsi over the ice in her glass.

"But he could be alive," Terry said, expressing the fear that nagged at him. "If he tells the police?"

"I think we would've heard, don't you?" Donette said. Such stories didn't take long to circulate. "Besides. They would be looking for a blonde, right?"

That did not mean Terry would be safe from then on. While neither one wanted it to be true, they knew Terry would have to leave New York.

"Now. Let's figure this out," she said.

First they gathered his skirts and scarves, his other two wigs, and his makeup kit. Donette said she would burn it all later in the incinerator out back with the rest of their trash. He told her about the keys and the knife.

"Good thinking," she said. "They'll just sink into that stinking muck like every other evil thing people dump into that river."

He told her about the money clip, about how much money he had in all. "I'm going to pay my rent share for a few months. I don't want you to suffer because of me."

She shook her head. "No, no, no," she said. "You going to need that money. Maybe more. But you better give me that clip. I think that thing ought to go in the river too."

Terry slipped the clip off the money and handed it to her. "Too bad," he said. "I think it's gold. Probably worth a bundle on its own."

"That's all right," she said. "Better it disappears."

She sat on the edge of the bed next to Terry. "You kept out enough makeup for that neck, right? It's going to be a while before those bruises heal. It's probably best you take a late bus. If it's dark, people won't be able to get a good look at you, if they cared to."

Terry was grateful Donette was there, helping him think logically. His brain still refused to focus. His nerves refused to calm.

"And the hardest part, you need to figure out where to go. If I were you, I'd head home. You're going to need your family."

She put her arms around him and pulled her to him. "It's going to be okay. I just know it will."

After Terry had gone to bed, Donette got ready for work. She met Maureen on their usual corner. If Maureen had heard about a stabbing, she'd be dying to tell Donette the news.

Donette gave her friend a hug. "You smell good," she said. "What's new?"

Maureen lit a cigarette. "Heard last night a wagon took in those girls who work near the pawn shop," Maureen said. "They'll be right back, though, so same old shit."

"Yeah," Donette said. "Same old shit."

A car pulled up and Maureen leaned in. A moment later she stood up. "He say he want the tall one," she said, glancing back at Donette.

"Unh uh, Sugar," Donette said from the curb. "Not tonight. Got me a ragin' headache."

The man drove off.

"Well, thanks for nothing, girl," Maureen said.

Donette apologized, then played up the headache. "I guess I better get on home," she said. "Let you earn some spendin' money."

"Go on then," Maureen laughed. "See you tomorrow."

On her way home, Donette threw the empty money clip into the river. "Someday, somebody's going to find a whole lot of crazy down there," she said out loud.

The next afternoon while Terry organized his things one last time, Donette made fried chicken.

"Gotta put a good meal in you before you leave me," she said.

Terry picked at his food. He just wasn't hungry. They talked about what Terry would do when he got home.

"Go back to school and get your diploma," Donette said. "You go on and be a writer. Tell my story maybe one day."

Terry told her he liked that idea.

"I mean it, though," she said. "Sometimes people say they gonna do things, but then they don't."

At eight, Donette went with Terry to the Port Authority bus terminal, waited while he bought his ticket, then sat with him until boarding time. She ruffled his hair, which she had trimmed that morning.

"You look a little like Bob Dylan now," she said. "You're skinny like him." She smiled. Her Terry had grown into a good-looking man when nobody was looking, she thought.

When it was time for his bus to depart, they stood aside while other passengers boarded.

"Honey," she said. "You were never meant for this life. No one is."

Tears welled in his eyes. It was all he could do to hold back sobs. Donette meant more to him than anyone he had ever known, and he did not want to leave her.

"I will call," he said, picking up his bag.

In her pocket she touched the paper with the address of Terry's father's house that she had forced him to give her.

"You better. Don't you become a ghost to me," she said.

Terry chose a window seat four rows behind the bus driver. His duffle worked well for a footrest. The late bus to Chicago filled up quickly, but there were still a few vacant seats and Terry was grateful no one had taken the one next to him. When they arrived at Union Station in Chicago the next afternoon, he planned to take a train to Elmwood Park and wander around his old neighborhood. He hadn't planned everything out yet, but the eighteen-hour trip would give him time to think.

The bus driver closed the door. "Just sit back and enjoy the ride," he said to his passengers." He turned the coach lights off and pulled out of the terminal. From the platform, Donette waved.

Terry was full of adrenaline and possibility. As they entered the Lincoln Tunnel, he was just as amazed as the first time he had seen it, amazed that humans could build such a thing, a steel and concrete passage under water that would awe even the ancient Romans.

When they emerged from the tunnel, they were in New Jersey, a state Terry knew little of, beyond eighth grade social studies and geography—Washington's victory at the battle of Trenton, Aaron Burr and Alexander Hamilton's duel at Weehawken, Edison's inventions at Menlo Park. He knew that Allen Ginsberg was from Paterson, where William Carlos Williams also lived and worked.

Terry had first become familiar with Williams in ninth grade English, when his teacher handed out short poems for the class to memorize. He had been given Williams' poem, "Blizzard." The day he was to stand at the podium and recite the poem, school had been canceled due to an actual blizzard.

When he laughed at the news and tried to explain to his mother why it was funny, she did not appreciate the irony. Instead, she told him

"If he thought he was just going to lay around the house all day, he had another think coming."

As Terry shoveled the driveway later that morning, it came to him that Williams' description of trees matched what he saw—black, wet bark, the long-fingered boughs of wide elms arching over the street, dark against the blue-gray sky, and he spoke the lines of the poem into the cold air.

"Hairy looking trees stand out
in long alleys
over a wild solitude."

His teacher had told them that when they memorized a poem, it belonged to them forever. "Blizzard" belonged to him then and it belonged to him now, especially the last line. Terry had often felt himself in "a wild solitude," even before he had words to express it. He had been alone most of his life, one way or another, but the last few years at home—the place where you're supposed to belong—were the most isolating of all. When you can tell no one what is happening to you or how awful it makes you feel, that's another kind of blizzard entirely.

The bus stopped at a traffic light. The taillights of nearby cars glowed orange-red. Across the aisle, a woman spoke to the man seated next to her.

"Did you know we're on The Lincoln Highway?"

"Yes, Dear," the man said impassionately.

"It goes all the way to California," she said. "I just find that interesting, is all."

The man patted her on the hand, then pressed his head back on the headrest. The woman shifted her body toward the aisle, where she noticed Terry and smiled. The bus engine chugged and they were moving again.

There are a lot of ways to be lonely, Terry thought, before covering his shoulders with his jacket and closing his eyes.

Rivals

Vivian apologized to Marion, saying she had hoped they would have been able to sit out on the porch after dinner and enjoy a nice summer night. She built a fire inside instead. A cold front from Canada had dropped the temperature by thirty degrees.

"You can't control the weather, Viv," Marion said.

"I know that," Vivian said, her tone sounding more hurt than it should have.

Sensing the tension, Marion said she didn't mind being indoors. "At least indoors, we won't have to fight off bugs," she said.

"True enough," Vivian said, then insisted Marion sit and relax while she got dessert and coffee.

With Sarge at her heels, Marion headed to the living room, clicked on a lamp, and chose the peach and green floral armchair she favored. In some ways Marion envied Vivian's elegant but comfortable living room. She envied her whole house, for that matter. Vivian had a knack for decorating, a fact Marion often stated and Vivian always diminished. In many ways Vivian's life had been picture perfect, scenes from a magazine.

Marion didn't like being envious. She didn't like that she often felt at odds with her older sister. They had been close as girls, closer as teens. It was Vivian who taught Marion how to drive their family's Model T when Marion was only fifteen. It had scandalized their mother but had brought the two sisters closer than ever.

Then a stupid thing pulled them apart. A new boy in school had started to show interest in Marion, but Vivian interceded and took him for herself. "You're far too young for boys, anyway," Vivian had told Marion. It had hurt then, and it hurt for years afterward. Then Vivian married Carl Michaels, a lawyer from a well-to-do family. Their mother praised the match and said Marion could only hope to do as well. Vivian was often considered the better looking of the two girls, and apparently their mother thought so too. Later, when Marion brought Harvard Goodman home to meet her parents, her mother's stiff, polite manner, opposite to the effusiveness she had shown Carl, made Marion resent her sister even more. Vivian could hardly be accountable for their mother's pettiness, but old wounds heal slowly.

Vivian served the coffee and tea first, then came back with dessert plates. "I know you like mother's chocolate walnut cake."

"I do," Marion said. "Thanks, Viv."

Vivian set a large dog biscuit in front of Sarge. He nosed cautiously at the treat before pawing it toward himself, licking it, then crunching it in a manner of seconds.

"So sweet of you to remember the dog, Viv," Marion said.

"He's growing on me, I guess. I suppose I ought to show him I'm a friend."

Marion reached down and rubbed the dog's neck. "You like Vivvy, don't you, boy?"

"I haven't heard that name in a long time," Viv said. "Harve always called me that. Remember? Though I think when he said it he was teasing me."

"Oh, I don't think so Viv. He was fond of you."

"I suppose. He was a nice man." Vivian set her empty plate on the table and picked up her teacup. The fire crackled as the logs burned. Sarge, who had been lying near the fire, moved away from the intense heat.

"You were lucky," Vivian said.

"How's that?"

"You married the man you deserved, instead of the man you fell in love with."

Marion frowned. "I was in love with him," she said, not at all sure what her sister meant by the remark.

"That's not—. I don't quite know what I mean." Vivian turned her teacup in her hand. "Harve was a good man and he loved you," she said. "It was plain for anyone to see. He loved you with all his heart. And I doubt that man had a selfish bone in his body. And you, my dear sister, are a good person, and you deserved a good man."

Marion saw that her sister's cheeks were splotched red, her eyes welling with water. "Well, thanks Viv. But you—."

Sarge gave a low chuff, a precursor to a warning bark. He had heard something outside that alarmed him and now he stood at the front door, whining to be let out.

Vivian got up to open the door for him "You go on out now and see what all the fuss is about."

She turned to Marion. "He won't run off, will he?"

"If he does, he'll find his way back. I wouldn't worry about him."

"While I'm up," Vivian said, "I'll unplug the coffee pot, unless you want another cup?"

Marion said no, any more would keep her awake all night.

When Vivian returned, she heard Sarge already back at the door. She let him in and returned to her chair. The dog followed her, and this time when he nudged her hand, she petted him. Then feigning annoyance, she told him to lie down. She was pleased he obeyed her.

"Who would have thought it, Viv, but you really are getting soft on that dog."

"Well, he's a good boy, aren't you?"

"I thought you and Carl were happy, Vivian. You always seemed so," Marion said.

Vivian smiled. "He made a good living. Gave me everything I ever wanted, even things I had no use for." She tipped her cup to her lips even though it had been empty for some time.

"I have come to realize," she said, then paused, as if the words she wanted to say were probably best left unsaid, "that Carl's death was the best thing that ever happened to me."

"Viv. you don't mean it," Marion said.

"I do. I mean it with all my heart. You don't know what it was like, Marion. I was a good wife. I did what was expected. I gave him everything, but he was never satisfied. I was never good enough. He could be unkind. Out of the blue he'd say my cooking was horrible. Or he'd tell me I was getting fat and ought to exercise more. But worst of all, he ignored me."

"I'm sure it wasn't that bad," Marion said.

Vivian looked into her sister's face. She shook her head. "No, because he was charming to you. And Mother loved him. I guess I just had to work harder at being happy in my marriage than you did."

"Not this again," Marion said. "Aren't we too old for such petty rivalry?"

"I'm not jealous, if that's what you think," Vivian said. "That's not what I meant."

"Well, what did you mean?" Marion insisted.

"Nothing. I didn't mean anything."

"Come now, Viv. Tell me what this is all about." Marion stared into her sister's eyes, willing a truthful answer.

"I guess I just wanted you to know—."

Vivian rose and gathered her dirty dishes. "I suppose you'd better be on your way Marion. I hate you have to drive home in the dark."

Marion got up, went to her sister, and put her arms around her. "I love you, Viv. I really do. You deserve to be happy. I'm sorry if you weren't."

Vivian squeezed her sister tightly, then stepped away, and wiped her eyes. "Let's just stop this now. We're foolish old women, aren't we Sarge?" Vivian said.

Minutes later, with Sarge in the passenger seat and extra cake on the floor in a Tupperware container, Marion started her truck. She thanked her sister for a nice evening.

"We'll talk again soon," Marion said.

Vivian nodded. "Yes. Soon."

After Marion's taillights were no longer visible, Vivian closed the door and locked it. She drew the living room drapes and turned out the lights. In bed, she spoke into the darkness. "I can never tell you, Marion, the worst of it, but you must know people aren't always what they seem." Maintaining the pretense that she was living the perfect life had worn her down. Of course she had been jealous of Marion. How could she not? But she had come to realize more and more that she needed her sister. Throughout her marriage to Carl, Vivian had been lonely. She was tired of being lonely. It would be hard to mend old grudges, but she was going to try.

Elmwood Park

Chicago Suburbs 1968

The train to the northwest suburbs rocked and clacked against the rails. At each stop, new passengers filed down the aisle and found their seats, filling in the empty spaces around Terry. Others gathered their things and exited. Then the train lunged ahead. There were only four more stops before the station in Elmwood Park and Terry had still not decided what he would do. When he left New York, the assumption was that he would go home to his father's house. But Terry had not spoken to either of his parents in two and a half years. He was no longer the child he was when his father had last seen him. The longer Terry was away from his family, the easier it was for him to push them out of his mind. He thought it was possible that his father would be glad to see him and be grateful that Terry had chosen to return to him and not his mother. Over time, Terry realized his mother had treated his father unfairly, exaggerating his faults.

Terry's stomach churned with anxiety at the inevitability of having to explain where he had been, though he had already calculated his response. It would not be lying to say he'd been rooming with friends in New York, making ends meet. He would say he'd worked at a little grocery store, which was partially true, since he had helped out at Sanchez's bodega now and then. They didn't need to know the rest.

As the train approached the station, it slowed, and summer life in

Elmwood Park came into focus. A boy popped a wheelie on his bike. A woman in a polka dot dress hurried behind a dog that looked to be dragging her. A group of teen girls stood in a circle on a street corner. A young child in a red ball cap held his mother's hand as they waited to cross the street. But this was not New York. Despite what had happened there, the East Village felt like home to Terry, while Illinois had become a foreign land.

A sandwich board on the sidewalk outside Wingate's Diner advertised *Tuesday's Special: Polish Sausage and Sauerkraut.* A bell rang as he entered the diner—only the waitress in her pale blue uniform looked up to acknowledge him. He slid into a booth, took a menu from the holder, and looked over his other choices.

The waitress set a glass of water on the Formica-topped table, a gray and green pattern that looked like interlocking boomerangs. If she questioned the overstuffed duffle bag on the bench next to him, she didn't ask. He told her he'd take the special. She scribbled on her pad, gave him a wink, then went to the raised counter by the kitchen to hand the slip to the cook.

Terry observed a group of noisy teens crowded into the corner booth near the front window. A muscular, sandy haired boy told a joke. They all laughed as if they had nothing to fear, nothing to worry about.

Before the food came, Terry went to the pay phone near the restrooms and dialed Donette's number.

"I made it, Donnie. I'm safe."

"Oh, Terry honey. It's good to hear your voice. I'm so glad you called to let me know. You at your daddy's?"

"No, not yet. Tonight. When he gets home from work. Probably."

"Now, don't you change your mind and start wandering all over."

"Is there any news?" Terry asked.

"Not a thing. No mention of a stabbing. I been thinking. What if that crazy bastard got up and walked out of that alley and never even called the police?"

"Why would he do that?"

"East Village hookers aren't the only ones who'd rather not have dealings with the police," she said.

The operator broke in and told Terry to put more coins in the phone. He dropped the coins in the slot.

"Guess I better go," Terry said.

"You just take care of yourself."

He promised her he would then set the receiver back in the cradle. Ten cents fell into the coin return.

Terry returned to his booth and ate. He found he was famished, finally. It was a good, safe feeling to be hungry, he thought. Even so, he turned down a piece of apple pie. At the cash register, as the waitress readied to count back his change, Terry told her to keep it. She'd been kind, and Terry knew how hard she worked.

"Thanks," she said. "Have a good evening."

"You, too," Terry said.

He walked along the main drag for a while. He passed a young couple out for a walk. He didn't recognize them, but why would he? He hadn't lived in this town for over eight years. Before long, the streetlights lit his path over heaved-up sidewalks, crowns of concrete over tree roots. Terry was now in a neighborhood he knew. One of his sister's friends had lived in a small white house he recognized. The house looked the same. All the houses looked the same.

Terry thought it was possible there were neighborhoods like this in every town. Blocks and blocks of one-story homes in the suburbs, built after the war, now dwarfed by giant elms and maples, inhabited by families who hoped to send their kids to college. Strict but loving parents, copies of Ward and June Cleaver. Or was that all an illusion? Maybe some of the fathers were more like his own, running away from something they couldn't fathom. You can't see happiness, Terry thought, by how nice a house looks.

A subconscious impulse steered Terry down Niagara Street. The houses glowed with yellow lamp light. In the middle of the block, Terry stopped and stood on the sidewalk outside of his father's house. The living room drapes were drawn, but dim light shone through the front door sidelight. There was no way of knowing if his father was awake.

"Not yet," he said, the night insects his only audience. "I can't. Not yet."

Fifteen minutes later, he strode across the high school baseball field, then down the steps into the home-team dugout. Terry lay on the bench and rested his head on his duffle. He looked across the field, the infield grass green, even in the moonlight, the curve of the mound obscuring a billboard on the outfield fence. Terry smiled. He remembered the night his friend Dennis and he had found a firecracker on the sidewalk. Dennis was thirteen, Terry nine, friends because their fathers worked together.

"Let's light it," Dennis said. "We'll find a place after dark."

Terry was unsure. He said firecrackers were dangerous and could blow your fingers off.

"That what your mother told you?" Dennis said. "You chicken?"

Terry shook his head. They would meet near the ball field after dinner.

The boys stood near home plate. A full moon was rising in the east. Dennis showed Terry the book of matches he had taken from his father's desk. On the cover was a dark-haired girl in a grass skirt. "Hula dancer," Dennis said, smirking, then rubbing his hands over his chest, alluding to her flower-covered breasts. Out on the field, Terry set the firecracker on the pitcher's mound, embedding it in the dirt like a candle on a birthday cake.

"After I light it," Dennis said, "run like hell." The match flame lit the twilight, then the fuse, sending sparks into the dark. The beauty mesmerized them.

"Run," Terry screamed.

They weren't even close to the dugout when the firecracker exploded. At the sound the boys fell to the ground pretending they'd been shot. They rolled in agony until their groans turned to laughter.

Afterward Dennis and Terry huddled in the dugout in the dark, each knowing their mothers had been out on their front stoops calling for their sons to come home. Mocking their mothers, the boys shouted "Dennis" then "Terry," their voices fading over the field. For the rest of that summer, Terry remembered, he had kept his eyes on the ground, searching for another firecracker.

Settling In

AMES, IOWA 1968

Six and a half hours after he had stolen his mother's car and most of her money, Rob pulled into the Hawkeye Motor Inn, just north of Ames, Iowa. He signed the register using his mother's maiden name. The motel manager, a woman in her sixties who wore her long gray hair straight down, noticed Rob's fatigue jacket.

"Army?" she asked.

"Yeah," he said. "Just got home a couple of weeks ago. "I'm out on the road trying to find myself."

"There's a lot of that going on with young people these days," she said, "though I'm not sure what it means. I never once thought of having to go looking for who I am." She winked when she said it and told him that she hoped he'd be comfortable and to let her know if he needed the slightest thing.

Bob Rogan's room, #5, came with a kitchenette, which was just a small refrigerator and counter with a single sink, a hot plate, and an electric coffee pot. The lower cabinet was stocked with white china, four plates, four bowls, four coffee cups, and a mishmash of silverware. A shelf above held salt and pepper shakers and a framed needlepoint canvas that read *"Home Away From Home."*

The room was stuffy, but otherwise clean. It smelled like furniture polish and scouring powder. A square picture window gave Rob a wide view of his car in the gravel parking lot, the highway, and a vast corn field west of the road. To each side of the big window were narrow casement windows, which he cranked open, grateful for the fresh air. He clicked on one of the bedside table lamps. An oil painting of snow-covered mountains hung over the double bed, which passed a quick test for comfort. After washing up, Rob walked the quarter mile down the road to Millie's Home Cooking for supper. The special was her "world-famous" meatloaf and mashed potatoes, which was surprisingly good. Much better than what his mother made.

Back in #5, Rob turned down the dark gold bedspread and pulled back the blanket and sheet. In bed, the lamp off, Rob stared out the window and watched the sky turn from deep pink to black. He had never been alone like this before, not just away from family, but away from everyone he knew, away from everything he knew. It wasn't a bad feeling, just disquieting. It also empowered him, knowing he could remake himself however he wished.

The next morning Rob slept late. Back at Millie's, he ordered the Wednesday lunch special, a breaded and deep-fried pork tenderloin sandwich. After lunch, Rob drove into town to reconnoiter. That had been his father's word for exploring a new town, and instantly Rob regretted using it. Rob discovered that Ames was a college town, a fact that seemed advantageous, as he would easily blend in with others his age and be less likely to raise suspicion from local residents who might otherwise notice a stranger. Downtown, he stopped at a crosswalk and watched a clutch of college-age girls cross the street. Dressed in plaid shorts and sleeveless blouses, ponytails bouncing as they walked, they moved like a school of fish, darting in unison whenever anything got in their way. They seemed like the girls he had known in high school, all planning to be secretaries, or nurses, each one as cold as the next.

Near campus, summer workers were busy mowing the expansive lawns surrounding Lake LaVerne. From Union Drive he spotted a group of teenagers idled on a blanket near the shore. Rob considered parking nearby, so he could casually wander past them and ask if they had any pot or knew where he could score some. But he thought better of that plan. Keeping a low profile, at least for now, was what he needed to do.

After filling up with gas, Rob pulled into the parking lot of a Hy-Vee supermarket. Midmorning, the store was loaded with women who looked like his mom, from their floral dresses belted tightly at the waist and their short, curled hair to their cat-eye glasses and gold-clasp purses. They smiled kindly at Rob as he pushed his cart and pulled things from the shelves—a loaf of bread, a jar of mustard, a package of bologna, a bag of potato chips. Behind him in line at the checkout, two women nattered on about the price of pork loin.

By Friday, Rob was bored. All he did was spend his afternoons in the motel, watching soap operas on a little black and white TV. *As the World Turns* was the show his mother liked best, and he had seen parts of it his whole life. He knew the main characters and their ongoing problems. The plots had changed very little over the years, much like his life, until now.

So far, there had been no police at his door, no news in the local paper, nothing on the radio to make him think anyone was after him. Rob thought his parents might just let the matter go, figuring that sooner or later their son would return. He hoped that would be the case, but another, more likely notion, continued to nag at Rob. It would be just like his dad to casually show up at the draft office, just to inquire about whether or not a Robert W. Lang, Jr. had received a notice. And the bastards might just tell him how they had sent a second notice— and were, in fact, expecting the young Mr. Lang to report any day now. And his dad just might tell the army that even though Robert W. Lang, Jr. was his son, the boy had been missing for several days. "AWOL. Isn't that what you fellows call it?" his dad would say. Yeah, Rob, thought bitterly, that's probably exactly how it would go. Rob calculated he had about three weeks until he officially became a draft dodger.

Around eight p.m. Rob dressed in a striped t-shirt and jeans and drove out to the roadside bar he had passed on his way into town.

"Popular place," he said, as he pulled into the nearly full lot at The Wagon Wheel. On the sign advertising live music, a cowboy boot was lit in neon lights. He squeezed into a spot under a pole light swarming with insects. He had never been a fan of country music, but his mother loved it. He thought about how she had constantly played her favorite Hank Williams record on the Hi-Fi, not even caring that "Your Cheatin' Heart" had a scratch in it. When it skipped, she just went over and manually moved the tone arm. It was kind of annoying.

Tonight, as advertised, a live band was on stage. The Barroom Boys were full-out country, with their elaborately stitched and polished pointy-toed cowboy boots, Levi's, and western shirts—the yokes embroidered in flowering cactuses—and of course, bolo ties. Rob thought they must be sweaty as hell under their ten-gallon hats, or whatever they were. A few people were dancing close to the stage, mostly older couples, and one couple was showing off with twirls and fancy moves. Rob hated that crap. His mother had always tried to make him dance with her in the living room when he was little and it had embarrassed the hell out of him.

Rob wedged his way through to the bar and stood next to a cute, curly blonde, who moved to make room for him. He smiled and waited for the bartender. He could see how much the girl liked this band, so when they finished their mediocre version of "Lovesick Blues," Rob clapped hard and put two fingers to his mouth and blew a shrill whistle of appreciation.

"Aren't they great," said the blonde.

"Amazing," Rob said.

She nodded, then sipped her drink, some pinkish thing with a long straw.

"You need another one of those?" Rob asked. "I'd be happy to buy it for you. Or are you here with someone?"

"I came with my roommate, but, you know."

Rob ordered himself a tap beer and "whatever that is," he said, nodding to the girl's drink.

"A Miller and a Sea Breeze. Got it, Joe," said the bartender, a paunchy older guy with a crew cut.

A Sea Breeze. Rob was amused. Smack in the middle of the Midwest about as far from an ocean as you could get. Well, it didn't matter.

"What's your name?" the girl said.

"Donovan," Rob replied.

"Like the singer?"

"Yep. Co-inky-dink, huh," Rob said, "seeing as how we're listening to music and all.

"Do you sing, too?"

Man, this chick would probably believe it if he told her he did, Rob thought.

"Unfortunately, I was not blessed with that gift." Rob offered his hand. "And you are—?"

Giggling, she said, "I'm Mandy" and held her hand out, limp at the wrist.

"Nice to meet you, Mandy."

He declined her suggestion that they dance, saying he didn't want to step all over her feet.

"You're funny," she said.

They sat at the bar, listened to the music, and watched the crowd swell. He told her he was new in town, that he would be a transfer student when the fall term started. He said he was looking for a job in the meantime.

"Too bad there's not an opening at the record store where I work," she said. "But I'm sure you'll find something."

"Thanks," Rob said. "I'm sure I will." When the band played the first few notes of a song he didn't recognize, he said, "I dig this one, don't you?"

She leaned into his ear, so close he could feel her breath hot against his neck. "Yeah. It's great," she said.

After the bartender sat Mandy's fourth Sea Breeze on the bar, the band took a break. In the relative quiet, Mandy's roommate and a long-haired young man in a weathered jean jacket wound their way to the bar.

"Thish is Carol," Mandy said. "And Gary."

Rob said hello.

"How ya doin' man," Gary said, taking Rob's hand in an amiable grip.

Carol said hello cautiously. Then she took Mandy's hand and leaned in. "You've had a few, huh?" she said.

Rob thought Carol was the kind of girl who already looked like she was someone's mom and acted like it, too. But the four of them conversed casually, despite the tension and once the music started up again, there was no need to fill the silence.

Twenty minutes later, Mandy leaned over to Carol and told her she didn't feel so good. Carol led Mandy to the ladies room. When they rejoined the guys at the bar a bit later, Carol told Gary they needed to get Mandy home. Carol thrust Mandy's purse into Gary's hands and pulled her friend toward the door. Mandy did not want to leave.

"Bye, Donovan," Mandy said, with a flaccid wave. "Maybe I'll shee you around?"

Rob said he hoped so, then watched as Carol maneuvered Mandy through the crowd and out the door. After one more beer and no other prospects, Rob drove back to the motel.

Reunion

Terry woke up cold and stiff and walked out to the pitcher's mound to loosen his joints. Back in the dugout, he ate the rest of the of cookies he had bought the day before. It was early, and he had an entire day to fill before finally facing his father.

During the night he had decided to find his old friend, Dennis. It might be nice to have a friend. Terry was eight years old when he met Dennis Madson, the son of his father's co-worker. Dennis's family moved into Terry's neighborhood when Dennis was twelve. Not only was Dennis older, but he was a natural athlete, whereas Terry was a natural bookworm.

When the families got together for a picnic or a work event, Dennis's latest athletic achievements were presented to Terry as a model to follow. It helped on Terry's end to know that Dennis was humiliated by his father's constant fawning. Dennis told Terry once that he thought his dad was more excited than he was for Dennis to play football in high school because his dad had been a perennial bench player. When the head football coach pulled Dennis off the freshman team to practice with the varsity team, Terry heard about it for weeks from his own dad, who admired things like that.

The two boys got along well, despite their differences, and they stayed friends when Dennis started high school. Dennis would drop by Terry's house sometimes after school and the two would hang out in Terry's basement, playing board games, talking about what they would like to be when they grew up. Dennis never said so, but Terry got the feeling that Dennis really didn't enjoy playing sports as much as everyone thought he did. After Terry's mom took him and his sister away from Elmwood Park, Terry knew about his friend only through the Christmas cards Dennis's mother sent. But a few years later, those stopped coming. It was likely, Terry thought, Dennis would not remember him at all.

Dennis would be twenty-two now, Terry thought, as he ventured towards his old friend's house. Terry stood on the stoop and rang the doorbell. A woman Terry recognized answered the door. It was ten a.m., but she was still in her bathrobe, unbelted and loose, revealing a floral nightgown underneath. Terry kept his eyes on hers.

"Hello, Mrs. Madson," Terry said.

"What do you want?"

"I'm an old friend of your son."

"Humphh," she said. "That one—." The woman inhaled her cigarette. "Who are you?"

"Oh, sorry ma'am." In that moment, Terry decided against giving her his own name. Terry's paranoia had worsened since arriving in Elmwood Park. Irrationally he imagined Mrs. Madson slamming the door on him and hurrying to call the police. He borrowed a character from *The Catcher in the Rye* instead. "My name is Carl Luce. Dennis and I were friends in high school," Terry said.

The woman dropped her chin and looked over her glasses at Terry. "He doesn't live here anymore."

"Is he still in Elmwood—?"

"Hold on," she said abruptly and let the aluminum screen door close behind her. She returned a moment later and handed Terry an address scrawled on a piece of ruled paper.

"Over off Belmont Avenue, Carl. You know where that is?"

"Yes. Thank you," Terry said. "I hope you have a good day."

Without responding, she closed the door.

Terry folded the piece of paper and slipped it in his wallet. He wandered around a bit. Walked to his grade school and stood across the street. Not a thing had changed. The sign out front read, *"Happy Summer Vacation!"*

Terry squinted to make out a cluster of windows on the second floor. His old sixth grade classroom. Mrs. Greene was his teacher. She was the first person to tell him he was a good writer. She encouraged him to write stories and poems. At that time, he could think of nothing to write about. His mind was full of stories now.

Terry was still hungry, so he went back to the diner from the day before and had lunch. He tried to scribble in his journal while he nibbled his food, but his growing anxiety over facing his father scrambled his thoughts.

"You want another Coke?" the waitress asked as she cleared his plate away.

Terry nodded. While he sipped the soda, Terry tried to write in his journal, but not finding the words, he scratched out every line he wrote. He was fully aware he was only delaying the inevitable.

Stanley Abbott opened his front door. "Yes?" he said. "Can I help you?"

Terry brushed the hair from his eyes. "Hi, Dad. It's me. "

"Terry?" Stanley Abbott shook his head. "I can't believe it." He motioned for Terry to come inside.

Terry dropped his bag on the floor just inside the door.

Stanley moved to put his arms around his son, but then dropped his arms and took Terry's hand, shaking it as if Terry were a co-worker he hadn't seen in a while.

"I'm glad—."

"I hope it's—."

Terry began to wonder if this was a good idea.

"Well, this is a surprise. How are you?" Stanley said.

"I'm good. You look good."

Stanley laughed. "I look older, you mean."

"A little. But you look good."

"What are you doing here? I mean, where've you been?" Stanley shook his head. "Jeez Terry. I got a lot of questions."

"I know," Terry said.

"Does your mother know you're here."

"No. And she doesn't need to know."

Stanley laughed. "But when she finds out, it'll be my fault all over again. I suppose you better call her sometime soon."

"Maybe," Terry said.

"Yeah, I get it," Stanley said.

Terry rolled his shoulders. He was tired. The dugout was safe but uncomfortable. For that matter, a bus seat wasn't the best place to sleep either. "I was wondering if I could stay with you, for a while, anyway. I—. I guess I don't have any place else right now. But, if you don't want me here, I understand."

"Not want you. No, no. That was her. She took you. I always wanted you. I tried to get you kids back. To hell with her, but I tried." Stanley's jaw tensed. "Don't ever think I didn't want you."

Terry nodded.

"You can sleep in your old room, if you want," Stanley said.

"Thanks. Dad." The word did not come easily.

"Why don't you get unpacked while I make dinner? I guess you remember the way." Stanley laughed.

Terry put his things in his old room, which had not changed. The carpet showed marks from being recently vacuumed, the furniture dusted, but nothing else moved in all that time. He looked in the chest of drawers. It was empty, except the bottom drawer, which was filled with neatly folded pants and t-shirts. Clothes he had worn when he was twelve, clothes his mother didn't have room for or overlooked when she packed. The fact that they were still there gave Terry an eerie feeling, as if time had stopped for Stanley Abbott.

Terry just tossed his duffle on the bed for now. Depending on how things went over the next day or two, he may or may not stay much longer. Terry used the bathroom, then went to ask his dad if he could help.

"I've got it under control," Stanley said. "You just relax and make yourself at home."

It was an odd thing to say, Terry thought. It was his home. Or it used to be. Remnants of his childhood were everywhere. His third-grade spelling trophy and Linda's kindergarten painting of a cat were still displayed on built-in bookshelves next to his grandmother's Hummels—five pieces his dad said would be worth real money one day. Next to the little German figurines was a baseball, supposedly autographed by Andy Pafko. If Terry had been interested in baseball, things like this would be something Terry could talk about with his dad.

Stanley Abbott didn't have many books, but those few he did have were well read. Terry pulled a worn copy of *A Farewell to Arms* from the shelf. Maybe Terry would ask to borrow it. He had never read it, even though his dad had often told him what a great story it was. For now, Terry returned the book to its place between two cast iron book ends, lions entangled in climbing ivy.

His attention was drawn next to his father's Purple Heart displayed against black velvet in a gold frame. All he knew about the medal was that it had been given to his father as he lay in a field hospital in Korea with seven bullet holes in his body. Three months later, Stanley Abbott was discharged from the army and returned home to his wife and two-year-old daughter.

In a memory, Terry saw his father asleep in his chair, snoring softly, Linda lying on the floor looking at *Mad* magazine, and himself, only six, looking up at the medal, gold and shiny, a thing he wanted to hold in his hands. His mother, out from the kitchen, wiping her hands on a dishtowel, had come up behind him. "He was my sweet boy, and they stole him from me," she said.

At dinner, Terry asked his dad about Sandra, whom he had met the time she and his dad had showed up in Milwaukee with a present for his thirteenth birthday. At that time Terry and Linda were living with their mom in a run down two-bedroom house. It wasn't perfect, but it was better than living at his aunt's house, and Terry had his own room in the basement. His dad had driven up in a brand-new, yellow-finned car, and Terry was excited to see him, but his mother ruined everything when she flew out of the house and started screaming at his dad.

At the time Terry hadn't understood his mother's remarks at dinner that evening when she wondered what Stanley thought he was doing with Marilyn Monroe. But later on he did and the comment intrigued him. He had to admit that his dad never seemed like the kind of guy a woman like Sandra would be interested in.

Chewing with his mouth open, Stanley waved his hand dismissively. "Too flighty that one," he said. "She had her head in the stars. Wanted to be in the movies. Not sure how she thought being married to a plant foreman from the Chicago suburbs was going to advance her career. Anyway, she's gone."

Stanley turned then to Chicago sports and jabbered on about how the Cubs season was shaping up. "Too bad about the Bears last year, though, right?" Stanley said. "Damn Packers stole the division again." Terry did his best to pretend he was part of the conversation.

"What I want to know," Stanley said, popping the last bite of meatloaf in his mouth, "is where the heck you've been for two years."

Terry spun his rehearsed tale.

"Well, it sounds interesting. New York seems like a place a kid like you would like to be. You know, theaters and things like that. But did you finish high school out there?"

This was a question Terry hadn't counted on. "Uh, no. I read a lot. Does that count?"

"Maybe to an English teacher, but I don't think a principal would give you a diploma for that. Are you—? Do you think you'd go back now? The high school here would probably take you. I suppose you could take some tests or something to show them what you know. I don't think they'd make a sixteen—."

"Seventeen," Terry said.

"I don't think they'd stick a seventeen-year-old in with the sophomores, do you?"

"Probably not. But I've got the rest of the summer to think about that."

"Sure. I just thought I'd mention it. And you know you'll never get anywhere without a good education," Stanley said.

Not knowing what else to say, Terry said, "That's true."

Terry cleared the table and told his father to go in the living room and relax. "I'm used to doing the dishes," Terry said. But Stanley pulled a clean dishtowel out of the drawer. As his son rinsed a plate and held it for him to dry, Stanley mentioned how tall Terry was.

"You were a puny kid. I wasn't sure you'd sprout out of that, but look at you now. Maybe taller than your old man?"

"Maybe," Terry said. The small talk was difficult. With Donnie, their conversations were effortless. Even from the first.

Stanley stacked the dried plates in the cupboard and hung the towel on the handle of the oven door.

"I thought we might drive into the city this weekend. You up for that? We could go to that Italian place we used to go to when you were a kid. Get some spaghetti or something."

"You don't have to go to any trouble for me, Dad."

After saying goodnight to his father, Terry closed the bedroom door and undressed. He stretched out on the twin bed and thought about how odd it felt being in his childhood bedroom. It was exactly the same as he remembered. Wood paneling, navy blue ripcord bedspread, matching drapes on two crank-out windows facing the back yard, and a cowboy lamp on the bed table. On a wall shelf, artifacts of his early life had been preserved. A stack of childhood books, a plastic model rocket ship, a coin bank shaped like mailbox, and a piece of feldspar he had found near Lake Michigan. Terry held the jagged pink-gold stone in his palm and its gold flecks glimmered in the lamplight.

He recalled the family outing to a white-dune beach in northern Indiana. Mother had packed a picnic. Linda played catch with him, and afterwards the two of them hunted for shells and stones. Linda collected a lunch sack full, but Terry had taken just this one stone. He thought it looked like gold and held it up to show his mother who had told him it was just a useless, ordinary rock. She took it from his hand and dropped it on the sand.

On the ride home Terry stared silently out the window. His mother's cigarette smoke made his eyes burn. It was late when his father pulled into the driveway. Terry and Linda were ordered straight to bed. Terry's light was out when Stanley came in to tell his son good night, but Terry had pretended to be asleep. Stanley closed the door as he left. Terry remembered staring in the dark, watching wall shadows as the night breeze lifted the drapes and let in the moonlight. In the morning, those phantoms were replaced by sun and heat, and under the cowboy lamp, a piece of pink feldspar.

Waif

This time the girl knocked at the back door, presenting herself in sun-filled daylight. In Marion's hand was a straw hat, not a rifle, but the girl cowered, nevertheless. Sarge whined to be let out. She opened the door for him. He sniffed at the girl's legs, and she dropped her hand to pet him.

"Who's this, then, Sarge?" The dog looked up at Marion as if to say, "I like her."

She was a tiny thing. Five feet tall, if that, maybe a hundred pounds. She had a sweet face, long stringy strawberry blonde hair, flushed, freckled cheeks. Her dirty blue jeans were torn in one knee. She wore a loose smock blouse and had a backpack strapped to her shoulders.

"I suppose you're not here to buy eggs, are you?"

"Are you the lady I can stay with for a little while?"

Marion recalled how she had scoffed at Vivian's comment about her being a target for vagrants, and now, here was this waif. She also remembered Roger's stern order, so instead of opening the door wide for the girl, Marion went outside. She motioned for the girl to sit.

"What's your name, honey?"

"Lily. Reynolds."

"How old are you, Lily?"

"Seventeen," she said, looking down at the porch floor.

"How old are you really?" Marion said.

"Fourteen."

Marion nodded. "I would have guessed twelve."

"I'm fourteen."

"Well. Okay." Sarge sniffed at Lily again. He looked up at Marion and barked once. "I see. Yes. There's a girl here. Yes, I know." Sarge's tail wagged wildly. "He likes you."

"He's a nice dog," Lily said.

Marion smiled. Just before Lily knocked at the door, Marion had been ready to walk on her meadow path, a Sunday ritual, particularly after her husband died. It was her meditation. A time away from the house where there was always something to do. When Harve first mowed a meandering walking path through their north field and planted its edges with a myriad of wildflowers, she was delighted. Over the years, he kept it neatly mowed, built her a bench, and added houses for a variety of birds. It wasn't church, no. It certainly was not that, but in her solitude in the wildflower meadow she sometimes spoke to Harve, sending her voice across the wild bergamot.

"I guess it's no accident that you found my house? Did Bridget tell you about me?"

Lily's eyes narrowed in confusion. "Who?"

"How is it you got here, Lily?"

"There are notes, on bathroom walls," Lily said. "Says you'll take care of runaways. Says you're nice."

"Notes on walls?" Marion interrupted. "My name is there?"

"Not your name. Stuff about you. Directions."

"Good grief," said Marion. "Am I to understand that I should expect a steady—flood—of others, like you? I'm not UNICEF, for goodness sake." Marion said the last part with more anger than she intended.

The girl stood up, held her backpack close, and quickly made her way down the steps.

Marion watched her scamper away. Lily was nearly to the road

135

when Marion started off in her direction, calling for the girl to return. "Come back. I'm not going to hurt you. I can give you something to eat, at least, before you run off again." Maybe the last phrase wasn't worded well. She hadn't meant anything by it. After all, she knew there had to be a reason this child was out in the world alone. Lily stopped and looked back but stayed firmly planted. Marion saw she would either have to go all the way down to where Lily stood or let her go.

"I meant what I said," Marion said, face to face with the girl whose cheeks were even more flushed than before. "I want you to come back with me. I'll get you something to eat and drink and whatever else you need." The girl hung her head in shame. "I'm not going to beg. It's up to you."

The sun beat on Marion's uncovered head. Days like this she envied those who had air conditioning. A stifling heat had risen with the sun. Marion realized she would not have spent much time in the meadow after all.

"Okay," sputtered the girl, who nodded her head in agreement.

Indoors, the girl asked for a bathroom. Marion motioned down the hall. After Lily closed the door, Marion composed herself and thought that it must have been Bridget who'd written those things. Who else? No good deed goes unpunished, she thought. She filled a glass with water and set it on the table. She returned to the sink to refill Sarge's water bowl. "What's taking so long?" Marion wondered out loud.

In a moment, the girl emerged from the bathroom, but instead of pink and flush, her face was pale, her skin perspiring.

"Goodness, child. You're white as a ghost."

"I got sick."

Marion steered the girl down the hall into the living room, where she threw the afghan down to cover the sofa. "Sit here," Marion said, then went to get the glass of water.

"Were you sick this morning?" Marion said, handing Lily the glass.

"No. Just now," Lily said.

"Heat stroke most likely. Or dehydration." Marion got an old towel from the laundry room to cover her pillows. She set an empty dishpan on the floor. Marion took the water glass from Lily and set it on the end table. She helped Lily take off her shoes.

"You just lie down and rest. I'll close the drapes and turn on the fan. You'll be feeling better in no time. If you need me, you call out. I won't be far."

Later that afternoon, Lily woke and found her way back to the bathroom. Marion was in the kitchen humming an old tune.

"That was quite a nap," Marion said, when Lily shuffled into the kitchen. "Feel better?"

Lily nodded. "I'm thirsty," she said.

"How about lemonade?"

"Yes," said Lily. "Yes, please."

Marion put a pinch of salt in Lily's glass, her mother's old remedy for overdoing it in the heat. Marion brought out a bologna sandwich from the refrigerator and handed the glass and the sandwich to Lily.

"Shall we sit out on the front porch? I believe it will be cooler than this kitchen is."

For a few moments, neither spoke. The air was dead still. Marion studied a yellow butterfly on the porch railing. Even that tiny thing seemed worn down by the day, Marion thought. As was typical of weather in Wisconsin, if you didn't like it, all you had to do was wait an hour for it to change. That was the old saying anyway. Then as if on cue, as if the day knew that Marion Goodman had had about enough of the heat, the wind shifted. A cooler breeze blew in from the northeast.

Lily took a small bite of the sandwich, then reached down to pet Sarge on the head. He brushed his dry black nose against her leg, and she smiled.

"He's been worried about you," Marion said.

Marion sipped her lemonade. She noticed a faded bruise, a tinge of yellow encircling the girl's wrist, blotches still faintly purple creeping up the inside of her sleeve as if the arm had been wrenched viciously, and not long ago. The marks were alarming. How had Marion not noticed them earlier?

Here was another reason to report this girl to Roger, which she still had not done. Why she was hesitant, she wasn't sure. Maybe she felt it better to get to know Lily first, in case she needed to advocate for her. Now that Marion had seen the bruises, she felt even more protective of the girl.

"Your glass is empty," Marion said. She handed Lily the glass pitcher, which the girl attempted to take, but her weak arm struggled to hold it. Marion saw the muscles quiver as the girl worked to transfer the pitcher to her other hand.

"You better tell me about that arm," Marion said, taking back the pitcher.

Lily squinted in confusion, tilted her head like Sarge sometimes did when Marion spoke to him.

Marion took the girl's hand, then the other, which was also bruised, though not to the same degree. She pushed up Lily's shirt sleeves and saw, not just the purple blotches but small half-moon wounds. I'm no detective, Marion thought, but those marks were made by fingernails digging in.

"Who hurt you?" Marion asked a bit desperately, staring into the girl's deep green eyes.

"I am fine," Lily said, but turned away from Marion.

For the time being, Marion let the lie go, but when she went inside to get a plate of sugar cookies, Marion dialed Roger. She told him the girl's name and asked him to find out what he could. She was planning chicken salad for dinner and said it might be a good idea for him to come.

Roger arrived at 6:00 p.m. He was out of uniform, dressed in dark gray slacks and a sporty knit shirt.

Marion introduced Roger to Lily. "I hope you don't mind, Lily, but

I invited Roger a few days ago for dinner. We're friends. You'll be happy to know, he doesn't bite."

Roger gave Marion a wry look, then turned to Lily, smiled, and said that it was nice to meet her.

Lily said it was nice to meet him, too.

Marion offered Roger a gin and tonic before dinner, but he said he'd be fine with iced tea, if she had it. She brought his tea to where he sat in the living room with Lily, who focused all her attention on Sarge who nestled near her feet. Roger took the glass from Marion.

"Thank you," he said. Roger observed Lily, who spoke to Sarge in quiet tones, as if she spoke to a sleeping baby.

"You're a good boy, aren't you?" she said. Sarge looked into her eyes. Roger thought he heard the dog purr.

"I think you have made a friend," Roger said.

Lily smiled. "I love dogs," she said.

Marion announced dinner was ready and the three of them sat in the dining room, with a tablecloth and Marion's best dishes. The Irish lace curtains billowed.

"That breeze feels wonderful, doesn't it?" Marion said. She took her cloth napkin, shook it open to her side and laid it on her lap. Lily, watching her, did the same.

Marion told Roger to start. He picked up the crystal bowl of chicken salad.

"Looks great, Marion," he said. He spooned a generous amount onto his lettuce-lined plate. Then he passed the bowl to Lily, who took it with both hands. After he took two dinner rolls, he passed her the basket. Once they all had their plates filled, Lily bowed her head and waited.

"Well, go ahead everyone," Marion said with a wink in her eye. "I am pretty sure it's safe to eat."

Lily ate greedily, which Roger watched with amusement.

"She's a good cook, Marion is, isn't she," Roger said to Lily.

Lily, with her mouthful said, "Yes." Then to Marion, "Very good."

"I'm glad you like it," Marion said.

Roger knew he was there on business, but he could not help admire how adeptly Marion had managed the situation, as if the girl had been an injured fawn that she had not wanted to scare away. Lily didn't seem too skittish, at least not at the moment. Gaining confidence meant disarming. Getting someone to talk meant establishing trust. Marion was doing everything right.

After Marion had called that afternoon, Roger looked through his reports of missing children, and while most were for cases out of state, it had not taken him long to find the file on Lily Reynolds. The picture in the report was several years old, but the girl looked like the one Marion described. The report said the girl, fourteen, had gone missing from her foster home near Little Wing, Wisconsin on June 28. It was the second time she had run away.

Roger asked his secretary to look on the statewide microfilm reports for anything related to the surname Reynolds in Aspen County. He could have contacted the local Sheriff or called the Little Wing police department directly, but Roger liked to learn as much as he could about a case before he involved anyone else. He had learned over the years that not everyone gave you the information you needed.

While Margie searched the microfilm, Roger made a few notes.

"Eureka," Margie called out. "Want to know why she was in foster care?"

"I do," he said.

"I'm just putting two and two, mind you," Margie said, "but a Walter Reynolds, 42, was convicted in 1966 for felony battery. Five-year sentence, no probation."

Roger thanked her and said her math probably added up just right. Lily's father, it seemed, had a temper. Furthering the equation, Roger wondered if Reynolds had ever struck his own daughter.

While Roger and Marion spoke about the weather and the egg business, Lily slipped a morsel of chicken to Sarge.

"Delicious dinner, Marion," Roger said. "How about I help you with the dishes?"

"That would be nice," Marion said. "Thank you."

Lily offered to help as well, but Marion suggested she take Sarge out in the yard so he could water the yews. At first Lily didn't understand, but then she did, smiled, and said sure.

Once Lily was outdoors, Roger told Marion what he had discovered about Lily.

"Of course, if her father is behind bars," Marion said, "he's not the one who hurt her."

"There's always a reason these kids run away, isn't there?" Roger said.

"In foster care—so the mother?" Marion asked.

"Nothing in the records," Roger said. He was about to draw the obvious conclusion when Lily and Sarge burst through the door. Sarge went directly to his water dish, and Lily washed her hands at the sink.

"It's starting to rain," Lily said.

"Good thing we got Sarge out to do his business then, isn't it?" said Marion. "Want dessert?"

Lily smiled and nodded.

The three of them sat at the kitchen table, bowls of vanilla ice cream with fresh raspberries in front of them. Sarge curled under Lily's chair and let out a satisfied sigh.

"My mom used to make raspberry jam," Lily said eagerly. Then she looked down into her bowl as if she'd said something she should not have said.

"Where is your mother, dear," Marion asked.

"When I was nine," Lily blurted, "she got sick. And she died."

"I'm so sorry to hear that. You must miss her," Marion said.

Lily nodded. She scraped the last bit of pink from the bowl before setting her spoon down.

Then Roger got down to what he had come there to do. He spoke to the girl in the gentlest voice he could find, telling her first that he was the county sheriff. He told her what he had learned, and that by law she would need to return to her foster family. A fourteen-year-old could not be legally independent, he explained.

"Unless," he said, leaving a door open for her, "unless there is something you need to say? Something I need to know?"

Lily sat mute and tightened her lips. Tears filled her eyes.

Marion saw her clamp down. "Now Lily, if you won't tell us who hurt you, we can't help you. Roger and I only want to help."

"I know I said you'd have to go back," Roger said, "but if you're in danger there, you have to tell us."

"I can't go back," Lily said, her eyes wide with alarm. "They were horrible. She was—. I can't," Lily said, wiping her eyes.

"That's enough for tonight," Marion said. "We'll sort this out tomorrow. Don't worry, Lily. I'm not sending you anywhere, at least not tonight. And Roger's not either. Are you Roger?"

"You're safe, Lily. You don't need to worry," he said.

Moments later as he edged near the door to leave, Roger said, "I have my job to do, Lily, but more important than that, I want to do right by you. I hope you believe me."

Marion followed him out. She said she'd see him in the morning unless something came up before then.

"Probably best she sleeps for a while," he said. "Tough though, poor kid."

Marion reached out and touched his arm. "Thank you, Roger."

After a bath, Lily crawled into the same bed Bridget had slept in.

"Comfortable?" Marion asked. "Do you need anything else?"

"No. I'm fine."

"Just holler if you do. And if you feel sick again, remember, the bathroom is just right there." In the back of her mind, it occurred to Marion that another reason the girl had vomited was that she was pregnant. It was not an unreasonable conclusion.

"Thank you," Lily said.

"And don't you worry about Roger. He's not going to put you in danger, but he does have to do his job. We'll talk more in the morning about what comes next. All right?"

Lily nodded and slunk down into the covers.

Marion turned the light off and pulled the bedroom door nearly closed, leaving it open a few inches.

At five to six Marion awoke with a jolt. Her alarm wasn't set to go off until 6:30. She lay there a moment and remembered Lily. She might like to help gather eggs, Marion thought. Marion stretched, got up, made her bed, and got dressed. When she passed by Lily's room on her way to the bathroom, Marion stopped to peek in on the girl. But when she opened the door, Marion found the bed was neatly made.

Marion called Roger soon after. "She's gone," she said. "I've looked everywhere."

"I'll have to put out a bulletin—describe her as a runaway," Roger said.

"I wish you wouldn't Roger. Can't she be left to fend for herself? She left those horrid people weeks ago, and she survived."

"We don't know her foster family did that to her. It could have happened while she was fending for herself," Roger said. "She's not safe out there, Marion, and you know it."

She knew Roger had a point. "Well, you keep an eye out for her, Roger. And if you find her, bring her back here and we will figure out what to do."

A Rock and A Hard Place

ELMWOOD PARK 1968

It was bright daylight when Stanley Abbott woke, his head throbbing, his neck stuck in an awkward kink. He looked at his watch and grunted. A whiskey bottle, empty, lay on the floor by his slippers. He rolled over on his side. Noise from the neighbor's lawn mower jolted him fully awake. For a moment he thought he was late for work, but eventually he realized it was Saturday.

Terry would be wondering why he wasn't up yet. He slipped on the trousers that laid in a crumpled pile on the floor and put on a clean shirt. Then he plodded to the bathroom and splashed handfuls of cold water on his face. In the mirror, Stanley felt his shame looking back at him.

Terry was in the kitchen standing over the sink eating a piece of jelly toast.

"Sorry, son," Stanley said. "I was more tired than I thought."

"That's all right," Terry said. "I haven't been up that long myself."

Later they drove into the city. At the Museum of Science and Industry, they moved from exhibit to exhibit. Making small talk minimized the awkwardness they both felt. It would take time, Stanley thought, to get to know his son again. Over pizza, Stanley fell back to talking about the upcoming baseball season. He had no idea what else to talk about. On the drive home, Stanley reminded Terry that he ought to call his mother.

"You've been here over a week. I think it's time you called her."

Terry shrugged.

"Listen, I don't know what went on between you two, or why you left her, but she's still your mother and you should call to tell her you're here and that you're fine, that we're fine," Stanley said.

"Yeah. Maybe tomorrow. Or sometime next week."

"Or you could call your sister instead," Stanley said. "I've got her number."

"Maybe," Terry said.

"I wish you would, son. They've got to be worried about you. I'll bet they wonder every day if you're okay. I know I sometimes thought you might be dead, since you didn't call all that time. A person has no way of knowing, and not knowing kind of leads to thinking the worst."

The next day Terry called his mother. His dad was in the living room, the *Tribune* on his lap. The phone was in the kitchen, and Terry was sure his dad couldn't help overhearing. Most of the brief conversation with his mother was one sided. He didn't know what he expected. Maybe a grateful acknowledgment that her son was safe and well. But instead, she told him if he wasn't home in two days, she and Dick would drive down there and get him. Terry hung up on her after that. He stood at the phone, expecting it to ring, expecting it to be his mother again, or maybe his sister, who'd say she didn't appreciate being the go-between. But she did not call back. That didn't mean his mother wasn't serious about coming to get him, Terry thought.

By then his dad was in the kitchen, looking out at the back yard.

"Jesus," Stanley said, "I need to mow."

"You want lunch?" Terry said.

"Yeah. Sure," Stanley said.

Stanley opened the refrigerator and grabbed a bottle of Schlitz. After snapping off the cap, he held up the bottle opener. "Want one?"

"No. Thanks."

Terry finished the sandwiches and set the plates on the table. "Can you grab me another beer before you sit down?" Stanley said.

Terry handed his dad the beer.

"So, what did she say?" Stanley asked.

"Oh, you know. Get your butt back where you belong, or else."

"You don't have to do what she wants," Stanley said.

"I know," Terry said.

"I mean, things are great here, with us now. Right?"

Terry smiled weakly at his dad. "Yeah, Dad," he said.

The truth was, while his dad was trying, Terry could see that things were anything but "great." Stanley had been drinking, enough for it to be a problem. The past Wednesday he had woken up so hungover, he called in sick to work.

"They owe me a little personal time, eh," Stanley had joked.

But it didn't feel like a joke to Terry. The worsening situation conjured memories of his parents screaming at each other, slamming doors, his mother throwing things at his dad, Linda cradling Terry in her room until the house quieted down. Some nights she kept him with her till morning. It was clear to Terry now that his dad's drinking had been the reason his mother had taken them away. Terry wondered if it was also why Sandra left.

"Listen, Terry," Stanley said. "I'll do whatever you want me to. I mean, if you want me to drive you to Milwaukee so you can get back to school there with your old friends, I will understand. I mean, maybe you and your mom could work it out. You're older now. Things might be better."

Terry pushed the salt shaker back in line with the pepper shaker. Two little ceramic ears of corn. He had no intention of going to Milwaukee, but he wasn't sure what he would do.

"Okay. I guess I'll think about it," Terry said.

"Though she be but little, she is fierce"

WISCONSIN 1968

Roger saw her sitting under a tree near a little cemetery on a county road. He slowed the patrol car and pulled onto the gravel shoulder. When she saw him, she waved.

"You okay," he asked, climbing up the slope where Lily sat crossed legged.

"Is Marion mad at me?"

"No. She's worried. She's afraid you're hurt. Are you?"

Lily's eyes filled with tears. She nodded and started to cry, her chest heaving with helpless sobs.

Roger planted his feet and reached his hand out to Lily. "Come on, girl."

She took his hand, and they made their way down to Roger's patrol car. He gave her his handkerchief. She took it and wiped her eyes. She blew her nose, then wadded the handkerchief in her hand.

"Where are you hurt," Roger asked, aware that her wounds could be internal, invisible to him. "Were you? Were you molested?"

"No," she squeaked shyly. "I'm okay."

Roger exhaled his relief. He threw her bag in the back seat and opened the passenger door for Lily.

"Let's get you back to Marion's for now."

Lily nodded and blew her nose again.

Marion flung the door open and hurried out to the driveway. Lily got out of the car and ran to the woman she had known only for a day and threw her arms around her.

"You poor thing," Marion said. "I'm so glad you're safe."

Roger stood nearby, his hat in his hand.

Marion said, "Come on. Let's go in. I've got cookies fresh from the oven."

While Lily washed up in the bathroom, Marion spoke with Roger. "Where was she?"

"West of here, on Barton Road, near the county line."

"Did she tell you where she's been? Is she hurt?"

Roger shook his head. "She said she was not molested. It didn't seem like she was lying about that. I told her she didn't have to tell me the rest, that we'd wait till we saw Marion and then maybe she'd feel comfortable telling you."

Marion went to her old friend and slipped her arms around him. When she released him, she wiped a tear away. "My goodness. I don't know why, but that little girl has a grip on my heart."

Roger nodded. "I understand. There's something sweet about her, but you know she's had it rough, and you kind of just want to protect her."

"That's it precisely, Roger."

Lily came out of the bathroom and Marion invited them all to sit. She poured Lily a glass of milk and set the plate of cookies in front of her.

"Roger? Coffee?"

"A glass of milk sounds good to me, too," he said.

"Milk for us all," Marion said.

That night when Lily was ready for bed, Marion asked if she could sit with her a while. Lily pulled the covers up to her chest, and Marion sat on the bed.

"Can you tell me about it? I promise, I'll just listen."

Lily lay her head on the pillow and turned on her side, facing the door. Then she let the story spill out of her.

"I ran away because I was afraid you'd send me back to my foster family. But I got arrested and they sent me back anyway. In the police station, I told them about how Mrs. Uebel had hit me, but they didn't believe me. They said it wasn't nice to make up stories about people who were just trying to help me."

"Mr. Uebel, he came and got me. He pretended like he was worried about me. When he got me home, Mrs. Uebel said I needed to learn my lesson. She made me scrub the kitchen floor, but I think she put something in the water. It smelled really bad and made my hands red and itchy. The next morning my knuckles were bleeding. When I took the clothes off the line, spots of blood got on one of Mr. Uebel's shirts. Mrs. Uebel slapped me and told me to be more careful. I couldn't help it. Mr. Uebel came over. She told him I was an ungrateful girl and that I had called her a name she couldn't repeat because it was just too horrible. I never did that. She was lying."

"He took my arm and pinched hard and dragged me behind him. But their dog Lucky growled at him, and he let me go. They made me stay in my room and ate supper without me. After they went to bed, I stayed awake for a long time. Then before it got light, I left. I stuffed a bunch of food in my bag, then snuck out the door. Lucky didn't even whine as I petted him and whispered goodbye. I should have taken him with me."

"Then later, there was just—. Just a man who—. I thought he looked okay when I first climbed into his pickup, but after a few miles, he started talking—. He said dirty things to me. After a while, he stopped for gas, and when he was inside the station paying, I got out of the truck and went to the ladies room and locked the door. I was in there a long time. Then a woman knocked on the door, and I had to come out."

"At the gas pumps was a car and a man, her husband I think, and he was washing the windshield. In the car were two or three kids, kind of noisy and wrestling about. They looked like a nice family, but I know for a fact that you can't tell about people by looking at them. People who seem nice are not always nice."

"I got a map from the gas station, so I could find my way back. I was afraid to hitchhike any more. So then I just walked. I had nowhere else to go but here."

Marion wondered how it had happened that Lily had become the object of torment, not just from her father, but from this couple, the Uebels, as well. Then she thought back to something she had learned years ago that is as true for humans as it is for animals. Sometimes we attack the weakest. She had seen it among the children in her classrooms, boys in particular, singling out the smallest among them for jeers and taunts. And it was a tightrope she walked in protecting such children, for if the herd sensed her intentions, they would become even more cruel. She had learned that lesson the hard way. She could never be sure, but Marion felt that the most steadfast bullies were also the most ill-treated themselves. She knew no child was born with hatred in his heart.

"Please don't send me away," Lily said.

Marion squeezed Lily's hand. "I won't. And Roger won't either. You're safe here. Now, snuggle down and go to sleep."

Marion turned off the lamp and pulled the door not quite closed.

Little Lily, Marion thought. How strong the child was.

The first few days with Marion, Lily sought some kind of work from the moment she woke up until the moment she went to bed. At first Marion mistook the girl's industry, thinking Lily might be just like she was, unable to truly relax, always feeling that she ought to be doing something. But then Marion understood what was really going on. At the Uebels, Lily had been expected to work. She was nothing more to them than an unpaid servant. It was likely Lily equated her worth with usefulness. On the other hand, Marion also understood that it was important to a person to feel needed. Doing something of value for someone you cared about felt right, at least to most people. So, no matter how it pained Marion to see the girl so focused on work, she would not ask Lily to be idle.

Instead, on Lily's fourth day, Marion spoke with Lily at breakfast and told her as plainly and directly as she could that her safety and care did not need to be repaid with chores.

"You are not here as a serving maid. You are here because I want you to feel safe." Tears welled in Lily's green eyes. "If you want to do things, I want those things to be things you enjoy," Marion said. Lily's tears spilled out in a rush. Marion rose, went to the girl, laid her hand on her shoulder. "Think about what you'd like to do. We can talk more about it later."

From then on, an ease came upon the girl. She and Marion decided that Lily's domain would extend to the chickens and Sarge. Sarge had become Lily's constant companion, so much so that Marion felt a bit bereft of his company. Each Sunday evening, Lily, at her insistence, would also cook dinner for her new friends, Marion and Roger, who became a once-weekly part of the new family.

The only one with any reservations about Lily's presence was Vivian, who asked Marion over the phone if she was "completely nuts."

"Not completely," Marion replied dryly, going on to say that she appreciated her sister's concern, but there was absolutely nothing to worry about.

Roger, on the other hand, told Marion he was happy that Lily was living with her, and not just for the teenager's sake. He was fully aware that the first girl, Bridget, had declared Marion's farm a sanctuary, and he thought the more eyes on any potentially dangerous visitors the better. Reports of vandalism and unsolved thefts continued to populate the alerts to his office. It seemed like these once rare occurrences were becoming all too normal.

While initially she had been intimidated by Roger, Lily quickly grew fond of him. He treated her well—never like a child—and his gentle manner always put her at ease. And there were his corny jokes. "What did the chicken say to the egg? Hey, wasn't I here first?" An eye roll from Lily warmed Roger's heart in a way it had not been warmed in a long time.

On Lily's second Friday night at Marion's home, Roger drove the three of them to the Stardusk Drive-In Theater. They took a grocery bag full of popcorn and a jug of lemonade. Marion fell asleep halfway through the second movie, but Roger and Lily stayed awake the entire time. Lily enjoyed being on Roger's side as he teased Marion about it later.

What meant the most to Lily was how Roger never kept her out of the conversation when he had news about her case. Eventually the tangled story of Lily's parentage was set right. With her father still incarcerated, and her mother deceased, Marion was granted temporary guardianship. Lily's testimony as well as Roger and Marion's signed affidavits were enough to indict the Uebels. Their foster license was permanently revoked. Mrs. Uebel got probation, Mr. Uebel, six months in county jail, sentences that seemed backward to Lily. Of the two, Mrs. Uebel had been more cruel. Despite that last day when Mr. Uebel had struck her, it was Mrs. Uebel who constantly abused her.

One morning Lily came into the kitchen with seven eggs in her basket, from opalescent white to the palest blue to light-brick brown. "Mrs. Uebel is being stubborn," Lily said to Marion.

Marion's eyebrows arched with confusion. "Mrs. Uebel?"

"Your fat, red hen with the beady black eyes. She's kind of mean to me, so I call her Mrs. Uebel. There was no egg from her this morning."

The next day Lily saw that Mrs. Uebel was not out in the yard for the morning scattering of grain, so she ducked into the coop and found the hen on her nest, her head at an unusual angle. Lily, now fearing the bird was sick, called Marion.

"Remember that huge egg a couple of days ago?" Marion said, turning the chicken to look at her vent. It was red and swollen. "Poor girl. That egg hurt, didn't it," Marion said, soothing the feathers on the hen's head.

Lily was sent to the house for the jar of Vaseline. Lily watched Marion swab the vent, inside and out.

"We need to keep her away from the others for a while. They'll peck and make things worse. And we'll keep her away from the boys, too, won't we girl?" At Marion's cooing, the hen blinked. Marion took the hen in her arms and transferred her to a clean nest in the old coop in the barn, where Marion kept the incubator.

For the next two days, Lily fed the ailing hen from her hand. On the morning of the third day, Lily found the hen off her nest, sipping water from the pan on the ground.

"You feeling better?" Lily asked, stooping down to pick her up.

She carried the hen into the house where Marion was taking sheets out of the washer to hang out on the line.

"Who do we have here?" Marion said.

"Ginger," Lily said and announced that from this moment on, Mrs. Uebel was dead. The perky red hen would now be named after the movie star on *Gilligan's Island*.

Marion smiled and told Lily that Ginger was free to move back to the main coop.

"I'm glad we didn't have to cull her," said Lily. "That wouldn't have been right."

Marion agreed. In the past she had culled many hens. That was just what one had to do. But not this time.

Domestic Life

ELMWOOD PARK 1968

Terry arrived at the address Mrs. Madson gave him. The three-story pale brick building sat on the corner. On the street level was a dry cleaner. The entire block was made up of similar buildings, businesses on the lower level, apartments on the upper floors. A city bus whooshed by Terry, expelling black smoke. The traffic was incessant.

Inside the doorway that led upstairs, Terry found eight tarnished brass mailboxes. Dennis Madson's name was printed above the box for apartment four. It was several minutes before someone came to the door. Terry was about to knock once more when a dark-haired young woman opened the door.

"Yeah," she said, rubbing the sleep out of her eyes. "Can I help you?"

"Uhm. Yeah. Is Dennis home?"

The woman waved Terry in. The apartment smelled like onions and sour milk. Dirty plates and glasses had been left on a coffee table in front of a well-worn brown sofa.

"Dennis!" she shouted. "Get up. Some guy is here for you." The girl went into the bathroom and closed the door.

When she came out, Dennis had still not emerged, so Terry asked if he could use the bathroom.

"First door," she said, pointing. After Terry closed the door, he heard the girl again. Then finally Dennis's voice. "Who is it?"

"Get up and find out for yourself. I'm not Houdini."

Boy, Terry thought, these two were not a happy couple. Out of the bathroom now, Terry went back by the front door and stood, his hands in his pockets, his bag on the floor next to him.

Dennis emerged, his hair long and scraggly, an equally scraggly beard on his face. "Yeah?" he said, scratching his back, looking at Terry, confusion on his face.

Terry gulped, feeling he had made a huge mistake. "Hi, Dennis. I didn't mean to come at a bad time."

Dennis shrugged and went to the refrigerator. He took out a pitcher of orange juice and poured himself a glass. "What can I do for you," Dennis said.

"It's Terry. Terry Abbott. Not sure if you remember me. We used to hang out together when we—."

Dennis looked closer, then smiled. "Hey, yeah. Terry. Long time no see." Dennis motioned for Terry to sit on the couch.

"What brings you by Terry," Dennis said. "Oh, sorry. You want some juice or something?"

"Uh. No. Thanks. I'm fine," Terry said. "I was in town to visit my dad. We've been estranged for a number of years, but I guess he moved away. That's what the people living in our old house said anyway. So, I thought while I was in town I'd look you up."

"Wow. He didn't even tell you where he was going?"

"Well, as I said, we had been estranged."

Dennis laughed. "I remember that about you, now. All the fancy words."

Terry smiled.

"You met my spouse, Sharon? She's really nice, just grumpy in the morning." Sharon, who was in the tiny galley kitchen making toast, glared at the remark. "After she drinks about a whole pot of coffee, she'll be nice."

"You're married?" It was a stupid thing to say, Terry thought. Why wouldn't he be?

"Not married, married. Not with an official '*I do*,' but we get along."
Terry nodded.

"Listen, Dennis. With my dad not being around and all, I was
wondering if I could maybe crash with you for a while, until I figure
things out. The reason I came back in the first place—. Let's just say
things aren't great at my mom's either, so I'm sort of without a place to
stay at the moment."

Sharon looked at Dennis wide-eyed. She shook her head "No."

"A day or two. I mean, I don't want to be a bother."

Terry wiped the hair from his forehead, then looked at the floor.

"Sure. What're old friends for?" Dennis said.

Sharon shook her head and sighed.

Against Sharon's protests, Dennis opened his arms to his old
friend, and before long, a couple of days became a week. Dennis seemed
happier with Terry around, and that made Sharon happier. Soon the
three fell into a kind of normalcy. Just as he had when he had lived with
Donette, Terry did what he could to help out. While Sharon was no
June Cleaver, she started getting used to how neat Terry kept his own
space, so she made more of an effort on her end as well. She and Terry
joked that Dennis was a lost cause as a housekeeper.

Dennis worked part-time pouring concrete, a job he hated. When
Terry asked why, he just shrugged and said that it wasn't much fun.
Sharon worked as a receptionist at the same construction company.
Terry assumed she was the one who kept their boat afloat. Despite
Terry's first impression, Dennis and Sharon seemed happy most of the
time.

Dennis worked with a guy whose brother managed the A & P who
agreed to give Terry a cash job stocking shelves from eight to midnight,
a few nights a week.

"But we have to keep the arrangement confidential." Dennis said.

"That's what he said. *Confidential.* The guy's probably pulling all kinds
of things on the boss, but if it helps you out, who cares? Right?"

Terry laughed. "I sure won't tell anyone," he said. He knew all about cash economies.

One Saturday the three of them went down the street to Luigi's for pizza. Dennis bought a couple of pitchers of Old Style. While they ate, they talked about the upcoming Democratic National Convention and the anti-war protests that were bearing down on Chicago.

"It's supposed to be big," Sharon said. "The protest. And they say people will be coming from all over to be here."

"Yeah, man. Fucking Vietnam. We gotta go down there and make our voices heard," Dennis said, feeling easy after his third beer.

"You registered?" Dennis asked Terry. "With the draft?"

Terry gulped a doughy bite. "Not yet," he said.

Dennis looked at Terry closely. "You even 18 yet, man?" When Terry lied and said, "Of course," Dennis drained the last of the pitcher into his glass.

Two weeks later, Terry and Dennis sat on the couch, watching television. Dennis's job had been called off for the day. At noon, the morning's steady rain still had not stopped. Terry had been paging through one of Sharon's magazines, but he found it filled with mostly useless advice. He was further distracted by Dennis's sour smelling feet up on the coffee table.

"I'm bored," Dennis said, then he popped up off the couch as if he had just realized he was late for something important. He dug a wad of crumpled dollar bills from his pocket, holding them out for Terry to see.

"You got any cash?" he asked.

Terry had twelve dollars, two fives and two singles, neatly stowed in his wallet, and he wasn't too eager to hand it over, knowing it would go to Jerry, the guy behind the counter at Avocet Records who would sell them pot. But Terry felt he owed Dennis, so he couldn't say no.

At the record store, they also bought Steppenwolf's album and were playing it so loud, when Sharon got home from work, she could hear it from the bottom of the stairs. She was sure all the neighbors could as well.

Once inside, she looked at the two with mild disgust. Terry felt like a scolded child. He got up and took the bag of groceries from Sharon's arms and went to the kitchen where he put everything it its place. Then he folded the paper bag and tucked it between the trash can and the fridge with the others. He expected a "hard at work all day and this is what I come home to" speech, but Sharon didn't say a word. Instead, she went into the bedroom to change. When she came out, her hair in a ponytail, she started making spaghetti for dinner. It was her silence, not just then, but throughout dinner and until she went to bed that got to him.

When Terry woke the next day, Dennis had already left for work. It was Sharon's day off, so she was still sleeping. Terry made himself coffee and ate a bowl of corn flakes. After picking up the mess from the day before, he gathered laundry and headed to the basement to a rusty set of coin-operated machines.

When he returned with a basket of clean laundry, Sharon was up, sitting on the couch, feet on the coffee table, staring out the window.

"Sorry about yesterday," Terry said.

"Not your fault. That's just Dennis. He needs to kill the pain sometimes."

Terry's brows tightened. "Pain from what?"

"He didn't tell you? Dennis was in Vietnam. Went over in '65, when he was 19. Not like he wanted to, not like some, but his dad pestered him to enlist. Forced him might be a better way to describe it. He doesn't tell me everything, but I know of the eighteen men in his platoon, Dennis was one of only three to survive."

"What happened?"

"They were on patrol, trying to clear a supply route, and they were hit by a sniper. It was bad. The worst thing was that Dennis tried to carry his friend out, but he got shot in the leg and couldn't hang on. That scar on his leg is no concrete burn."

That evening, they ate Chinese take-out and watched television.

"Got any more soy sauce," Dennis asked.

Sharon said there wasn't any left.

"Get more next time," he said. "There's never enough."

"Sorry. I forgot," Sharon said, getting up to throw her trash away. "Anybody want anything while I'm up?"

"I'm fine, Terry said.

"Another beer," Dennis said.

The show they had been watching ended, so when Sharon returned with Dennis's beer, she changed the channel to a western she liked.

"She loves the main guy in this," Dennis said to Terry. "Don't ya, babe? Wishes she was with him and not me."

"Knock it off, Dennis," she said.

Dennis shrugged, lifted the bottle to his lips, took a long swig, then sunk down into the couch and closed his eyes. Terry and Sharon watched the show in awkward silence.

The episode was about a Civil War widow who had married her husband's younger brother, a man who had excelled at soldiering, but couldn't make a go of farming. His failure made him bitter and mean. Being saddled with a family that wasn't his made him feel trapped. At one point, he lashed out and struck the woman, so she took her son and ran away. When her husband caught her and brought her back, he warned her he wouldn't be so kind next time. The climax of the story came when the boy, trying to defend his mother, stood between the man and his rifle. It was then that the man saw, finally, through the fear in the child's eyes, just how far he'd fallen.

While the story had a typical Hollywood happy ending, it had made Terry think again about what Dennis had been through, about what he had seen in Vietnam. But not just Dennis's experience. His father had been through things too. He had wounds he still lived with.

The next day, Sharon and Dennis were quiet and kind to each other, but didn't joke around like they usually did. Terry wondered if the couple went through periods like this, now and then, when they had to work harder at getting along. He knew it probably didn't help that he was there as a witness. Terry had been with them for five weeks, but the longer he stayed with Dennis and Sharon, the more he felt his presence was an intrusion. Just by being there, he was staring through a window at an intimacy he had no right to see. Three days later, Terry left.

He Said

It wasn't hard for Rob to find Mandy the next day. He had been driving around town and had seen her go into a record store near campus and figured it was the one where she worked. A few minutes after she went in, he walked up to the front of the store to see when it closed.

He was waiting for her when she came out just after five.

"Hello m'lady," he said, taking her hand, which she withdrew in alarm.

She squinted at him and looked confused.

Rob feigned a stab wound. "You don't remember me? Donovan, from last night."

"Of course, I remember," she said defensively. "What are you doing here?"

"Ouch. That's cold. I thought you'd be happy to see me."

"I hardly know you."

"True. But we had so much fun last night, I thought I'd come by to see if you wanted to see a movie with me tonight. Would have been hard to call you up, since I don't have your number."

She nodded. "Yeah, but how'd you know where I work?"

"You told me last night. I guess you don't remember that, either."

"Guess not."

Rob sensed her hesitancy, but he remained confident. Girls were not so complicated. Just find out what they liked, what they wanted, then promise them things.

"Where do you live? I'll drive you home and we can make plans on the way."

"I guess so," she said, looking at her watch then back towards the store.

"Or if you would rather—?"

"A movie would be okay, I guess."

"Well, then. Your chariot awaits," Rob said.

"You're kinda weird," Mandy said, getting into to the car.

Rob and Mandy had been seeing each other for two weeks, and despite what Rob first imagined, she wasn't as easy to manipulate as he had counted on. And unlike that first night at the bar, she wasn't the lush he had taken her for. He couldn't quite figure her out. Sometimes she seemed wild and willing to do anything, but other times she was so quiet and withdrawn, it was like she hated being with him. He asked her once why she was so "crabby," and she almost bit his head off. He had to apologize like crazy to get her to calm down after that.

All she seemed to care about was California. Thinking a girl like her would be fascinated by how worldly he was, he told her he'd been stationed at an army base near the ocean. In their free time, he said, he and a bunch of other guys would go to the beach. Of course, it was all a lie, but spinning a tale was always pleasurable for him, and he tended to push his stories to the brink of believability. When he had casually mentioned taking her out there with him someday, he had no idea what an obsession the idea would become for her. She couldn't let it go. It was a good thing, he thought, that he had told her his name was Donovan. The girl seemed a little unstable, and he wasn't sure how much longer he wanted to put up with her mood swings. And yet, for the time being, she was still an amusement.

She Said

AMES, IOWA 1968

Mandy woke up and found herself alone in bed. She expected Donovan to still be there, and she wondered why he wasn't. When had he shown up at her work two weeks ago, he kind of freaked her out. But weird or not, he seemed harmless, so she agreed to go out with him. He was good looking and funny and would do for a while. Sure, he sometimes said things that she didn't know how to take, like if they were meant to be funny or if they were mean. She knew he wasn't her soulmate, but she wasn't looking for one.

Still, why hadn't he nudged her this morning? Why would he just leave? Reluctantly, she got up and started to make the bed. When she moved her pillow, she found a folded note underneath:

Hey Mandy, Had things to do and I didn't want to wake you. See you at the Wagon Wheel tonight? Donovan.

"Hmm," she said. "Weird." She folded the note and laid it on her nightstand.

"That guy stayed over again last night, huh?" Carol said when Mandy padded barefoot into the kitchen.

"Yeah. Did you see him? He didn't wake me when he left."

"I saw him creeping out the door when I got up."

"I'm sure he wasn't creeping," Mandy said.

163

"I don't trust him," Carol said, chewing buttered toast.

Carol had made her opinion of Donovan clear, many times. But Mandy ignored her. She didn't really care what Carol had to say, about anything. Mandy had moved in with Carol the past summer, and at first they got along great, but when Mandy was put on academic probation mid-year, Carol turned into a different person. Carol sometimes acted more like a mom than her own mom. It had become so annoying.

Mandy opened the refrigerator. "We're out of juice?" she said, noticing the empty pitcher on the counter. "We're always out of stuff."

"You know where the grocery store is, too," Carol said. "And if that guy, Donovan—what a laugh— comes back tonight, you can tell him to pitch in for groceries. I'm pretty sure he's the one who finished the juice."

Mandy rolled her eyes at Carol, then went back to her room. Last night she'd told Donovan she wanted call in sick today so they could drive down to Des Moines and mess around. It didn't have to be Des Moines. It could have been anywhere. Mandy had fallen asleep assuming that was still the plan. She picked up the note again and let out a frustrated groan. "Maybe I should just get on a bus and go somewhere by myself," she said.

Before she left for work, Mandy tore the grocery list off the notepad and stuck it in her purse. She hurried up the street to the record store. She was ten minutes late, and Todd, her pimply-faced manager, reminded her he had warned her twice before. Mandy apologized, though she knew today wouldn't be the last time she'd be late.

She waited on an older couple looking for a gift for their grandson and three local teens, boys she was pretty sure had stolen records before. But it wasn't her store, so why did she care? She was not looking to impress the owner like Todd always was. At the moment, he was struggling to set up a ladder so he could wash the front windows.

"You could help you know," he said when he almost lost his balance.

"Who would take care of all our customers?" she said, laughing. There had been no one in since the teens finally left an hour earlier.

This was going to be one of those days when she thought she could fall asleep standing up.

"Well at least straighten up. Do something," Todd said. "That's what you're being paid for, isn't it?"

Mandy plodded over to where the teens had been flipping through records, and she found a few out of place. She lingered longer than she needed to so she could appear to be busy. If she had enough money, Mandy thought, she'd quit this stupid job that moment. But she was strapped. It had been hard to save after her parents cut off her "allowance." They were furious she had not kept her grades up and said they'd only finance her education if things turned around. But Mandy had no real interest in any of her classes and had no idea what she wanted to do with her life. That was why she was desperate to get to California before everything changed. She had already missed The Summer of Love, and she was convinced the best part of her life was happening without her. When Donovan planted the idea in her head that they could go together, she had not been able to stop thinking about it.

After work, Mandy walked to the grocery store near where she lived. When she opened her wallet to pay the cashier, blood drained from her face and her heart pounded in her ears. Two dollars? Where was the rest of her money? She knew she had $17 when Donovan picked her up before they went to the concert in the park last night. She was even going to buy their beer, but he hadn't let her.

The cashier stared at her, tapping the keys on the cash register impatiently. The woman in line behind her sighed her annoyance.

"Is there a problem?" the cashier asked.

Mandy laughed weakly. "I guess I can only afford the juice and the bread," she said.

The cashier rolled her eyes, and the woman behind her muttered, "Dirty hippies."

Mandy's eyes burned in embarrassment as she stomped home. Did Donovan take the money? Carol wouldn't have. That made no sense.

She threw the grocery sack on the kitchen table, then hurried to her room, where she tossed things around, looking for the money. Maybe it had fallen out of her purse. She found nothing.

Carol stood in Mandy's doorway. "What's wrong?" she asked.

"I'm missing fifteen dollars," Mandy said.

"I told you that guy was no good," Carol said.

Instantly Mandy regretted saying anything.

"You don't know he took it. Maybe I just lost it," Mandy said.

"Your problem is you are so gullible," Carol said.

"I don't want to hear what my problem is, Carol," Mandy said, slamming her bedroom door.

Going to California

It took some coaxing on Mandy's part to get Carol to agree to drive her out to the Wagon Wheel that night. Carol was convinced Donovan had taken Mandy's money, but Mandy still hoped it was all a simple misunderstanding. When they arrived, Donovan wasn't there. At the bar Mandy ordered a rum and Coke, no rum, and Carol said she'd have the same. Then they listened the band, a bunch of local boys playing covers of popular songs. After an hour, Carol said she was tired of waiting and told Mandy they should leave.

"Not yet," Mandy said. "He'll be here."

Carol shook her head. "If he took your money, and you know what I think, then he's probably long gone."

"He wouldn't do that," Mandy protested.

"He wouldn't? What do you really know about him? You met him two weeks ago. He lives in a motel. He could be a criminal. I mean, how would you know?"

"But he's—." Mandy wanted to defend Donovan and prove Carol wrong, but it was true she didn't know that much about him.

"I don't want you here by yourself."

"I'm not a child. You don't have to babysit me."

"Fine," Carol said. "See if I care if he hurts you." She left Mandy alone at the bar.

The band was playing *Brown Eyed Girl* when Rob walked in. He saw Mandy at the bar and smiled. She waved.

"Whatcha drinking?" he asked, leaning in to kiss her cheek.

"A rum and Coke," she said.

"You gotta take it easy with those things," Rob said, grinning. "I'll take a beer," he told the bartender.

Rob told Mandy she looked pretty, and she said thanks. "Good song," he said. "You're my brown-eyed girl," aren't you?

She sipped her drink and stirred the ice and lime with the little cocktail straw. "Got your note," she said. "You should have woken me up."

Rob sensed she was annoyed. "Wanna dance?" he asked, thinking it might ease the tension. She said she didn't feel like it. He saw her jaw tighten. She obviously knew about the money. Why else would she be upset? He thought about what he had done that morning, how he had gone through her purse—. He didn't know why he had done it. It was like he couldn't control the impulse. He honestly didn't think she'd even notice or might think she'd just misplaced the money.

Fuck it, he thought. He wasn't planning to marry this girl, but he couldn't afford to make enemies either. He thought he'd better smooth things over. Rob smiled, took a swig of his beer, then nodded his head in time with the music.

"Hey, I totally forgot," he said, as if a lost thought had just come back to him. "I borrowed $15 from you this morning."

"You mean you stole it," she said.

"No—," he said, acting shocked that she'd even think that. "Borrowed. I was going to go to your record store and buy a couple of albums to surprise you. I knew I didn't have enough, so I thought I'd borrow a few bucks from you and pay you back when I could."

"I was at work. You never came to the store."

"I was going to, I said. Then I thought it was a dumb idea." He reached to his back pocket and took out his wallet. He paid for the beer, then took out fifteen dollars and handed it to her.

She clasped the money in her hand and sighed.

"Why would I lie? Aren't you my girl?" he said, taking her hand and squeezing it.

"If you say so," she said.

"I say so," he said. They sipped their drinks and listened to the band, neither attempting to talk over the music. Then Rob leaned in and said, "I gotta take a leak." He reached around to put his wallet away, waving to the bartender with his other hand. "Another round," he said before slipping off the bar stool.

When Mandy unzipped her purse to put the money away, she noticed Donovan's wallet on the floor and got down to pick it up. Driven by curiosity, she opened it. She gasped at what she saw. Fifty dollars, at least. "What the hell?" she whispered. She felt a lurch in her stomach at what she noticed next. The name on his driver's license was Robert W. Lang, Jr.

"Robert?" she sputtered. Mandy glanced over at the entrance to the men's room and saw him talking and laughing with a group of girls. What was she going to do?

The bartender set their drinks on the bar and smiled. Quickly Mandy laid the wallet back on the floor where she'd found it and climbed back on the stool. The cold glass felt good in her sweaty hand. Her heart racing, she sipped the drink. The bartender had remembered, just Coke and lime. Maybe Carol was right, she thought. Maybe Donov—, Robert, was someone she should be afraid of.

The band told the crowd they were going to take a quick break, but not to go anywhere because they'd be back soon to play some slow dance tunes. "All you ladies get ready," the singer said.

Mandy laughed. The singer was probably not even old enough to order a drink. "Ladies," she scoffed.

Rob was back at Mandy's side now. "Miss me?" he said, moving her ponytail to kiss the back of her neck.

When she flinched, he frowned. "What's wrong?"

"Nothing. Just tickles," she said.

He shrugged and sat on the bar stool. "Hey, you know those girls over there?" Rob asked, pointing behind him.

"Where?" Mandy said, coughing as she spoke.

"By the restrooms. They kind of ambushed me when I came out. Guess you better hold on tight to your man." He laughed.

He had a cover story for that, too, she thought. Was everything about him a lie?

"Never saw them before," she said, coolly.

"Everything okay?" he said.

"Of course."

Rob reached for his beer, but the bartender reminded him it would be a buck and a half.

"Unless the lady wants to pay," Rob joked, "cuz I'm about broke now."

Mandy couldn't control her face. Was he for real?

"Just kidding," he said. Rob reached back for his wallet and realized it was gone. He looked quickly around him and saw it on the floor. "Man, that's not good," he said, reaching down to retrieve it.

"What's not good," Mandy said.

"I dropped my wallet," he said, laying two dollars on the bar. Then he slipped his wallet in his pocket, feeling again to make sure it was secure.

"Good thing you found it," she said.

Rob nodded. "Seriously," Rob said, "about the fifteen bucks. I just wanted to do something nice for you. It stinks not having enough money sometimes."

It took all her will to listen to him and not confront him. "Yeah. I know what that's like," she said, hopping off the bar stool. "I gotta go to the ladies room."

Mandy sat on the toilet and clutched her purse in her lap. Outside the stall, girls chattered and laughed, turned faucets on and off. If a person lied to you all the time, Mandy thought, were you even safe?

She wished Carol were still there to drive her home. Even so, she could just sneak out and walk home. Maybe there would even be someone in the parking lot she could get a ride from. But what if Dono—. Ugh. Robert. Robert! She couldn't get that through her head. What if he drove after her? What would he do? She knew she wouldn't be able to fight him off if he tried to force her in his car. Mandy shook her head. You're letting your imagination get away from you, she thought.

Mandy heard the band warming up and realized she'd need to decide soon what to do. She fumbled in her purse for her house key and was relieved to see it where she expected it to be. The money Robert returned to her was still lying loose. Instead of putting it in her wallet, she decided it would be more secure in the small pocket of her purse, though he'd have to be a real idiot to try to steal from her again. She slid open the zipper. Lying in the bottom of the otherwise empty pocket was a small white pill. Mandy lifted it out and held it between her thumb and finger. "I forgot all about this," she said.

At a party the previous summer, she had been given the pill. A girl from one of her classes had a baggy full of them. "Downers," she said. "It'll mellow you out, man."

Mandy accepted the pill but instead of swallowing it, she dropped it in her purse. Later that night, drunk and disoriented, Mandy wobbled into the bathroom and saw that same girl on the floor, her head hanging over the edge of the toilet. Mandy told Carol about the girl the next day. While Carol could be an insufferable know-it-all, she had probably been right when she said that girl was lucky they didn't have to take her to the hospital and pump her stomach.

Mandy held the little pill in her hand and thought of all the money in *his* wallet. She returned it to the zippered pouch along with her cash. She stood at the sink and washed her hands. When she lifted her face to the mirror, she smiled. Robert had no idea, but he was going to be her ticket out of Iowa after all.

Back at the bar, Mandy put her arms around Robert.

"Hey, there you are," he said. "I thought maybe you ditched me."

She lowered her eyes demurely. "I was thinking we could go to your motel tonight. I've never slept in a motel bed before."

"That's more like it," Rob said, chugging the rest of his beer, before leading her out to his car.

At the motel, Rob told Mandy to make herself at home.

"Want a beer?" he asked, pulling two bottles from the refrigerator.

"Sure," she said. "Does that thing work?" she said, pointing to the old radio on kitchenette counter.

He tuned the radio to the local college station. Then he snapped the caps off the beers and handed one to her.

Mandy took a sip, then set her beer on the bedside table.

"I'll be right back," he said. "Gotta pee again, but you can get comfortable," he said, patting the mattress.

When the bathroom door clicked, Mandy retrieved the little pill, crushed it, and dropped the powder into Rob's beer, swishing the bottle a bit to help it dissolve. Then she placed her purse on the chair by the door. After, she sat on the edge of the bed and listened to the radio. Her foot tapped from nerves, not the music.

"Hey, cool," he said, now out of the bathroom. "Glad to see you're making yourself at home."

Mandy said it was a nice room. "Almost like an apartment."

"Bed's comfy, right?" he said, then guzzled his beer. "Ah," he said, letting out a small belch afterwards. "How's yours? You like this brand?"

"Yeah. I guess."

"It's cheap, but it's got a bit of an aftertaste. Sorry I can't make you a rum and Coke," he said.

"That's all right. This is fine." She took small sips and tried to look relaxed.

Rob lifted his bottle and emptied it. "Ugh," he said. "Bitter. Want another one?"

"I'm fine," she said, but you go ahead.

He went to the refrigerator. *Mellow Yellow*, he said, indicating the song currently on the radio. My favorite, right? He laughed.

"Too bad you didn't really write it," she said. "We'd probably be in a nicer motel right now."

He took a long drink from the bottle then set it on the table opposite where Mandy sat. He sat on the bed, took off his shoes, and put his feet up. He patted the bed again.

"Come on. Lie next to me," he said.

"I will," she said. "But I should use the bathroom first."

She sat on the edge of the bathtub and let the minutes pass. Then, she got up, flushed the toilet for effect, and ran the faucet. When she opened the door, Rob had pulled the bedspread down and was lying on the sheets, his shirt off. He had turned off one of the lamps and the room was dim. He yawned wide and shook it off.

She could see that she would have to lie down next to him for a while. She put her shoes under the chair where her purse lay and took off her sweater.

"Let's just talk for a while," she said, climbing onto the bed next to him. "or just relax and listen to the music."

Later when Rob pulled Mandy to him and kissed her, he said his lips felt numb. "Did you put a spell on me?" he joked.

Mandy stroked his head and rocked against him, kissing him softly, now and then, humming to the music, lulling him to sleep. And before long, just as she had hoped, Rob was out.

Mid-morning Rob woke, his head groggy, but he was otherwise happy, remembering Mandy was lying next to him. He reached out to touch her, to tell her good morning, but the bed was empty. Opening his eyes, he saw only rumpled sheets. He lay there and listened, thinking she was probably in the bathroom. When he opened his eyes again, he saw the bathroom door was open. Where'd she go? he thought. He got up and went to the window. He opened the drapes and the sun flooded into the dark room, stinging his swollen eyes. When his fuzzy brain connected, he looked back out to the parking lot. Where was his car?

"What the hell?" He glanced at the nightstand where his keys should have been, where his wallet was. He opened his wallet—not a single dollar left.

His mind raced to his duffle that he kept stuffed under the bed. It lay unzipped on the floor. His clothes and papers were strewn about. And the small bag where he kept his extra cash was on the floor, open, and empty.

"Fuck!" he yelled.

"Hi. How ya doin' Carol," Rob said with forced good humor, his hand sweaty as he gripped the phone. "Is Mandy around?"

"No idea where she is," Carol said. "She must have left during the night. All her stuff's gone. I mean all of it." Carol made a loud tsk sound that hurt Rob's ear. "I figured you two were running off together." Her mocking laugh made him slam the receiver.

Now what? he thought. How would he go after her? And where would he even begin to look? After all their talk, she was probably on her way to California, but she could be headed anywhere. Rob sat on the edge of the bed, holding his pounding head in his hands. She had his car, she had his money, and she was hours away.

The manager was wiping down the glass counter when Rob came into the office, wearing the same fatigue jacket he had on the day he'd checked in. She smiled and asked how his day was going. When he told her that he'd be checking out, she said she was sorry to hear it. Rob said his plans had changed and he needed to leave today. He asked if it would be possible to get a refund for the amount he had paid for the upcoming week.

She seemed reluctant, but agreed, and counted the cash into his hand.

"You can leave the key on the kitchenette counter," she said.

He asked about the road maps in the wire rack by the door.

"Free as can be," she said.

Rob was really broke now, and the $42 refund wasn't going to last long. He realized it was not enough for the extravagance of bus tickets or motels. Food would be his priority, and a half loaf of bread and an almost empty jar of peanut butter would not last long. He'd have to hitchhike, figure out some way to get money. Get a goddamn job. He sure couldn't go back home. He had both dismantled that bridge and burnt it to a heap of ashes, not to mention he'd probably be thrown in jail.

Out on the road, no longer within sight of the motel, Rob stuck out his thumb, something he had never done before. In the past he had driven by hitchhikers and laughed at them, calling them dumb suckers, sometimes out his open window loud enough for them to hear. Now he was the sucker, and he felt every bit of the humiliation.

The sun burned against his neck and intensified his headache. An old truck puttered by leaving a trail of blue exhaust. Several more cars passed before a black sedan pulled onto the shoulder.

Rob tossed his things in the back seat and slid into the passenger seat. "Thanks," he told the driver.

"Sure. Glad to help," the driver said. "I'm Fred, by the way."

"Mark," Rob said.

"Vietnam?" Fred asked.

"First Brigade. Fifth Infantry Division," Rob said, not sure where such a precise detail had come from. Probably from his father who was always talking as if he'd been in the thick of it, but no more a veteran than Rob was.

"Korea for me," Fred said. "Air Force. I'm headed to Rochester. It's in Minnesota. That direction okay with you?"

It was way too close to home, but Rob told Fred he was just wandering, so it really didn't matter. "Trying to get my head right, you know—."

Fred told Rob there was no need to explain. Fred smoked one cigarette after another and honked at slower cars as he pushed past the

175

speed limit.

Just like my dad, Rob thought. He hated being reminded of his parents, who barged into his thoughts no matter what he did to try to keep them out. Rob imagined them at the table after lunch. His father would be talking, his mother listening, her fingers tapping the table, his father yelling at her to cut it out. "It's been two weeks, Arlene," he'd say. "You don't honestly think he's coming back, do you?" She would burst into tears and wonder how her life had come to this.

All the "what ifs" continued to nag at Rob. What if they had finally found his mother's car at Lucky Lou's? What if old Glen had described the car he had sold that poor widower, Robert Lang? What if they tracked Mandy down somewhere, zipping along the highway in the Falcon? What would she say? She knew how to hurt him.

As Fred drove, Rob watched the miles, fields green with corn, and tried to calm his mind, which was so much easier said than done. If I ever, Rob thought, see that bitch again, she's going to regret she was ever born.

Part Three

The Crazy Train

NEWTON, IOWA 1968

It was quarter past nine at night, and Terry had been walking for an hour since his last ride dropped him off. He had been passed by so many times, he had almost given up. But the ache in his legs told him to keep trying, so he adjusted the strap of his bag on his shoulder and turned to face the headlights of the oncoming traffic, thumb raised in weary hope. Ten minutes later, just south of DeKalb, a van pulled to the shoulder. A tall man got out of the front to open the side door. He was thin and his blond beard and beginning-to-bald head made him look older than he probably was.

"I'm Jim," the man said, extending his hand to Terry. "Welcome to the crazy train."

"I'm Terry. Thanks for stopping."

Terry was swept into the van as if he were the lost lamb they had all been searching for. Everyone greeted Terry cheerfully, then rearranged themselves to make room for him. Besides Jim, there was the driver Ritchie, and in the back with Terry, three others, a young, bearded man named Paul, who was with a dark-haired girl named Karen. Terry settled himself close to the back of the driver's seat, near a blonde girl named Bridget who rested in a nest of blankets. Moments later they were back on the road.

"Where you headed, man?" Jim asked, handing Terry a freshly lit joint.

Terry took a hit and handed the joint to the blonde girl. She took it, inhaled, then passed it on.

"Nowhere, I guess," Terry said.

Jim waved his hand over the others in the van, six of them now, with Terry aboard. "We're all on that same journey, man. Just out there trying to find where it's at, you know? Does anyone really belong anywhere? Or do we all just belong everywhere?"

"That's deep, man," said Richie.

Terry lifted his chin and studied the roof of the van. In the dim glow of the dashboard lights, he could see it had been painted in a rainbow swirl, kind of like Van Gogh's *The Starry Night*, except instead of blues and golds, were all the colors of the rainbow. Jefferson Airplane was on the eight-track player, "Somebody to Love," a song Terry really liked.

He waved off the joint when it got back around to him. His head was already woozy enough and at some point, he was going to have to think about where he would go next. After he left Dennis and Sharon's, Terry had planned to head north to his sister Linda's place, but he had since decided not to. What would it solve? He would only be closer to his mother and going back to her house was something he would not do. So, he'd been thinking maybe Canada, though he was in no danger of being drafted yet. His eighteenth birthday was still months away.

Vietnam weighed on him though. The specter of war was everywhere, from photographs in newspapers to actual film on TV news. Terry thought about what Donette said when they'd watched in horror the footage of a South Vietnamese general putting a revolver to the head of a prisoner and shooting him. "This shit ain't no good," she'd said. "President Johnson thinks people are against the war now? Showing this on TV is just going to make it worse. Going to be more protests. Going to get real ugly."

It might be smart to head north and cross over into Canada before he had no choice, Terry thought. He had no wish to end up like Dennis. Terry probably wouldn't be that lucky, though. He imagined himself suited up in army green, but instead of being out on patrol, he'd be at the edge of a rice paddy with a bullet in his brain. That's about right, he thought. I would get killed looking up at the stars. I'd be thinking how beautiful it all was, and before I'd finish the thought, the bullet would hit. And it would be a hairy situation, so the platoon would just let me lie there in the mud, my eyes wide open, still staring at the sky.

Maybe Jim knew something. He seemed like a guy who had been around. How does someone get close enough to walk into Canada? Then once you are there, how do you get by? It wouldn't be like going to France where it would be obvious you were a foreigner, but still, would Canadians just take him in? And he would have to get a job, a real job, no more hustling. Contemplating the unknown made his chest hurt. If he thought too long about it, that sick taste would rise into his throat. He rested his head against the steel wall of the van.

The blonde offered Terry a small macrame covered pillow and he accepted it gratefully. "Thanks," he said. "You're Bridget, right?"

"You remembered my name," she said, sounding pleased. "I won't bother you anymore, so you can sleep," she said.

"You're not bothering me," he said. "Thanks again for the pillow." Terry laid his head down. He stared at the silhouettes of the driver and Jim, before finally succumbing to the hypnotic rhythm of the road. He did not feel the van slow down for a stop at a wooded rest area at two a.m. or the engine start up a few hours later.

When they pulled into a gas station on the outskirts of Newton, Iowa, the sun was pink in the sky behind them. The driver's door squeaked open and startled Terry awake. The others stretched and yawned.

"Holy mother," Jim said, grinning to the sleepy-eyed crew in the back. "I can't believe we made it. I wasn't too sure for a while. Ante up boys and girls."

In what Terry decided was a ritual, everyone threw a few coins into the leather coin purse Jim passed back to them. Terry added two dollars, and as he did so, Bridget looked as if he had exposed a million dollars.

While the station attendant finished filling the tank, Ritchie helped by washing the windshield of the velvet green VW bus. When he saw the attendant's confused expression, Richie said, "It's okay, man. I did your job when I was in high school. People used to expect everything from me—check the tires, change the oil, put on a new wiper blade, wipe my ass. Christ. That's what garages are for, right?"

The attendant laughed.

"That'll be $3.85," the attendant said, adjusting his glasses that had slid onto the bridge of his nose. Jim counted bills and coins into the young man's outstretched hand.

The crew settled into a large corner booth at the Pine Breeze Diner near the gas station. Wide windows looked out onto the parking lot and the highway. Terry thought of how ironic the name of the diner was, since all he could see for miles were flat corn fields.

"Mornin' folks," the waitress said. Dori, according to her name tag. She looked fifty, was heavy-hipped, and her salt and pepper hair was curled in a tight style.

Dori set glasses of water all around and told them the special that morning was biscuits and sausage gravy.

"That sounds great, Dori," said Jim.

Terry was starting to realize that Jim was a bit like Gandalf, the one who disarmed the suspicious, cajoled the wary, and lighted the path through dim forests of wandering.

Dori smiled and left them to look over their menus.

"We're sixty-five cents ahead in gas money," Ritchie said. "It's a beautiful day."

"That it is," Jim said.

When Dori brought plates and plates of biscuits and gravy, eggs runny or scrambled, bacon, stacks of toast, and waffles, Terry commented on how much food there was.

"Breakfast is cheap" Jim said, "so we load up."

Terry liked Jim. He could tell that everyone felt the same. And Terry hadn't forgotten that at some point, he wanted to feel him out about what it would take for him to cross over into Canada. In the booth opposite Terry was the married couple, Karen and Paul. They'd been further back in the van and hadn't spoken to Terry beyond saying hello. This morning Terry noticed that Karen was pregnant. As she poured syrup over her waffles and sausage, Terry wondered how she managed being on the road.

After breakfast, the crew got back on the road, with Paul driving and Karen with him up front. Ritchie tossed a stack of road maps into Terry's lap—Iowa, Wisconsin, Minnesota, Nebraska, South Dakota. "I overheard you say you weren't sure where you were headed yet," he said. "These might help you figure things out. In case you don't want to go all the way to California with us."

The van hit a bump in the road and tossed the loose passengers in the back against each other. Jim grabbed a nearby sleeping bag and fitted it under his head as a pillow. He turned on his side toward the wall. Paul turned up the radio to hear Cream's *Sunshine of Your Love.* Terry looked at the cover of the Wisconsin map—the state that held so much pain. He tucked it under the others, opened the Iowa map, found Newton, where they'd just been. It was a little town almost directly in the center of the state. He'd never been to Iowa before today. It seemed like an okay place, but it didn't call to him. Some places had a pull. Iowa did not.

"You been on the road a long time?" Bridget asked.

She'd been quiet at breakfast, and it was nice to hear her voice again. She'd been singing along with the radio last night and it sounded pretty. If he had known this girl in high school, he would have asked her out, he thought. Then moments later, he realized he wouldn't even have had the courage to talk to her. But he wasn't that boy any longer. He wasn't sure who he was. But he hadn't been that boy for a long time.

"Things got weird at home about two years ago," he said.

She said she understood. They took turns telling each other about their interests. Bridget said she liked to work in the garden and grow flowers.

"That's cool," Terry said. "I'm more into imaginative gardens."

"What?" she said, not understanding.

"Books. I read a lot."

She asked him what his favorite books were, and when he mentioned *The Catcher in the Rye*, she shook her head. "Don't know how you can stand that book," she said.

"Whattya mean?"

"Holden. He's such a whiney baby. Phoney this and phoney that."

"But he's an allegory—."

She eyed him skeptically.

"I mean, he stands for all of us, you know, anyone who thinks the world shouldn't change. Kids ought to be able to believe that all those things they hope for in life are going to be there when they grow up."

"Yeah," she said, "but that is never how it really is." She turned away, pulled the window curtain aside, and stared at the road.

Terry turned back to the maps. If he were really serious about crossing into Canada, it wouldn't be smart to go much further west. If he left the group soon, he could proceed straight north, pass through Minneapolis, then veer east toward Duluth or west toward Bemidji. But then where? On the map, Ontario appeared to be one tremendous forest. Terry thought of Tolkien's maps. Wasn't he looking at much the same? True, Superior National Forest wasn't Mordor, but if he found himself at its edges, Terry realized he would have just as much trepidation about where he was going as Frodo did. In contrast, Manitoba looked like it might be similar in landscape to North Dakota. And a real city, Winnipeg, was not far from the border. Terry felt a paralyzing state of indecision. He shoved the maps into his duffle and closed his eyes.

When a person belongs nowhere, he thought, anywhere is as good a destination as the next. But anywhere is never home. He missed Donette, his life with her. Amid all that was not normal in how they lived, they had their normal, their routines. Life with her felt like what life should feel like. Home, meals together, even cleaning. He missed vacuuming. He missed the lemon oil smell of a freshly dusted room. He missed jokes only they understood, the knowing looks they gave each other. He missed not having to consider every little word he said and how someone else might be offended or confused.

Help Wanted

Marion studied the wooden extension ladder propped up against the wall in the barn near the tool bench. Just like some of the tools hanging on the pegboard behind the bench, spiders had used it more than she had. She brushed away a sticky web and pulled the round-runged ladder from the wall before realizing its unwieldy length also outweighed her. Lily was out in the drive leading her new nanny goat around on a leash. The goat had been a present for Lily's fifteenth birthday the previous Saturday. Marion didn't have the heart to break Lily's blissful moment to ask for help. She set the ladder against the wall, consigning it back to the spiders for the time being.

"How's your new girl doing," Marion asked Lily.

"She's wonderful," Lily said.

"Does she have a name yet?"

Lily said she was thinking about Mildred.

"I had an Aunt Mildred," Marion said. "She was the sweetest person. Always sneaking me sweets when we'd visit her. She died when I was about your age. I haven't thought of her in a long time, but I think she'd be tickled to have a darling goat named after her."

Lily beamed brightly. "Then she's definitely going to be Mildred."

Marion bent to pet Mildred on the head. "I can see you're going to be a spoiled child, but that's just fine by me."

Lily led the goat into the barn to the chicken-wire pen they'd made for her in the northeast corner. Bales of straw banked the front edges. The man who sold them the goat had explained how she would sleep best off the ground, so Marion and Roger built a ramp that went up to a four by six wooden platform that Lily covered in loose straw and an old plaid blanket.

Marion had almost given in to Lily's plea to stay out in the barn with the goat on her first night on the farm. She hated her words later. "That would just be silly," she had said. Why demean the child for a clearly loving impulse? But Lily had not argued back. And the next morning when she found her goat down from the platform munching straw, as happy as ever, Lily decided the goat would be safe in the barn alone each night.

With garden gloves on, Marion ran the paint scraper against the peeling clapboards. Flecks of sun-bleached paint landed below on an old sheet covering her dahlias. She scraped and scraped. The job was slow going. She'd rather paint. Honestly, she wouldn't mind painting if all this before-hand work could be done by someone else. Looking up at the peeling gable, thinking of that old ladder, she realized she had no desire to climb such heights even if she could maneuver the ladder by herself. In such moments, she felt her age. And it did not help that her sister emphasized that point.

"Some tasks are just too much for a 62-year-old widow," Vivian told her a few weeks earlier. Marion rejected the comment.

"You know what I mean," Vivian said.

Marion did know. It's just that sometimes Vivian's well-meant comments got under her skin, especially when her sister was right.

"The whole thing needs painting," Vivian said later as they sat in the shade on the front porch. "You ought to put an ad in the paper. If you buy the paint and supplies, you could have it done inexpensively. You see ads for painters all the time."

Tossing the scraper to the ground, Marion wiped the sweat from her forehead and decided her sister was right. Again.

After dinner, Lily and Marion sat in the living room, the television off as it was most nights. Marion preferred to read or work on hand embroidery. Besides, there was too much bad news these days, and comedy or variety shows did little to wipe it away. She preferred silence. Silence and the occasional snorts of contentment from Sarge.

In Lily's lap lay a steno pad. At dinner she had told Marion she wanted to write the ad for the painting job and Marion said she would appreciate it. Lily lifted the pencil, moved her lips as she read what she had written, then erased, then wrote again.

"How's this sound?" Lily asked a few minutes later.

"Wanted. Capable painter to scrape and paint exterior of two-story farmhouse. All supplies provided. Contact M. Goodman."

"I especially like the phrase 'capable painter,'" Marion said. "I think you better add my phone number, but other than that, it's very well done."

When Lily had gone up to bed, Marion glanced at the steno pad on the kitchen table. Not only had Lily the loveliest cursive, penmanship an old teacher could be proud of, but she also had begun to sketch a rough portrait of Sarge at the bottom of the page. The details were so tenderly rendered that Marion wanted to tear that part away and keep it for herself, a symbol of the growing love she felt for Lily.

"It's time to file formal guardianship papers," she whispered out loud to herself as she crawled between her own sheets. "I don't know what I would do if I lost her now."

Wisconsin Map

IOWA 1968

Before the van of wayfarers crossed the Missouri River into Nebraska, they stopped at the edge of town for gas and bought bottles of pop from the machine outside the station. Terry pushed the root beer button and his bottle clunked to the slot below.

Bridget lifted the fluted green Coke bottle to her lips. "Ah," she said. "That first fizzy sip. So good." She smiled at Terry. "Come sit with me at that picnic table." She took Terry's hand and pulled him with her to a little space of grass at the edge of the pavement. She sat with the sun at her back and the afternoon sky lit the ends of her hair. Terry had never seen anyone so beautiful. He wanted to ask Bridget so many things, but he could not make one question form in his mouth.

"Sorry about before," Bridget said.

"Before?" Terry said, confused.

"When you were telling me about Holden. That's what my freshman English teacher said, too. And all that stuff about his hunting hat being on backwards. I get it. But how does it help me find my way? Reading a book about a boy who can't find his?"

Terry considered her question. It was a good question. At the moment he had no idea how to answer it.

"If you find your place in a book, though," she said, "I think that's cool."

"Where will you find your place," he said. "California?"

"You never know." She smiled and finished her Coke. "For two days at the beginning of summer, I thought I found it at a farm in Wisconsin. A woman named Marion took me in. If you had seen me then—." She rolled her eyes and laughed. "I was really lost. See, Holden, he's got a nice house, a sister who loves him. She adores him. And his parents give him everything. So what if they're detached? He's a rich kid. He's got the whole world waiting for him. But not me. I had none of that. And my parents were horrible. But at Marion's house—." She looked off into the open prairie beyond the gas station. "I felt so safe. I could have stayed there forever."

"Why didn't you?"

"How do you just tell someone who's not your family that you wish they were?"

Terry understood better than he could say.

"I think about her though, Marion. All the time. I lie awake at night and imagine my life in California—or wherever I end up. When I picture my house, it's her house. A big farmhouse at the top of a long steep driveway, a red barn, neat garden, wide front porch under shade trees, hens clucking in the driveway. I imagine I become just like her, just as kind and thoughtful."

"She sounds like a great person," Terry said.

"She's—. Well, she's more than that," Bridget said. "Have you ever known someone who knew what you needed even when you didn't?"

Terry was about to answer when Paul's voice raised everyone's attention. He and Karen had been leaning against the van, but now he had her by the arm as she attempted to get away from him.

"Just listen to me," Paul shouted.

"No," Karen cried. She wrenched her arm away from him and climbed into the van. Paul went in after her.

Bridget and Terry went to the opposite side of the station to where Jim and Ritchie sat on a berm under the weak shade of a young oak tree.

"Those two can't seem to get their shit together," Ritchie said.

Jim remained silent.

"When we were in the restroom earlier," Bridget said, "Karen told me she wants to go home. She said if Paul didn't take her back to Terre Haute, she was going to leave him and go by herself."

Before long, Paul emerged from the van with the couple's bags. Karen, red-eyed, went to Bridget and the two embraced. Terry felt the need to step away, but he was penned in, so he stood next to Ritchie and listened as Paul explained the situation to Jim.

"We're not—."

"No need, man," Jim said. "You gotta do what you gotta do."

"It's just that Karen, well, she misses home."

Jim looked down at his shoes.

"The worst part," Paul said, "is that I hate to leave you strapped for gas money."

Jim shook his head. "Don't you worry about that. We'll pick up someone new. We always do." Jim shook Paul's hand and held it a moment, as if to reinforce what he said next.

"It'll be okay, man," Jim said. "It's always okay."

The gesture hit Terry as a sudden profound truth. All he'd been through—. And here he was, safe, fed, among people who were kind. Maybe the world was a place where no matter where you went you would be okay. Like moving through water, it never left you, but always came to buoy you and carry you within. Terry knew, finally, what he would do.

"Seems we're losing everyone in a single day," Jim said when Terry told him he would be leaving the group too. "Though I didn't expect you'd be going along much farther. There's something holding you close to home, I think."

Terry smiled and shook his head. "Not home, but something," he said.

"We better get on the road," Ritchie said.

"Yep," Jim agreed.

Terry shook Jim's hand, then Ritchie's. "Thanks for everything," he said.

"No sweat," Ritchie said.

Jim just gave Terry a nod.

Before she climbed into the van, Bridget put her arms around Terry and hugged him fiercely. "You go get 'em Holden," she said. "Find what you're searching for." She tucked a folded note into Terry's hand, then turned and walked to the van. Once she was inside, Jim shut the door and got in the front seat.

"Take it easy," Jim said from the passenger side window to the three still standing on the gravel driveway of the gas station.

"You too," Paul shouted.

Karen waved as Ritchie drove away. When the van was a green blur in the distance, Karen asked Terry where he would go.

"North," he answered.

"Guess we're on our way to the bus station," Paul said.

Karen wrapped her arm around his waist. From Paul's expression, Terry sensed her gesture felt like a lasso.

"Best wishes on the baby," Terry said. Then he picked up his duffle and walked along the shoulder in the opposite direction. It felt good to stretch his legs, felt good to have a destination. Terry stuck out his thumb once again.

"Where you headed, son," the trucker asked.

"Wisconsin," Terry said.

"I can take you as far as Cedar Rapids," the driver said.

"Thanks! I appreciate it."

The driver, who wore a green plaid shirt and a seed-corn cap was a tall, thin man who didn't look much older than Terry. But he moved older. He spoke older. And he shifted the gears and turned the wheel like he had been doing it forever. When the driver turned to offer Terry a smoke, it was hard not to notice the star-shaped scar below the ridge of his sunburned collar bone. Terry's guess was Vietnam, but he didn't ask.

"No thanks," Terry said. The driver smiled and tucked the pack of Camels in his shirt pocket. Instead, Terry appreciated the silent space between them, and he leaned against the window. He thought of Bridget's note. He had taken it out to read three times while he walked along the road.

Use your Wisconsin map. East of Fond du Lac, west of Plymouth, south of Highway 23. On Summit Road. Look for the egg sign. She'll cook for you and help you on your way. Her name is Marion.

Terry never did ask Jim about Canada. The idea was a possibility too remote, even for Terry's imagination. In the two years Terry had been on his own, he had never truly been alone. He had—one way or another—found himself in the company of others. He thought Canada would mean isolation, and he was not sure he was ready for that kind of life. The camaraderie of the "crazy train" only reinforced his sense that he was not a loner.

Bridget had begun to tell him a story, and he wanted to know the rest. There was a woman named Marion who raised chickens. Her farm sat on a mile-long road, alone but not lonely, and had long views of the sky—blue in the morning, purple in the evening. She lived in a big house. In one room there was an entire wall of books. It was a house that felt, from the moment you stepped inside, like it had always been your home.

He would go there. Find what he could find. Maybe he would walk through a door that would lead him to where he was always meant to go. If not, it would be a door to another door. He had no idea what he would find when he got there, whether Bridget's memory or his own invention. But he was not worried. Like Jim said. It'll be okay. It was always okay.

The Hired Hand

Lily ran her hands over the siding on the hen house, checking to see if the second coat of butter yellow paint was dry enough for her to add the floral embellishment she had been fussing over for weeks, drawing, erasing, crumpling paper, and starting over again. She wanted the design to be perfect, for Marion.

"Looks like an Amish hex sign," Marion said when she first saw Lily's sketch.

Lily had seen such circular ornaments in the gable peaks of some of the houses near where she used to live. The nice houses, not the one she lived in before her father went to jail.

Lily decided to place the design about eight inches below the sloping roof, between two divided-light windows that faced the garden. She tied one length of twine to a pencil and the other to a sharp tack she'd found in Marion's "you-never-know-when-you-might-need-it" drawer. Eyeing the center space between the windows, Lily pounded the tack end into one of the wide planks of the hen house wall. Then pulling the twine taut, she drew a circle. She jiggled the tack loose to remove it. She used a ruler to dissect the circle in four equal quadrants. Each quadrant would contain a replica of her design—a long stemmed, drooping tulip with a single leaf. She would paint the stems and leaves dark green, the flower itself, deep blood red. She would paint the dissecting lines as well as the center circle and the outside border black. She would paint hearts at the top of the lines, and they would lie within the circle. Those would be soft green, like the fragrant leaves of Marion's lavender plant. Once the outlines were drawn, she laid the paper flower, an inverse stencil, on the siding and traced carefully.

She had completed the first quadrant when a noisy, dark green pickup pulled in and idled at the end of the driveway. Lily had never seen the truck before. It did not belong to one of Marion's regular egg customers. And because she had promised Roger to take note of anything odd, she wrote the license plate number in a corner of her stencil. She waited, anxious to get back to her project, but no one got out of the truck. She wondered if the driver might be lost, but she did not feel comfortable venturing down the driveway to ask if she could help. While she knew there was no reason for it, Lily felt a sense of dread. She shook off the feeling as a silly notion. She was safe now, here with Marion. Lily knew that in her head. But knowing something and feeling something were not the same thing. Lily glanced at the house, wondering why Marion hadn't come out as she usually did when someone pulled in.

Just as Lily heard the porch door squeak, the truck drove off in an impatient thrust of gravel. In the settling dust, a tall young man with a duffle bag slung over his shoulder stood looking up at her. He smiled. She did not smile back. Marion and Sarge were at Lily's side now as the young man approached them.

"I'm here about the ad," he said, climbing the driveway.

Her ad. A house painter needed for an old, two-story farmhouse. Lily remembered after the ad came out in the paper, Marion said they were likely to attract a school teacher with too many mouths to feed. Lily was not prepared for this dark-haired young man in an army jacket. She had never seen a boy with such beautiful eyes. He stood only a few feet from them now. He smelled like mown grass and cigarette smoke, Lily thought.

Marion extended her hand, and the young man shook it.

"I'm Marion Goodman, and this is Lily."

Marion gave no other details beyond Lily's name. Lily said nothing. Sarge nosed curiously around the young man, who reached down and pumped three short flat-palmed pats on the dog's head. Lily noticed the gesture. It was as if he had never petted a dog before.

"Robert—Rob—Ames," he said.

"Robert?"

"Yes, ma'am, or just Rob."

"Why don't we all head up to the house and we can talk about this?"

Marion led the way, Rob after her, and Lily and Sarge lagged behind.

Inside, they sat at the kitchen table. Sarge sprawled on the floor at Lily's feet. Rob asked Marion if he might trouble her for a glass of water. She offered lemonade instead. She also put out a package of sugar-dusted vanilla cookies. Rob grabbed two and ate the first in one mouthful.

Marion offered the package to Lily who waved it off.

"You're not quite who I expected when I placed the ad," Marion said bluntly. "You're awfully young."

"I hope you won't hold that against me," he said with a confident laugh.

Marion let silence hang between them as an invitation to hear more.

Rob explained that he'd been a bit restless after the army. "Vietnam, you know."

He gulped his lemonade and shoved the other cookie into his mouth.

Marion nodded her awareness of the fact that there was a war going on. But my God, she thought, had he been in a uniform only days after turning eighteen? Or before?

"I'm sort of out on a—. What would you call it? Before I begin college in the fall, I thought it would be good to travel around for the summer, work my way from one place to the next."

"You don't live nearby?"

"No ma'am. My folks live in Nebraska."

"But the green truck?" Marion said, confused. "Who dropped you off."

"Just a guy who gave me a lift. I hitchhike now and then. When I earn enough money, I treat myself to a bus ticket. As I said, I'm out to see this great country of ours."

"I don't suppose you have any references?" Marion said.

Rob pulled a crinkled envelope out of his jacket pocket and handed her the note he had written the day before.

She read the brief note that looked to have been written in the chicken scratching of an arthritic widower. The note attested to the fact that *"Robert Ames did a fine job at our place and was a trustworthy employee for the two weeks he stayed with us. Sincerely, Marvin Osterberg"*

"I see," she said, handing back the note. So could you start any time?"

"Yes, ma'am. Only—."

"Yes?"

"Well, as I said, I'm not from around here. And other people I've worked for have given me a room—and my meals."

"I see," Marion said, again. Marion knew she couldn't possibly offer him a room in her house. Especially not with Lily there now. And yet the young man appeared to be in earnest, had a positive reference, looked clean and well fed, in no way desperate like some of the vagrants Roger continued to warn her about.

She pulled a cookie from the package and held it, rubbing her fingers over the rough sugar. "I'm not sure —."

Then in answer Marion's evident quandary, Lily said in a quiet voice, "He could stay in the farm hand's quarters in the barn."

Marion considered the peeling paint on her poor old house and the fact that no one else had answered the ad.

"Yes," she said. "That is exactly the place. Thank you, Lily."

The three of them stood inside the cool shade of the barn. To one side was the goat pen, which Lily planned to paint when she was finished with the hen house, for they had recently discovered the doe was pregnant, and Lily wanted her to have a pretty place for her baby.

Lily introduced Rob to Mildred.

"Will there be other animals in the barn, too?" Rob asked.

"Just the goat," Marion said. "And a cat or two. Does that bother you?"

"No," Rob laughed uneasily. "Of course not."

They turned their attention to the farm hand's quarters. Just as with the goat pen, the structure sat back from the big barn doors about fifteen feet. Marion and Harve had never hired anyone who needed the use of it, but they had never torn it down either. It looked like a tiny house built into the corner of the barn and was even covered by a shingled sloping roof. The lap siding had been painted red, which matched the outside of the barn. There was a concrete threshold at the base of the door, a sort of front porch, and one large window to the left of the door.

Marion pushed the door open and led Rob inside. She clicked the switch by the door and was glad to see the ceiling light worked. The glass cover was filled with the black carcasses of insects.

"It could use a good sweep," Marion said. "And it's small but looks like it was pretty homey at one time."

The cabin's interior walls had been finished with lath and plaster and painted mint green. Cut into the side of the barn were two double hung windows that looked down the sloping lawn to a willow tree at the mouth of the driveway. Under the windows lay a steel spring single bed. Marion remembered the corresponding mattress was rolled up in her attic. She told Rob she would get it later and air it out for him.

A small rusted-iron wood stove sat upon two concrete blocks in one corner, its tall chimney pipe escaping out the ceiling, then far above out the barn roof. A couple of fires would reduce that rust, though Marion hoped her painter would be gone before the evenings cooled enough to warrant its use. To the side of the stove along one wall was a set of cabinets topped by eight feet of kitchen counter, and in the middle a shallow enameled sink sat under a hand pump, which connected to the well. The young man would have clean water.

She opened the small medicine cabinet mounted on the wall over the sink, the edges of its mirror beginning to lose their silver. She noticed an old safety razor, a package of blue blades, and a half bottle of Old Spice after-shave. How long had all that been in there, she wondered. War times or before? Though these were also war times, she thought, and he is a veteran, young as he is.

"Well, it's not much," she said, "but it's cozy. I'll get bedding and some soap and towels and then I think you'll have everything you need."

"A restroom?" he asked.

Marion smiled then led them outside to the north end of the barn to the old privy. It stood as if it had been built to withstand an apocalypse. Unlike her house, the blue paint on the cedar-shingled outhouse showed not a single chip or curl of decay. Harve had used the privy regularly after they first bought the farm. In a moment of urgent need, Marion still did. She kept it swept of spiders and stocked with paper.

"You've used one of these before?"

"Worse than that in Vietnam."

Marion said she didn't doubt it.

Out of barn now, they looked over at the house.

"It's big, I know," she said, "but I hope it won't be too much of a job, that is, if you're still interested."

Rob nodded. "Yes, ma'am. Ready and able."

"I supply the paint and brushes, and room and board, of course, and when the job is finished, one hundred dollars cash," Marion said.

"Thank you," Rob said. "I really appreciate it."

"I'll go fetch that mattress," Marion said. "You might want to sweep a bit before you make up the bed later. There's a broom near the workbench."

Marion laid the mattress across two sawhorses. When she began to hit it with an old wire rug beater, Sarge ran from the noise and dust. As Marion wielded the tool, she was glad she hadn't thrown it out. She was no hoarder, but she didn't see the sense in tossing out something that someday might be used in one way or another. She thought of the oldest tools in the barn, created when horse-drawn plows dragged over the clay-clodded land. Most were silly to use now, with modern versions so much easier, and faster. But one tool she still used regularly was an old reaping hook—a short, wooden handled scythe. The curved blade sliced easily through clumps of withered perennials. Sometimes old things worked just as well—even better, maybe—than new ones, she thought.

Sarge padded along with Lily who waited outside the farmhand's cabin, her arms loaded with bed linens. Rob opened the door.

"My first visitor," he said.

Lily swallowed. "Marion says if you find something in the barn you want to use, to go ahead." Her throat contracted as the words escaped. She had never felt comfortable talking to boys.

Rob reached out to take the bedding from Lily, lingering just long enough for her to feel her cheeks begin to burn.

"Thanks," he said,

She was about to squeak out "you're welcome" when he went back in the cabin, letting the door bang behind him.

Mildred bleated. "Oh, you," Lily said, stroking the goat's head. "What would you know about it?"

Sarge bounded out of the barn and Lily led the goat over to where Marion was finishing up with the mattress.

"How's your little mother doing today," Marion asked.

"She's great," Lily said with enthusiasm, putting her embarrassment behind her. "I've been reading that book we got at the library," Lily said, "and I don't think she will kid until October or November. And from what I can tell, she's healthy as can be."

"She couldn't be in better care. That's for certain," Marion said.
Lily smiled, grateful for the compliment.

"All right," Marion said. "I'm going to take this mattress to our new hired hand. Make sure he's not up to any mischief." She winked at the goat. "That's your department, isn't it Milly Mae?"

Rob had unpacked his bag. An orange crate slid under the bed held his few folded clothes. His jacket hung on a nail to the right of the door.

"How's it going?" Marion said, sticking her head through the cabin door. She stepped inside and looked around. "I thought now would be a good time to show you where the painting supplies are, and then we should look at the house and talk about what I'd like done. That way, you'll be all set to start tomorrow."

"Yeah, sure," he said. "Good idea."

Marion led Rob over to a large tool bench that sat under a pegboard hung with tools. Next to the bench was a deep wooden closet with large double doors secured with an iron latch. On the bottom shelves, Marion had stacked eight gallons of "Doe Gray" latex paint, a collection of old cloths and rags, and two new paintbrushes.

"These cans will need a good shake," she said. "I bought this paint last year thinking I would be able to manage the job myself." She laughed. "My sister has since talked me out of that idea."

Rob caught a glimpse of a little three-legged table lying under the bench. He picked it up and examined it.

"That could be useful," Marion said. She pulled a rag off a peg and handed it to Rob.

He wiped off the top of the table.

"I've got an old lamp I could let you use."

On their way out, Rob set the table on the concrete stoop.

Before they left the barn, Marion pointed to a small door to the right of the big barn doors. "At night I close the big doors," she said. "So, you'll have to use this door when you need to go out. And when you come into supper later, I suggest leaving your lamp on out here.

Otherwise, it'll be dark as pitch when you make your way back."

"Would you have a flashlight?" he said. "For later, for the outhouse."

Marion shook her head. "Oh, sure. Of course," she said. "Come on. I've got one inside."

Robert Ames

SUMMIT ROAD 1968

When Rob woke the next morning, it took him a minute to remember where he was. In the middle of the night, a dream had startled him awake—the sirens and lights in his subconscious so real his skin was wet with sweat. Afterwards, he lay awake in the moonlight, staring at the ceiling while his heart calmed, and he thought about how lucky he had been yesterday, how easily Marion had hired him, offered him this little cabin, provided him good food. It sure beat trying to get by hitchhiking, not knowing where he'd end up next. Plus, his new story was solid. As Rob Ames from Nebraska, no one would be looking for him. A few weeks settled in one place, safe—it was exactly what he needed.

Still, he wasn't really there to paint. He'd do what he could with it, of course, and gladly take what she was paying him. But there had to be some other way he could make out here, some other opportunity to make money. Of course, not right away. He didn't want to make anyone suspicious. But he wouldn't mind having a look inside the house. There had to be stuff in there worth a bundle.

Washed and dressed, Rob was about to head outside when a blinding light filled his cabin. Lily stood silhouetted in the open space of the big barn doors. She had come to tend to her goat. Rob stepped out onto his stoop and said good morning. She told him that Marion was

203

hanging out laundry. His cue, he guessed, to go find her. He realized he had no idea what time it was other than morning, so he would ask Marion for a clock.

He found her east of the house, hanging sheets on the clothesline. She said there were boxes of cereal on the table, milk in the fridge, coffee on the counter. She'd be in momentarily.

While he ate a bowl of cornflakes, she sat opposite him and filled out a grocery list. When she asked what he liked to eat, Rob said he wasn't particular.

"Anything you fix will be fine," he said.

"That makes things easy," she said.

Rob smiled and poured more corn flakes into his bowl.

Marion got up, looked in a cupboard, came back to the table, and wrote "macaroni" on her list. She cleared her throat.

"You're sure you—know what to do?"

Rob told her not to worry. "The summer after my sophomore year," he said, "my friend and I worked for his dad. He's a painter."

Marion nodded. "Glad to hear it," she said. "More coffee?"

He shook his head. "Better get to work, right?"

She smiled and held out her hand for his empty bowl.

In the barn, Rob loaded a wheelbarrow with supplies. Before heading outside, he paused near the goat pen, where Lily was brushing Mildred.

"Your mom is nice," Rob said.

Lily nodded. Mildred rubbed her snout against the leg of Rob's pants, and he backed away.

"You can pet her," Lily said. "She's really gentle."

Rob had never touched a goat before. This place was crazy with animals, he thought. Rob petted the goat. "She's sweet. Just like you."

Lily colored bright pink and Rob thought, girls are so easy. So ridiculously easy.

"Well, take it easy there Mildred," he said. "Got to get to work."

Minutes later Rob looked up at the sheer height of the side of the house. Scraping was one thing, but how he would manage his balance and hold a bucket and a paint brush, he had no idea. He started up the ladder, his legs rubbery with apprehension. It was a hell of a way to earn a few bucks, he thought, and at that moment, Rob wasn't sure it was worth it.

Tether

"Terry, honey," Donette said when she answered the phone. "It's good to hear your voice. I been thinking a lot about you, wondering how you been getting on."

Terry apologized. He thought of telling her he had been too busy helping his dad get the house in order, about his new part time job, how he was studying for his GED, then college if he could manage it. But even if it was a story she'd be happy to hear, he couldn't lie to her.

"You still at your dad's," she said.

"No. I think my being there made it harder for him. I don't know. He's still messed up."

Donette said she was sorry to hear it.

He told her about Dennis and Sharon. "Dennis and I got along okay, but I think there's just a lot going on in his head," Terry said. "He was wounded in Vietnam."

Donette made a tsking sound with her teeth. "Too many boys killed or hurt. Too many," she said.

"Sharon was the one who told me. I think Dennis tries to pretend it never happened. At least it seemed that way to me. Anyway, I guess I just felt like I was in the way."

"If I thought this was the right place for you, I'd tell you to get back on that bus. Still, I don't like the idea of you having nowhere to go."

"Donnie, you think Dennis and my dad are the same?"

"How do you mean?"

"They both were hurt in a war."

"Seems like all that death would be hard to forget," she said.

"Yeah. Maybe each one in his own way is trying to kill their pain."

"They're not the only ones doing that, though, are they honey?"

Terry said he guessed not.

"Are you safe? Are you eating?"

He said he was. "How are you, Donnie?"

"Oh, you know. Pretty much the same. Maureen moved in. We're trying to make it work. But we got along better when we just saw each other out on the street. She's not as neat and tidy as you were, that's for sure."

Terry laughed. "Still nothing about that man?

"There never was. It's just the strangest thing. Guess that means you don't have to let it worry you anymore," she said.

"I'll try not," he said.

"You know, Terry, maybe you could give your dad one more chance," Donette said.

"I don't know," Terry said, hesitancy in his voice. "He's the one who's supposed to take care of me, not the other way around."

"I know you think he ought to be stronger," she said. "But we both know how hard it is to get by sometimes, especially alone."

Terry said he would think about it.

"Everybody needs somebody," she said.

"I better hang up," Terry said. "I'm almost out of change."

"You be safe," Donette said. "And call me again."

"I will. I promise," he said.

Terry held the receiver in his hand a moment or two before setting it down. How easily her voice had tethered him to a feeling of love and home.

Blood

SUMMIT ROAD, WISCONSIN 1968

The paint job was progressing faster than Rob expected. Even though he had no experience as a painter, he realized he was learning just by doing the job. And he didn't hate the work. It was mindless and gave him time to think things out. Sometimes he thought about where he'd head next—out to the east coast, maybe. He hoped he wouldn't need to flee to Canada, but he knew it was a possibility if he got wind of someone looking for him. An old road map he found in the barn showed him a logical route, closer than he thought, up through the upper peninsula of Michigan, crossing over at Sault Ste. Marie.

He felt pretty sure he was in the clear, but he kept wondering if Mandy was mad enough to turn him in. Still, he wasn't too worried. If she went to the police, they'd notice the car. Good luck, Miss Mandy, explaining how you came to be driving a stolen car. Rob laughed out loud.

"Everything going okay?" Marion called up to him.

"Yeah. Going great. Thanks."

The old lady kept a close watch on him, too. He was still waiting for an opportunity to get into the house. She'd gone into town yesterday, but Lily was around, so he couldn't chance it. All this space and sometimes he felt like he was in prison.

The sound of a sputtering engine roused Rob from a fitful sleep. His eyelids felt glued together and every joint in his body ached. His throat hurt and his skin felt hot. He sat up, looked out the window, and saw a biplane climbing into the clouds above the field across the road then disappearing from his sight. It had been a bad night. At about two that morning, he'd woken, sweaty and freezing cold. He stumbled out of bed, out the small barn door to urinate at the side of the barn. Back inside he had quickly pulled on more clothes and climbed under his blankets, every inch of him shivering. An hour later, he was burning hot again. At dawn he woke, cool, but tangled in damp sheets. With effort he went back to sleep. His eyes stung now as he opened them and struggled to clear his focus. Rob glanced at the clock. Seven thirty. He should be finishing breakfast by now. He quickly got to his feet, but a lurch in his stomach forced him back onto the bed.

"What the hell," he said. "What's wrong with me?"

He lay back down and drew his knees up. A cool breeze blew across his bare chest. He stared mindlessly out the window. Before long, his stomach quieted, though not enough to get him back out of bed. Rob wondered why he'd not seen a single truck or tractor pass on the road.

"Sunday," he muttered. He had forgotten.

Rob woke an hour later, a hot breeze blowing through the windows, the aluminum drinking ladle banging against the sink wall.

"Christ," Rob said. It was nearly noon. At least he no longer felt sick to his stomach. At the sink, he filled the ladle and drank greedily, then rinsed his face and neck. He looked in the mirror and almost didn't recognize the face looking back at him. He needed a shave, but it was more than that. This past year, he had seen his face change. No longer a child, he looked more and more like his father.

He poured a ladleful of water over his head, let it drip into the sink. Without lathering, he scraped quickly at his face with the razor, until he felt the sharp nick. "Damn it," he yelped, tossing the razor in the sink. He pressed at the cut with a towel, leaving it a blood-stained mess.

"This fucking place," he said, pulling on his shirt. "I've gotta get out of here pretty soon."

Stepping out his door, he saw Lily at the goat pen.

"We thought you were never going to wake up," she said.

"Just tired, I guess." He asked if Marion was home. Lily craned her neck toward the house.

"She's inside. Plucked a chicken this morning. She's finishing with that. Roger's coming for dinner."

Rob gave Lily a puzzled look but didn't pursue his question. In the kitchen he found a bologna sandwich made for him, covered in waxed paper. He asked Marion for a Coke and she said she thought there was a bottle in the fridge.

Her hand inside the chicken, she pulled out a mess of bloody organs. "You feeling all right?" she asked. "You look a bit peaked."

"I have a headache," Rob said, "but I'm okay. Maybe I got a bit too much sun yesterday."

Marion pointed to her own chin.

"Yeah," he said. "Shaving accident."

She dried her hands on her apron, went to the half bath, and returned with the aspirin bottle. He slugged back two tablets with the last of his Coke. Back at the sink she lifted the chicken by its now-bare legs.

"Who's Roger?" Rob said.

"A dear friend. He comes for dinner every Sunday night."

Rob looked confused. It had been just the three of them the previous Sunday, when she made meatloaf for dinner and a huge bowl of mashed potatoes. He remembered because he had been so hungry, he thought he might eat the entire bowl.

"But last Sunday—."

"Last week he was in Madison," Marion said. "It was the annual meeting of county sheriffs. He says he always hates those things, spending three days talking about nothing, but I know he has a good time."

"Sheriff's meeting?" Rob asked, his throat sore again, but this time, it was an anxious twinge.

"Roger is the county sheriff. Has been for many years. He'll be by at five. I'm sure you two will get along fine. He's not much of a talker, but then again, I'm not either, which you probably noticed. On the other hand, I know he's going to want to know more about you."

"He already knows about me?"

"He knows I have a hired man who's living in the barn and painting my house. Roger's kind of protective of us, Lily and me, so I'm sure he's going to have to satisfy himself that you're no one we need to fear." She laughed and then looked at him intently. "You're not some escaped murderer are you?"

"Me?" he laughed. "How'd you figure me out?"

Marion waved off his nonsense. She ran a sudsy rag around the inside of the sink then rinsed it clean. "Since it's Sunday, you don't have to work on the house, but if you felt up to it, even a little? The weatherman says we're likely to get rain most of the day tomorrow, so make hay—, right?"

Rob said he supposed he could put in a few hours, though his joints still ached like crazy. He thanked her for the sandwich, then headed to the barn to gather his supplies. When he got there, he was disappointed to find that Lily wasn't there. He was hoping to find out more about the sheriff. A fucking sheriff, he thought. He took a deep breath. It would do no good to overreact. He reminded himself, no one was looking for Robert Ames.

Rock Bottom

ELMWOOD PARK, ILLINOIS 1968

Stanley Abbott, who was halfway to pass-out-drunk, strained to recognize the man at his door. It was Lenny Johnson, a guy from work. What does he want? Stanley wondered.

"Got a minute, Stanley?" Lenny said, scuffing his shoes on Stanley's frayed welcome mat. "Wondered if you were ever going to answer the doorbell."

"Oh. Len. Hi. Kina bishy right now," Stanley slurred.

"I see that," Lenny said, pushing his way past Stanley.

"Hey, what're you doing?" Stanley said.

"I'm just here to help, Stan," Lenny said, shutting the door. "And you're going to help me help you, aren't you?"

Stanley stood in a daze, then made his way unsteadily into the kitchen where he watched with bewilderment as Lenny searched the cupboards for coffee and a couple of clean mugs.

"You heard what they did?" Stanley said.

"Uh huh," Lenny said. He filled the carafe with water and flipped the brew switch. "They had no choice, Stanley."

"I gave that company everything," Stanley said.

While the coffee brewed, Lenny rummaged through the rest of the cupboards and found at least part of what he was looking for—a half-empty fifth of gin and an unopened bottle of bourbon, which he poured down the drain despite Stanley's wide-eyed protestations.

"You've had a bad day, Stan. This ain't going to make it better. Trust me," Lenny said.

An empty six pack carton was still in the refrigerator. Lenny crushed it and put it in the garbage where he found the empty bottles.

When the coffee was done, the two men sat at the table under the glaring light.

"You gotta get that coffee in you, Stan."

"D'rather have a beer. Doan you want one?"

Lenny shook his head and took up his mug. "Just drink your coffee," Lenny said. He said nothing after that but kept Stanley's cup filled. The men's silence magnified the drip of the kitchen faucet, which became like a metronome for an inaudible opera.

Before long, Stanley's head began to clear and he remembered what Lenny had done.

"It wasn't necessary," he said.

"What's that Stan?"

"You—. You didn't have to—."

"Didn't have to what?"

"What I mean is—. You can go now. I'll be fine."

"Sure, Stan. I understand. Listen. It's late. Why don't you go to bed? I can let myself out."

Stanley nodded. His brain still too dulled to comprehend the logic of the situation, he plodded down the hall to his bedroom.

The aroma of coffee woke Stanley the next morning, and his first thought was that Terry had got up before him and had put the coffee on. Stanley's smile faded quickly when he remembered Terry wasn't there. When he opened his eyes, he saw that he'd slept in his clothes. Stanley massaged the kink in his neck and rubbed his tongue over his chalk-covered teeth. As he rose to his feet, Stanley could feel sickness rise. He hurried to the bathroom, where luckily the wave of nausea passed. He had learned over time how to breathe that feeling back down. He splashed cold water on his face but dared not confront himself in the mirror. There would be enough to face that day without having to stare into his shame.

"You're here early," Stanley said to Lenny, who slid two pieces of bread into the toaster.

Lenny smiled. "Never left," he said, setting a cup of coffee on the table for Stanley.

Stanley shook his head. "I don't really know why you're here, Len," Stanley said.

"Well then. Have a seat and I'll tell you."

"I was in a hell hole before Bridger hired me. Rock bottom. So don't think I don't know what you're feeling. I understand, believe me. I saw this day coming a mile away. Why? Because I used to be you. What's your trigger, Stanley?"

Stanley looked at Lenny as if he spoke a foreign language.

"What's the thing that sets you off, pushes you down into your darkness? We've all got that one thing. For some guys it's the war. You a veteran, Stanley? For some guys it's a secret they can't tell, something they did when they were younger that they've never faced and never atoned for. That was it for me. I used to hit my wife. Can you believe that? I was a rotten son of a bitch. I don't know why I did it. But I did. Then afterwards, I just had to blot it all out." Lenny burst into a laugh. "It's a goddamn cycle. And once you're in it, you're spinning, and you can't get out.

The idea of not being able to escape his troubles made sense to Stanley.

"There's more of us than you think, Stanley, at Bridger I mean. Even the boss. Why do you think he kept you on as long as he did? My guess is he kept hoping you'd turn things around."

"You mean everyone knew? You were all talking about me?"

"No. That's not what I meant. I'm guessing about the boss. But you know the saying, it takes one to know one? I had you figured years back, Stanley. But until a month ago, you never missed work, right? You made it work. Then all of a sudden, it didn't work, and I could see you had taken a leap off the high dive. Something happened, right? Something that changed everything?"

Stanley nodded. He had relived the scene over and over, waking up midday, so hungover he could barely think, padding out of his bedroom, the house as quiet as a graveyard, seeing the emptiness and knowing that Terry would not be back.

"How'd you do it?" Stanley asked. "How'd you get past it all?"

"Not by myself, that's for sure," Lenny said.

It took Lenny several days to convince Stanley to go with him to an AA meeting. They stood outside the church now and watched men and women climb the broad stone steps and enter by a side door.

"I can tell you're nervous," Lenny said, "But remember, everyone in there tonight has either been in your shoes in the past or is standing in them with you right now."

"Not sure I can do this."

"You only have to listen if that's all you can do. Sometimes that's enough for your first meeting. But, and you gotta hear me," Lenny said, "if you want to get better, one day you're going to have to take the first step. And you gotta do it alone. I mean, I'm here to listen and support you, but I can't do it for you. Hell, I can't fix a goddamn thing for you, Stanley, much as I would like to. If I could wave a magic wand to keep you from buying your next bottle, don't you think I would? And don't think I don't know that's exactly what you would do if you walked away from here right now."

Stanley looked as if he'd been suddenly stripped naked. How well Lenny knew him. Stanley nodded and followed Lenny into the church and down to a basement room where a half dozen people mingled near a coffee urn and a tray of cookies. Thirty or so wooden folding chairs were set up facing a podium. Behind it hung a large banner embroidered with the serenity prayer.

"Take a cookie," Lenny said. "It'll help with the shakes."

The two men sat in the back, and as Stanley ate the cookie, he stared at a broken floor tile at his feet.

A man who had been speaking ended his remarks and returned to his seat. After him, a woman told about her recent lapse. Empathetic murmurs filled the room. After she took her seat, no one rose to speak. Stanley mistook the silence for pressure, and he slid down in his seat.

Then Lenny stood and walked to the podium. "Hi. My name's Leonard, and I'm an alcoholic. I've been sober seven years. I took my last drink the night my wife left me."

Stanley listened to Lenny tell his story. When he finished, the others in the room clapped for him, as they had for all the others.

All Stanley could think about was Terry, if he was out there somewhere, wishing his dad had been a better man. Did he wish that? Does he think I'm weak like his mother does? And Linda. Did she think so, too? Did his children despise him? Stanley's chest heaved and he felt the heaviness of his life crush against him.

After Lenny returned to his seat, another man told his story. "I'm the same as you," Stanley wanted to shout. Except he wasn't. This man had been sober for three years, not three days. And he had made amends with the son he had hurt, while Stanley, who had only just accepted his life was in crisis, was terrified of moving an inch forward. But if AA was the way to get Terry back, what was he waiting for? "If you've got something hard to say," Stanley's father had always told him, "Don't think about it. Just spit it out. If it's important. If it's not. Keep it to yourself."

Maybe he'd done too much of the latter in his life. Maybe he'd kept too much inside where it taunted and gnawed at him.

Lenny leaned over. "You don't have to—."

Stanley Abbott stood. He felt his knees go weak as he tried to say, "My name is." He coughed and started again. "My name is Stanley and I'm an—." He looked down at Lenny, then ahead to where the leader of the group stood facing them. They all waited, though not impatiently,

Stanley realized. They had all shared this first moment and knew how hard it was.

"I'm an alcoholic. My last drink was three days ago, the day I lost my job."

It was all he could say. He slumped back to his seat, his body shaking, his forehead gleaming in sweat. The soft applause of recognition from the group sounded far off, as if he heard it in a dream.

Minutes later, everyone rose to their feet. Some shook his hand as they made their way to the exit. One man spoke to him on his way out. "First time is always the hardest. Takes a lot of courage, but you did it."

Out in the evening air, Stanley felt the lightness of being that comes from standing on the other side of a moment one has long feared. The dread that he had carried with him that entire day was gone.

"It'll get easier," Lenny said. "It just takes time."

Sentry

Tonight, like most nights, Rob couldn't relax. He often sat on his bed in the dark, looking out to the road, alert for police cars, or Roger's white Impala. Constant in his mind was the sense that Minnesota would catch up with him.

A faint, familiar odor drew Rob's attention to the road, where he saw a shadowy figure standing a few feet past the edge of the driveway.

Moments later, as Rob approached, a small red glow lit a boy's face.

Rob stood face to face with the boy—sixteen at most. "Hand it here," Rob commanded.

"Hand what here?" the boy said.

Rob reached out, but the boy took several steps backwards, holding the joint behind his back.

"I said. Give. It. Here."

"Fuck you," said the boy.

Rob lurched forward and grabbed the boy by the arm, twisting it. "I said hand it over."

The boy yelped in pain and relinquished the joint.

Rob let go. "Who are you?" he said. "What are you doing here, anyway?"

The boy sniffed and rubbed his arm. "I heard the lady who lives here will give you a bed for the night and feed you."

Rob laughed. "You've been misinformed."

"But," sputtered the boy.

"You got more than that one joint?"

The boy backed away.

"You do, don't you?" Rob sneered. "Hand it over."

"Or what?" the boy said.

"Or what? Or I'll haul you up to the house and call the sheriff. He's a friend of the lady who lives here. They don't like trespassers."

"Come on, man," the boy said.

"Come on, man," Rob mocked.

The boy reached in his jacket pocket and retrieved a plastic bag. He held it in front of him.

Rob took the baggie, opened it, sniffed its contents. "It's not much, but it's better than nothing."

The boy hung his head.

"Well. What are you waiting for?" Rob said.

"But maybe I could just—."

Rob held out his arm stiffly. "Move on," he said.

The boy cocked his head like a puppy. "What?" he said.

"You stupid? I said move on."

"Asshole," the boy said, walking away.

When the boy was out of sight, Rob climbed the driveway back to the barn.

Blueberry Pie

Tuesday morning after Lily gathered eggs, she painted the last quadrant of her design on the hen house. It had turned out better than she hoped it would and Marion said the painting was the cheeriest thing around. It had been a long time, since her mother died, that Lily had felt such kindness. Marion was not her mother, but Lily loved her as if she were. Memories of her father and the Uebels still nagged at Lily, but more and more, she was able to dismiss her dark thoughts.

School would start soon, and though she was anxious about making new friends, Lily felt excited about the future. She realized she had a chance to start a new life. She no longer wanted to be the poor girl whose mother had died. Or the foster child others stared at. Lily had begun to imagine that in her new school, she might make friends with the pretty girls, the girls whom others followed, those who had shunned her in the past.

Lily drew a clean brush from her box of paints and unscrewed the cap from the tube of Mars Black. She dabbed the brush into the glistening paint and touched up a scratch in the center circle.

A rasp of gravel drew her attention to the driveway. It was Roger. She smiled widely and shouted, "I finished it."

"It's a fine job, Lily," he said, now standing at her side. "More than fine."

Lily felt her cheeks turn warm.

"Maybe soon you could paint one on my garage," he said.

"I can do that."

Roger smiled. "My neighbors will be envious. Maybe you'll get other requests. Become our local Picasso?"

Lily shook her head. "I'm not that good," she said.

Roger pulled his handkerchief from his back pocket and wiped his forehead. "Where's the boss?"

"I think she is making a blueberry pie."

"Without telling me?" He gave Lily a wink and headed toward the kitchen.

Lily rinsed out her brush and dried it on a rag. She dumped the bowl of dark gray water on the driveway.

In the kitchen, Roger peered over the cooling pie, sitting on the counter on a wooden trivet. Deep purple jam was still bubbling in the vents of the sugar-sprinkled crust.

"Pie on a Tuesday, Marion? Life is just a bacchanalian riot around here, isn't it?"

She waved her arm at him dismissively. "If you must know, Vivian stopped by with six pints of berries yesterday. So, voila."

"Well, it smells wonderful," Roger said.

"Your back still bothering you, Roger?" Marion asked, noticing the wince as Roger lowered himself to a chair.

"I think it's a disk. I almost called the doctor yesterday, but I've had this trouble before. It will go away. Comes from these bumpy country roads. Or maybe I'm just old."

"Let's blame it on the car," she said with a wink. Marion picked up a magazine and waved it like a fan. "What on earth was I thinking, turning on the oven on a hot August day?"

"You'll be glad later, when you cut into that pie," he said.

Marion smiled. "I do love blueberry pie."

"Talked to Lily," he went on. "That design she painted on the hen

221

house is something special."

Marion agreed. She sipped her water and laid her cold wet hand on the back of her neck, which she rolled to release the heat tension that had begun to settle there.

"I didn't see the young man—."

"Robert."

"Yes. Robert. Ames. I can't find anything on a 21-year-old veteran of that name. There are a few Roberts we ought to be aware of, particularly one who appears to have stolen and sold his mother's car. A nineteen-year-old from Minneapolis. A draft dodger, too."

"Well, that's not our Rob," Marion said.

"Likely not," Roger said. "The description matches just about anyone of that age, so it's hard to say. There are a lot of Roberts in the world. Your young man seems to be working steadily, not bothering you, right?

"Right."

"And he's not ingratiated himself into your home life? Keeps to himself out there?"

"Yes."

Roger readjusted his back.

"He comes in for meals," Marion said. "And I wash his clothes. Got him a few work shirts at the secondhand store so he wouldn't ruin his own with paint. But no, he has not ingratiated himself." She didn't like what the word implied, people who were conniving, calculating.

Roger said he was only concerned for her welfare, and now Lily's welfare, too.

"I know you are. I appreciate it," Marion said. A brief silence hung between them.

Roger finished his water.

"If you can stay a while," Marion said, "the pie might cool enough for you to have a piece."

"Thanks, but I've got a few other stops this afternoon. Rain check?"

"Of course."

Roger said goodbye and left the house. He looked for Lily, but she was out of sight. As he drove slowly down the driveway, Roger looked back at the house and saw Rob on the ladder near the roofline. With the paintbrush in his hand, Rob waved at Roger. Then Roger turned onto the road and drove towards Greenbush.

He was on his way to meet his deputy Arnie at a gas station in the little town. The owner had reported shotgun damage to his new sign advertising live bait. "Muskie got a hole right troo da eye," Arnie had said on the radio, mocking the owner's speech. "Be nice, Arnie," Roger replied. But later as Roger pulled into the gas station and saw the damaged sign, he chuckled and said to himself, "Troo da eye."

Meadow

After Roger left, Lily decided to take Sarge for a walk on Marion's winding meadow path. Besides being with Mildred or the hens, it was Lily's favorite place to be. When Marion had first shown her the path, Lily had seen a red fox cross the path several yards in front of them.

"What was that?" she asked, fearfully.

"Just a little fox."

"Do they bite?"

"They won't hurt you," Marion said. "They're much more afraid of you, a big giant, than you are of them."

Later, Marion gave Lily a book about Wisconsin wildlife. "It's their world, too. It was theirs first," she said, handing Lily the book.

In time, Lily was eager to learn about fox, opossum, bats, and even snakes. Knowing about each species made her less afraid. Her mother had been terrified of bees, so Lily had been, too, but now she appreciated the honeybees, busy in the blossoms, doing their important work.

It was the butterflies Lily loved most, especially the indigo blue swallowtails with their teardrop wings. Once she'd stopped by a clump of coneflowers and held out her hand, hoping a one would land on it, but it fluttered off to another blossom, then another. It was enough just to watch him, she thought.

Sarge nosed at the edge of the path, his thick tail wagging as he sniffed the complex summer scents. Lily followed the flight of a blue heron overhead, his long legs tapering behind him as he crossed the clouds that dotted the bright sky.

Spontaneously Lily began singing the lines about clouds from "Both Sides Now." The sound of her own voice surprised her. She felt embarrassed for a moment, but soon realized there was no one there to laugh at her.

Lily and Sarge turned onto a broad sweep of yellowing grass where a lurching grasshopper nearly hit her in the face. Startled, Lily leaned back. "Did you see that, Sarge?" She reached down and joggled the furry neck of her companion. "You're such a good boy." Sarge looked into her eyes, his tail swooshing side to side.

"I like your singing," came a sing-songy voice behind her.

Lily was startled to hear Rob's voice. What was he doing out here? Had he been following her all along? She turned and saw his tall, dark shape emerge around the bend.

"You following me?"

"Just out for a walk," he said. Rob bent down and petted Sarge on the top of his head. Sarge did not wag his tail but stood at Lily's side.

"What do you want?"

"What do you mean?"

Lily shrugged. "Why are you following me?"

"Are you trying to get rid of me?"

"I just like to be alone out here." She still felt embarrassed that he had heard her singing.

"Sorry to disturb you, your majesty."

"You don't have to be mean," she said, walking away from him.

"Oh, come on. Can't you take a joke?"

"It didn't feel like a joke," she said, picking up her pace.

Rob continued to follow her. At a clump of red bee balm, he reached down to snap off a blossom.

"For you, my queen," he said in a mock bow.

"Why'd you pick that?" Lily said. "Now it's dead."

"I just wanted to pick a flower for you. Jesus, you're ungrateful."

"Why does someone need to hold one? They're everywhere if you haven't noticed."

"You don't have to be mean," Rob said mimicking her tone from a moment before.

Rob dropped the flower to the ground.

Lily walked away with deliberately longer strides.

"You are trying to get away from me, aren't you?" Rob said, keeping up with her pace.

"I told you. I want to be alone."

Back at her side, he leaned close to her, and whispered in her ear, "but you didn't mean it."

Sarge made a sneezing sound, then a low guttural expression of anxiety.

Rob moved in closer now and put his hand on Lily's waist. He pulled her to his body. It was warm, solid. It felt good, but wrong. Her body prickled with anxious excitement. She did nothing for a moment, not sure if she should feel afraid.

Rob took advantage of her motionless posture. With his right arm he seized control of her, turned her toward him, and locked her in his grasp. He leaned into her face, smiled, his white teeth exposed, and spoke quietly.

"You've got pretty eyes," he cooed. And your freckles, they kind of make you look like a kid. But you're not a kid, are you?" He drew his left hand across her chest, gazed down at her breasts. "Not a little girl, are you?"

Lily tried to wriggle out of his hold, but he clasped onto her even tighter.

"Aww, come on. Don't you like me?"

"Let me go."

Rob leaned down, pressed his face into the curve of her neck, kissed it once, then bit it, not hard, but enough that she felt his teeth. "We're just getting started."

She mewed in fear, and Sarge reacted. He jumped up on Rob, growling a warning growl. Rob kicked the dog sharply, and Sarge let out a wincing yelp.

"Stop it," Lily cried. "You hurt him."

Rob ignored the dog and thrust his hand up under Lily's blouse. He crushed her breast with his hand. The pain made her shriek. Her eyes filled with tears.

Sarge barked loudly. Rob kicked the dog again.

"Stop it. Stop it," Lily screamed, her face hot and red. She panted in fear, struggling now with all her strength to get free.

Rob did not release her, but he pulled his hand out of her shirt and allowed a space between them. "You telling me you didn't like that?" Their faces were only inches apart. "Girls like you always want it."

"I'll tell Marion."

"Go ahead. I'll tell her you teased me. You asked me to kiss you. You were the one flirting with me. Who's she going believe? Girls always flirt with me."

Lily's eyes burned.

Rob whispered in her ear. "If you say one word, your little Millie Mae will pay." Then he released her.

With Sarge at her side, Lily ran toward the house. Even when Rob was out of sight, Lily could still hear him laughing.

Another Journey

After dinner one Sunday night, Marion and Vivian sat on Marion's back porch listening to the sounds of the evening. They watched the roof of the barn, which stood against the sky in silhouette, turn from blue to purple to black. Rob had gone back to his cabin, and Roger and Lily were playing cards in the dining room.

"I was against you keeping that girl," Vivian said.

Marion winced at the word "keeping." Lily was not a stray dog.

"At your age, taking on a responsibility like that. But I was wrong. She's a loving child."

"She is."

"And you're happy. You and your little family."

Marion nodded. She was afraid she'd come to tears if she said anything more. *You and your little family* sounded so lovely. The sisters rocked quietly.

"I got a letter from Rachel this week," Vivian said. "She wants me to come for a visit. Asked if you could drive me to the train station in Milwaukee."

"I can do that, Vivvy. It's a grand idea."

"I'm just not sure how would it be, the two of us under one roof?"

"I'm sure it will be fine," Marion said.

"It's been a year and a half."

228

"But she asked you—."

"I know. But the last time—. I said things in anger. I know. Bite my tongue, right? I guess I never mastered that skill."

"I think that's something we could all do better," Marion said. A moth flitted near the porch light, then disappeared. A crescent moon crowned the horizon. "She's your daughter, Viv. You love each other. Tell her that. Be her mother, not her mom."

Vivian looked puzzled.

"You only need to love her. You don't need to raise her anymore."

"I suppose you're right."

"Well," Marion said, laughing, "there are four words I never thought I'd hear."

"Oh, you. Just stop." Vivian smiled, her heart full of what might be. She felt tears welling in her eyes and a weight lifting from her chest.

Burial

Montgomery, Alabama 1968

Summer had dragged on endlessly for Donette after Terry left. One day indistinct from the next. There was a tense undercurrent below the surface of things happening in the city. Everyone felt it. It seemed to Donette that ever since the big riot that April in Harlem, being black in New York felt more and more like a crime. Then a john beat up Maureen, split her lip, made her eye so puffy she couldn't see. Maureen said that even with one eye she could see the writing on the wall. When she healed enough, she boarded a bus back to Mississippi. "Least there I know who hates me," she said.

After Maureen left, a premonition woke Donette early one morning. Stifling heat had left her sleepless most of the night, but she rose with an urgency to call her mother.

"Not been feeling well," her mother said in a voice that sounded old and weak. "Mostly dyspepsi. But Bernice is taking good care of me."

A week later Donette's mother was dead. "Doctor say a heart attack," Aunt Bernice reported on the phone. "Nothin' they could've done for her."

The bus ride to Alabama for the funeral was long. It took Donette through parts of the country she had not seen for a long time, through long stretches of verdant woods in Virginia and North Carolina, through red clay fields in Georgia. It was a calming journey. She was grateful for the solitude. Everyone on the bus kept to themselves, women crocheting, men thumbing through magazines, mostly people just staring, like she did, out the window at the miles passing by. For a time, a sweet-perfumed lady in a pill box hat sat next to her. The woman paged through a small New Testament, not appearing to actually read anything, just touching the pages with her white-gloved fingers. After a stop in Atlanta, a wiry man with gray whiskers in a dark, sweat-smelling suit sat in the woman's place. He was on his way to Mobile, he said. "Visitin' his grandchild, new born."

At the Montgomery bus station, Bernice was waiting when Donette arrived. A young man was with her, leaning against a green Ford sedan. "This is Bobby. He's our neighbor, home from college." Donette said hello and Bobby put her bag in the trunk. He drove them directly to the funeral home.

A dark, red-draped room was lit by two floor lamps. Four mourners were seated on wooden folding chairs facing the casket where her mother lay. A brass plant stand held a spray of waxy gardenias tied with a white satin ribbon that read "SISTER" in gold lettering.

Bernice led Donette by the hand to the coffin. "Don't she look peaceful, now?" Bernice said. She bent down and kissed her sister on the forehead.

To Donette, her mother looked dead, a lifeless undertone of green in her skin, her lips pulled taut, not plump and pursed like usual. All the sass of her mouth was gone. All the fight taken from her.

Before the service began, a few more people came to pay their respects. To Donette's surprise, a few were white women.

"They the ones we clean for," Bernice whispered.

The minister spoke of Miss Caroline's steadfast faith in the Lord. Bernice sobbed an "amen." Donette was surprised to find she felt little.

After the service. a procession of four cars followed the hearse, not enough to stop any traffic on the cross streets to the cemetery. By four o'clock her mother had been laid to rest, and as Donette and her aunt walked back to the car, Donette wished she could twitch her nose like that blonde witch on TV and be back on the bus headed home. She was eager for the city again, if not her own apartment, which she feared would seem lonelier than ever, but for the world she called home.

In the car on the way back to the house, Bernice said, "Why don't you come down here and stay in your momma's room. You my last family, and you'd be good compny," Bernice said. She patted her niece on the knee. "I know we'd get along just fine."

"I am sure we would," Donette said. "But I've got my job to get back to."

"Sure, sure. I understand," Bernice said.

Donette thought of the letters she'd written, letters full of lovely lies she knew her mother would be pleased to hear. In her in letters back, Caroline Murray had told her daughter how proud she was of her, proud of how Donette had made things work on her own.

When Bobby turned the corner to their little house, Bernice said with a sigh, "I miss her already." Then she added, "You know, your momma missed you every day. Every day, till her last."

The skin on the back of Donette's neck turned cold. She knew what her aunt was up to, but Donette would not resign her life to taking her mother's place in her aunt's lonely life. She didn't know what she wanted, but she knew she didn't want that.

Part Four

The North Star

SUMMIT ROAD, WISCONSIN 1968

Marion studied the young man who sat with her at the kitchen table. His dark hair fell across his forehead, framing his chestnut eyes, and on his chin was the two-day beard of a boy. He looked road-weary like the others, but less ragged and forlorn than Bridget or Lily had been, and less ingratiating than Rob had been when he first arrived. The way he smiled when she spoke to him, never turning away, told her what she needed to know. He was not a threat.

"Terry," he said, when she asked his name. "Abbott. From Chicago."

"I have a feeling I know how you ended up here," Marion said. "A girl named Bridget?"

Terry nodded. "I met her in Iowa. She was with a few people driving out to California. I thought for a while I might go along," he said. "But it's a long way. She told me about your farm and about you—."

"And that I take in strays?" Marion smiled.

Terry sipped his water. "Yeah."

"Home is Chicago?" Marion said. "I would have guessed somewhere out east. What else did Bridget say?"

"I don't know," Terry said, pushing his hair out of his eyes. "She liked it here."

"And you want to stay? Until you figure things out?"

"Something like that, I guess," Terry said. "But I don't have to stay

long. A few days? Or not at all. I mean, I understand if you would rather
I move along," he said, setting the uneaten portion of his sandwich on
the plate. "I can work, though. I wouldn't expect to stay for nothing."

"But you're here because you don't have a place to move along to,
right?" She pushed her chair back and stood. She went to the sink to
finish washing the lunch dishes she'd let sit in the sudsy water when
Terry arrived. From the kitchen window, Marion could see Lily leading
her goat into the barn. Rob would be back soon. He had taken the
truck into town to buy another can of paint. Marion wondered why
the prospect of the three meeting one another worried her. Lily would
certainly be kind to a newcomer. But Rob, who'd lately developed sharp
edges, might not be.

"I suppose you could say I ran away from home," he said, "but I like
to think of it more as escaping a harmful situation."

"Harmful how?" Marion asked.

"I'd rather not get into that," he said.

She appreciated his forthright answer. He had every right not to
tell her. Terry was open in a way most adults were not. And because
such people were always guarding themselves, they were harder to get
to know, or trust. Terry had the honesty of a child, but he spoke as one
much older, much wiser.

"I need you to understand that I will call my friend Roger, the
county sheriff, and let him know you're here," Marion said, drying her
hands on a towel. "It's an arrangement we've had ever since Bridget
decided to place the north star over my house," Marion said. "Is there
any reason you wouldn't want him to know about you?"

"I guess I wouldn't want him to call my mother," Terry laughed.
"But if he does call her, I'll bet he'll wish he hadn't."

Marion smiled, though it was not a humorous situation. Another
Mrs. Uebel, she wondered?

"Also, I've hired a young man to paint the house, and he sleeps in
the farm hand's quarters in the barn. There's not room out there for
two, though I'm not sure he'd relish the idea of a roommate even if

there were. And there's Lily, my ward."

"I understand," Terry said. "I wouldn't cause any trouble, for you or for them. I wouldn't want to be in the way."

"What do you like to do, Terry?" Marion asked. A young man so earnest about his intentions made her curious.

The answer spilled out of him as if no one had ever asked him that question before. "I love books. Reading. And writing. I keep a journal. I guess that sounds dumb."

"Not at all. I admire writers," Marion said. "But I never felt the urge. I found it hard enough to write report card comments."

Terry looked confused.

"I taught middle school," she explained. "Sometimes what parents want to hear and what they need to hear are entirely at odds. It was a challenge to compose sentences that told the truth in a kind way."

Terry nodded as if he understood.

Marion knew the most sensible thing would be to send this young man away, perhaps give him a few dollars, certainly food. But something held her back. She was drawn to his gentleness, and however vulnerable he first appeared, she sensed he wasn't weak.

"I've got something to show you," Marion said. She motioned for him to follow. She led him down the hallway into the living room, then across the foyer to the library.

"She told me about this, too, Bridget did," he said, looking at the floor to ceiling shelves. He ran his hand over the top of a high-backed leather chair.

"When we first moved here, this room was an empty space. My husband loved to read, so it was his idea to turn it into a library. That was his chair."

"You have so many books," Terry said.

"More than I'll ever be able to read. That's for sure."

"I'd sure try though," he said.

Marion would lodge him in the smallest bedroom near the front of the house, farthest away from Lily's room, but close enough to her own that she could keep an eye on him. Bridget had sent him to her for a reason, as she had sent Lily for a reason. Marion couldn't turn him way, not yet.

"How about if we try it for a day or so? I've got a room for you upstairs. And you can come down here any time you like."

"Thank you," he said.

Marion could sense his relief. She left him gazing at the books, touching their spines like a pilgrim who has found a holy relic.

Introductions

After Marion left Terry alone to explore her library, he was reminded of his first year in high school. When Terry was fourteen, his mom and Dick moved to a new house, too far from the school where his middle school friends would go. Being the new kid in ninth grade was harder than being the new kid in grade school. In high school, cliques were already formed. Outsiders had to negotiate their way into a group, and a kid like Terry, who already felt like he didn't belong, had it rough. As a freshman, Terry had not yet begun to sprout out of his slight, adolescent build. His voice still sounded like a child's, and each attempt to make friends resulted in rejection, a problem compounded by the fact that he wasn't safe at home either. He was a stranger in a strange land.

To cope with his alienation, Terry began to leave the house earlier and earlier each morning that fall, walking the mile route to school slowly. September turned to October and on sunny mornings, when giant maple leaves cast golden light on him, Terry would recite poems he had memorized along the way. At times he caught himself verbalizing the words out loud. He would arrive early, before plaid-skirted groups of girls, before football-jacketed boys, even before most of the harried teachers who lugged careworn briefcases up the stone steps of the main entrance, and he would sit on the top step in leaf-filtered light, listening to the morning birds, and read. On one such morning, the school's

239

librarian stopped to speak with him.

"What's your book," she said.

Terry held up a worn copy of *A Separate Peace.*

"It looks like you've read that one a few times," she said.

He squinted up at her and smiled. She moved on into the building.

A few days later, she stopped again. "I think it's going to rain soon," she said. "Would you like to come inside with me?"

He followed her up the stairs, inside the quiet building, down the polished hallways to the library door. She unlocked it and they entered the dark, silent expanse of shelves. She flipped the switches, and the lights began to hum and glow. Terry never forgot that day, standing in the school library for the first time, not one among dozens of classmates, but alone. He felt as if he had been invited to a secret world. The next day when she reached him at his perch at the top of the steps, she smiled and motioned for him to follow.

"Come on then," she said.

And here he was, alone with books again. How could one person own so many? There were books and writers he knew and had read but so many more he had never heard of, and Terry realized how few books he had actually read. There is so much to know, he thought.

One shelf was crammed with children's picture books, and nearby was a collection of Nancy Drew mysteries and a set of *Little House on the Prairie.* Terry was excited to find a pristine copy of *A Wrinkle in Time,* the book that first gave him the feeling that if he was brave enough, he could do anything. The book cracked audibly when he opened it. Bringing it to his nose, he closed his eyes and breathed it in.

But a book, no matter how familiar, was not a place where one could find true safety. Neither was this woman's house, he thought, no matter how safe it felt. He was not home. He was only a visitor. A temporary guest at best. Terry shelved the book and sighed. Near the long narrow windows, dust motes danced in the light-filled room.

Terry stepped down onto the front sidewalk and looked up at Rob who brushed paint on the angled clapboards just under the soffit.

"Hi," Terry said genially. "I'm Terry. "What's your name?"

The painter ignored him.

"If you've got another brush, I wouldn't mind giving you a hand," Terry said.

Rob stopped in mid stroke and looked down. "No thanks. I've got it."

"If you change your mind, I would be happy to help," Terry said.

"I won't," Rob said.

"Well, see ya then," Terry said, the back of his neck prickling at the hint of conflict.

Terry found Lily by the chicken coop and introduced himself.

She smiled. "I'm Lily. It's nice to meet you. This is Sarge," Lily said.

Terry petted the dog, then scratched his ears.

"He likes you," Lily said.

Terry followed as Lily introduced him to the hens, naming each one as though they were her brood of unruly children, even embarrassing the youngest, an Austra White named Dorothy, who, Lily said, liked to wander off on her own.

"I guess she's like me, then," Terry laughed.

Lily smiled. "You're nice," she said. "Are you going to stay here for a while?"

"Not sure yet," Terry said.

She nodded and picked up the water pan. "You're so thirsty today, aren't you," she cooed to the hens.

Terry left Lily to her work and walked to the garden. He found Marion in her straw hat and mud-encrusted garden gloves retying a drooping cucumber vine. The gate had been left open, so Terry entered and looked around. He had never been in a garden in his life. His people got their beans and carrots from cans. He bent to pull a weed from the path.

Marion watched him pull stalk of pigroot from the top, snapping it in half, leaving the vigorous lower stem and root intact. She smiled gently as he pulled two more in the same manner.

241

"I don't know if I'm doing this right," he said.

"If you really want to show them who's boss," she said, grabbing a weeder from a basket and going to his side, "you've got to grab them down at their feet, wiggle a bit, then pull. And if that doesn't work, we use this." She showed him the wood-handled tool with a long, forked prong. She demonstrated how it worked. "Just jab this down alongside the root." In a fluid arc, Marion unearthed the weed, which lay on top the dirt path, its long, pink taproot exposed to the sun.

"Of course, it's foolish to believe we can ever win the weed battle. They keep coming back, again and again."

Terry tried the tool. After a few jabs, he got the hang of the motion, and soon he had freed a small heap of withering weeds. "Like I said, I would be happy to help out. Whatever you need."

"It's all I can do to keep a few steps ahead of all the chores around here," she said. "I'll see what I can find for you."

He hoped she would not suggest that he help with the painting.

At dinner, the four of them ate a simple meal of spaghetti and meat sauce. From Marion, Terry learned the painter's name. Rob had still not offered a friendly greeting.

"Everyone is awfully quiet tonight," Marion said.

Terry wondered if his presence had upset the group's balance.

"Lily, pass the salad bowl, please."

Lily handed Marion the glass bowl. She piled more salad on her plate then held the bowl out. "More for you, Rob?" Marion asked.

"No," he said.

"Terry?"

Terry took the bowl from Marion even though he didn't want any more. It seemed impolite not to.

"We grew everything that's in that bowl. Right, Lily?" Marion said. Lily nodded.

"Tell us about yourself, Terry," Marion said.

Terry struggled to tell a story that felt true. Born near Chicago. True. Parents divorced. True. Stepfather. Not the nicest guy. That was an understatement, but true. Been wandering, trying to find where he fit. True. All true. He would not elaborate further. He kept all of that inside, no matter how much it swelled and pushed against him.

"You're from Chicago?" Rob said. "That's a dirty city."

The other three looked at Rob, confusion on their faces.

Marion diffused the tense moment and said Chicago was likely no dirtier than any other city, though she had been there only once, long ago. She said she could not recall anything other than the scope of gray concrete scratching at the blue sky. It was lovely, she recalled, and she told them that.

The Hobbit

Lily woke in the middle of the night and kicked the sheet away. Her body was wet with perspiration, her heart pounding. When she calmed enough to think, she remembered the dream. She had been kissing the new boy, Terry. She had wanted him to reach up under her blouse. She had led his hand there. She had never had a dream like that before. It was an hour before she could get back to sleep.

In the morning, Lily dressed and remembered the feeling her dream had left her with. After breakfast she busied herself with her usual chores and tried not to think about the dream.

Mid-morning, Marion sent Rob on an errand. Lily was glad to see him leave in the truck. After that time in the meadow, she prayed each day that he would leave for good. A few hours was better than nothing. After Lily put Mildred in her pen, she searched for Terry. She found him on the front porch.

"What are you reading?" Lily asked. "Is that one of Marion's books?" Sarge came up the porch steps alongside her.

Holding up the tattered paperback for her to see, Terry said, "No. It's mine. It is called *The Hobbit*."

"The what?"

"*The Hobbit*. It's a book about a little person, sort of, named Bilbo Baggins, who has adventures with dwarves and elves."

"Like a little man?"

"Kind of." Terry described the human-like species in more detail. He told her hobbits exhibited some human traits, particularly their love of a cozy home and lots of food. "But they don't need shoes because their feet are covered in thick hair."

Lily laughed.

"It's not supposed to be funny. I mean, they look a bit funny, I guess, but it's a serious book. He's—. Bilbo Baggins is a hero. You should read it."

"It sounds like a boys book," she said.

"It's a book for anyone who has ever felt they're not good enough."

She looked away. She somehow felt he meant her, though he didn't know her at all.

Terry closed the book.

"I didn't want to bother you," she said. "I'm just kinda bored."

"You're not bothering me. Anyway, I've read it lots of times."

"You read it more than once?"

"I read lots of books more than once."

She eyed him curiously.

"You can sit here, too, if you want," he said.

Lily felt her breath catch. Terry's invitation made her feel the same way the dream had.

Terry moved to one side of the porch swing, and Lily sat on the other. After awkward attempts, they began to move their feet in unison, gently moving back and forth.

"I don't really read," she said. "I mean not like you do."

"If you don't read," he said, "how can you know about stuff?"

"Things like elves," she laughed.

"Like anything," he said.

She felt the need to defend herself. It wasn't that she never read. She just didn't enjoy it that much, and certainly not as much as he did. Such stories seemed useless to her. How could a book about elves and dwarves teach you anything about real life?

"I read. I learned how to take care of Mildred from a book I got from the library. But that's different. Books like that tell you things you need to know. I don't see how fairy stories tell you anything useful."

Terry told her she might be right.

"Pee-you," Lily said. "You smell that? Skunk."

"I kind of like that smell," Terry said.

"Are you a complete weirdo or what?"

"Only a partial weirdo."

"I think it stinks."

"I've smelled worse."

Lily nodded. "I guess I have, too."

They rocked while Sarge snored not far from their swinging feet.

"What do you think of Marion?" Lily asked. "Isn't she the best? I wish—." She stopped. She thought was she was about to say she would sound childish, and she did not want Terry to think she was a child.

"She's really nice," Terry said. "And it's so peaceful here."

"Yeah," Lily nodded. "At night, especially. Sometimes I don't even want to fall asleep because I like to listen to the sound of the night coming through the windows. What's best is when it rains," she said. "I love that sound." Lily looked at her feet. She felt embarrassed by all the words tumbling from her mouth. "Sorry. I talk too much."

"Don't be sorry," Terry said. "I know what you mean—about the sound of rain."

Lily thought about yesterday, when Rob told her Terry was a fag. Lily stuck up for the new boy and told Rob he was wrong. But Rob laughed and said she was naïve. She didn't know what that word meant, but when he said it, her body prickled with apprehension.

Gateway

When Donette got back to New York after her mother's funeral, she began buying the Chicago paper from the news rack in Sanchez's store. Even though her aunt wanted her to live with her, Donette knew she couldn't move to Montgomery. She couldn't live in the same house with her mother's ghost. But her aunt's invitation got her thinking. Just because she'd been settled for so long in one place didn't mean she could not make a life somewhere else. Maureen had done it, and she was getting along fine, according to her last letter. Why couldn't she do the same?

With all she'd saved, Donette figured she could rent a furnished apartment, maybe not far from Terry. Then she'd find a job. It didn't have to pay much, enough to cover the rent and groceries. She didn't need much.

"Ever been to Chicago?" Donette asked Sanchez, handing him the money for the paper.

"No," he said. "I went to St. Louis once. My cousin drove us there in his station wagon to see that big arch. You know about that arch?"

Donette said she had seen pictures in a magazine.

"I remember it being hot, there."

"It's hot here, too," she said.

"Is that where you want to go, querida?"

"What?"

He reached out and touched her arm. "I get the feeling you are going to leave me," he said.

She shook her head. "If I moved away, who would make you pies?"

"A lot of people can make pies. There's a truck that will bring me pies—not good ones like you make—but they're pies. You miss that boy. He was here, then he was gone. You've been sad ever since. I think you want to go see him."

"He went home," Donette said.

"This place is my home," Sanchez said, "but I think maybe you haven't found where yours is yet?"

She leaned over and kissed the old man on the top of his tanned head.

Chasms

Only once since Lenny had taken Stanley to his first AA meeting had Stanley fallen off the wagon. And he knew exactly why. Stanley had called Connie, his ex, to ask if she had heard from Terry. He had hoped she would let him know how to contact their son.

"I have no goddamn idea where he is," she said. "And if he ever shows up here, I might just remind him that he left me and send him right back to you." She hung up without another word.

She never used to be such an old shrew, Stanley thought. He wanted to blame her, but she didn't make him drive to the liquor store.

Stanley called Lenny the next day.

"We all stumble at first, Stan," Lenny said, no tinge of judgment in his voice.

He arrived later with a carton of Coca Cola and a pound of sausage to cook on the grill. The two spent the afternoon in Stanley's back yard listening to the Cubs on the radio.

"No one knows where he is," Stanley said, squeezing mustard on his sandwich.

"But he did call you, right, not long ago?"

"Yeah, but he wouldn't tell me where he is, only that he was traveling with some others. I told him he should come back here, that things were better, but he said he wasn't sure that would work," Stanley said, lifting the Coke bottle to his lips. "If he goes to California with those people, I may never see him again."

"They have trains and buses to California, Stan. And planes."

"It's my own fault," Stanley said. "Not his. Not even Connie's. My own damn fault."

Lenny got up for another bottle of Coke. "You remember when you were his age, Stanley?"

"Guess so."

"I sure do. I was chasing girls, saving up for my own car, and not thinking about much else. Then my older brother was killed in Korea. My parents were devastated by the news. I was too. But that telegram changed everything. My parents were so consumed by David's death, it was like they forgot they had a second son. I started doing a lot of crazy things just to get them to notice me. It took me a long time to figure out who I was after that."

"Connie and I started dating in tenth grade. By our second date, I think she'd already made our wedding plans," Stanley said.

Lenny laughed. "I knew girls like that. Couldn't wait to latch on to a boy. It's not like that now, though, is it? I mean getting married doesn't seem to be the first thing girls think of these days."

"Like my Linda. She just had a baby, but she's still not married to his father."

"So was it your plan, too, marrying Connie right after high school?"

"I don't know what I wanted. She was pretty and she liked me. She could have had any boy, but she said she liked my dark eyes and how quiet I was. She liked that I never bossed her around." Stanley laughed. "As if anyone could do that."

"Don't you think Terry might be the same?"

Stanley looked confused. "The same how?"

"Not knowing what he wants. Just trying to figure things out, like we all do. But he's not a helpless little kid. He's nearly the same age you were when you got married, nearly the same age as my brother was when he joined the army. Seventeen. Eighteen. What's the difference? Seems like we think there's this big chasm we cross when we turn eighteen, some giant leap from childhood to adulthood. But it's not like that. It's really just a moment. Who we are the day of our eighteenth birthday is who we were the day before."

"You're telling me he's not a kid and I shouldn't worry."

"I'm telling you he's probably more capable than you realize. And if he were not safe, or if something happened to him, you'd hear about it."

"No news is good news. Is that what you're saying?"

"Something like that," Lenny said.

"What if I never see him again?"

"You will, Stan. You will. And don't you want to be ready for him when that day comes?"

Stanley let his tense shoulders fall. He nodded. "I do. I can't stand thinking he's ashamed of me."

The two men fell to silence after that and listened to the call of balls and strikes and chirping birds. Learning to accept stillness while a storm raged within was the hardest thing of all.

Part Five

The Reaping Hook

SUMMIT ROAD, WISCONSIN 1968

Lily handed a dripping plate to Terry, who waited with a dish towel. They were nearly finished with the dishes, when Marion entered the kitchen.

"I think I'll take Sarge out on the path for an evening walk," Marion said. "He's been lying around a bit too much today." The truth was, she needed time alone. Dinner had been tense. Rob got under Terry's skin again, this time teasing him about being bookish.

Sarge bounded ahead of Marion and nosed at clumps of yellow coreopsis and blue chicory sniffing for rabbits. Back at her side now, she massaged the back of his neck. "You are such a good boy" she said and took a deep breath. The summer sun still burned, even at seven and the air was thick with humidity. Likely it would rain during the night. They could use it, but rain meant a delay in the paint job, and the past few days, Marion was growing more and more anxious for the job to be done. Mostly, she wanted Rob Ames to be on his way. Until Terry had arrived, Marion hadn't realized how abrasive Rob could be.

Terry told Lily he would finish up in the kitchen so she could go out to take care of her goat, which she always did after dinner.

"Aw, that's so sweet," Lily said.

"I don't mind," Terry said.

Lily was at the back door when Terry reminded her to get a carrot for Mildred.

"Oh, thanks. I forgot," Lily said. "I'll tell her you remembered her snack, and she'll love you even more."

Terry laughed. "She's smarter than I thought."

On her way to the barn, Lily stopped to pet one of the barn cats, who had been staying close to the house lately. If Marion was right, there would be kittens soon, and Lily couldn't wait.

"Hi, there, girl," Lily said, nuzzling her goat. "Look what I have for you." Lily held the carrot out to Mildred, who chomped at it eagerly. "Good, isn't it?" Lily said.

"Where's my treat?" Rob said, coming up behind her, slipping his arm around Lily's waist, pulling her tightly against him.

"Let me go," Lily said.

"I've been waiting for you, more than ever tonight," Rob said.

Lily tried to wriggle free, but Rob clenched on to her tightly.

"You bring that goat a carrot every night, but I know it's just an excuse to come out here, hoping I'll finally take you into my cabin." He bent to smell her neck. "Baby shampoo? Mmmm. Smells so nice. You're so nice."

"I said let me go."

"You don't mean that," Rob said. "No. I don't think you do," he said, fumbling with the zipper of her shorts.

After Terry finished in the kitchen, he went into the library. He wanted to see if Marion had a copy of *A Farewell to Arms*, the book his father admired so much. He found a copy and set it on the staircase to take up to his room later. Out on the front porch, Terry looked towards the road and the corn fields beyond. It was serenely quiet.

Then a cry pierced his skin. It was Lily.

"Help," she screamed.

Terry leapt off the porch and ran toward the sound. He found her in the barn, Rob lying on top of her, Lily kicking and fighting against him.

"Get off her," Terry commanded.

Rob twisted away from Lily for a moment, his weight still trapping her to the barn floor. He looked into Terry's eyes and laughed.

"I said—." Terry grabbed Rob's arm and yanked so hard he stumbled backwards, but Lily was able to squirm away. She got to her feet and ran into the dark center of the barn.

"You fucking fag," Rob shouted, now up and lurching towards Terry, who backed away.

They were on the gravel now, outside the barn doors, and Rob moved on Terry, his right arm ready to punch. Terry threw up his arms in defense, but Rob punched him in the gut instead. Terry reeled back, caught his breath, and came back with a punch of his own. Then another that split Rob's lip.

Rob touched his lip, tasted the blood. "That was a mistake." He sent Terry to the ground with a knee to his groin.

At that moment Marion and Sarge were at the edge of the meadow. They had both heard Lily's scream. Sarge barked and ran toward the fight. Marion ran after him. Coming around the garden, Marion saw Terry on the ground, Rob kneeling over him, pounding with his fists.

Then she saw Lily headed toward them, the curved reaping hook raised in her trembling hand.

"Stop it," Lily cried. "Leave Terry alone."

Sarge bounded onto the boys. Rob swung at the dog, hitting him in the neck. Sarge squealed.

"If you don't stop, I'll cut you," Lily screamed.

Marion had rushed into the house for her rifle. She fired into the sky. "This will stop now," she said.

Rob had not listened to Lily or seen the scythe in her hand, but Marion's gunshot penetrated his consciousness. Rob looked at Terry under him, blood gushing from his nose, his eyes glazed in pain. The sound of the rifle echoed in his head. He wobbled to his feet, stared at Marion and Lily, then ran to the truck parked near the barn. No time to gather his things. He turned the key and sped off down the hill and out onto the road.

Lily ran after him, Sarge by her heels.

Marion yelled, "Come back, Lily. He's gone."

Lily stood near the road. Her heart pounded in her ears and the damp of the evening grabbed at her throat. Her fingers grasped the reaping hook so tightly they began to hurt.

Marion was now at Lily's side.

"He's gone," she said softly. "He's not going to hurt you or Terry now."

Lily's chest heaved.

"It's okay, sweetheart. It's okay," Marion said.

Sarge whined.

"Give me that now," Marion said and took the tool from Lily's hand.

Sarge licked at Lily's bare legs. His wet tongue brought her into the present. Lily looked into Marion's face, then ran up the driveway where Terry struggled to sit.

"Are you all right?" Lily said, reaching out to him, afraid to touch his bloodied face.

"I think so," Terry said. He pulled the yoke of his shirt to his face and wiped his nose.

Sarge licked Terry's face. "It's all right, boy," Terry said. "I'm okay."

"You all right?" Marion asked.

"I will be."

Marion helped Terry to his feet.

"I'd run you right into the hospital if—."

"I hope I gave him worse than he gave me," Terry said.

"Even so. Let's get you inside." Marion and Lily braced Terry and they walked to the house. Inside, Terry sat in the kitchen. Lily filled a basin with water and got a clean dishrag from the drawer. With the cloth, she wiped the blood from Terry's face.

Marion laid her rifle on the table and went to the phone. She dialed the sheriff's office. The phone rang and rang.

"Answer, damn it," she said.

"You'll have a black eye," Lily said to Terry.

She rinsed the cloth and wrung it out. As she wiped the cool cloth across the back of his neck, Terry laid his hand over hers.

"He hurt you?"

"I'm okay now."

Marion hung up the phone. "I got that useless deputy," she said, then dialed Roger's number at home.

"Roger! Thank God."

Goodnight Stars

SUMMIT ROAD, WISCONSIN 1968

After Marion hung up the phone, she went to Terry, brushed the hair from his forehead, and grimaced. "That cut's not deep, but I think we should call the doctor," Marion said.

"I'm okay," he said, "just sore."

"Where else does it hurt?"

Terry's arm covered his ribs. "Here, mostly," he said.

"Hmm," Marion said. "I wonder if he broke a rib? Does it hurt to breathe?"

"No, not really. I don't think anything's broken."

She went to the medicine cabinet and got aspirin and a Band-Aid. "Here," she said. "This will help."

He swallowed the pills, then she washed and bandaged his cut.

"Do you have a clean shirt?"

"Yeah. I'll go—." He started to rise.

"I'll get it. Just tell me where it is."

She found a clean t-shirt in the top drawer. Before turning out the light in the small front room, Marion noticed how neatly the bed had been made, how conscientiously Terry's few belongings had been stowed. How wrong her first fears had been. And how wrong she was about Rob, whom she had trusted enough to leave on his own, enough to hand him the keys to her truck.

"Well Marion," she said out loud, "that was stupid."

Back in the kitchen, Marion helped Terry with the shirt. Gentle as she was, Terry let out an expression of pain as he lifted his arms. "If you're not better in the morning, I am definitely calling the doctor," she said.

Marion put the bloodied shirt into the sink and ran cold water over it. Lily was at the back door, peering through the screen. Marion went to her side.

"You doing okay?" she said.

Lily nodded. "Uh huh."

"What a horrible thing," Marion said, squeezing the girl's hand. After a moment, she asked Lily to lock the front door. "The screen door, too. Then close the drapes. I'm going out to lock up the barn," she said.

"No," Lily cried. "Mildred can't stay out there alone."

"She's a goat, dear. She'll be fine."

"It's not that," Lily said desperately. "What if he comes back? He'll hurt her."

"He wouldn't—."

"You didn't hear him, the things he said. I know he would—."

Marion could see there would be no consoling Lily's fears, which she knew were not irrational under the circumstances.

"All right, Lily. Let's go get her. We'll keep her in the kitchen. Though I'm afraid there'll be a mess in the morning."

"But she'll be safe," Lily said.

Marion nodded. "Yes. She'll be safe."

Marion held the back door open while Lily led the goat up the porch steps. What would Vivian have to say about this, Marion thought. She'd tell me I was daft, and she might be right. Once inside, Lily handed Terry the lead. While Terry held onto the goat, Sarge nosed about Mildred's belly, sniffing under her tail. Lily built a makeshift pen by laying the kitchen chairs on their sides. Marion brought blankets for the floor. Lily got another carrot from the refrigerator and used it to coax Mildred into the enclosure. The goat chewed. Then she folded her front legs under her and lowered herself to the floor. Lily sat on the floor outside the pen and gave Mildred the rest of the carrot. "I think she likes it," Lily said.

"Not too much, I hope," said Marion playfully. "I wish we'd hear something more from Roger."

"He's probably chasing after Rob right now," Lily said.

"I hope you're right, Lily."

"I hope they lock him up in jail for the rest of his life," Lily said.

Marion sighed. They'd have to catch him first. But Lily's sentiment felt just about right to her.

"All right now, Lily. Mildred will be fine without you by her side for a few minutes," Marion said. "Go on and wash your hands, then come sit with us. I think we should finish that peach pie."

Marion brought the plates and forks to the table. She put extra ice cream on both Lily and Terry's plates. "We look like refugees," Marion said. "But we're safe."

At ten o'clock, Marion said they should go to bed. As Marion assumed would be the case, Lily refused to leave Mildred alone in the kitchen.

"I guess that's for the best," Marion said. "I can't imagine the damage she'd do on her own."

Marion blew up an old beach air mattress for Lily to lie on, and Lily brought a pillow and blankets down from her room.

"All set then, girls?" Marion said. "Camping in the kitchen?"

Lily nodded. "Good night, Terry," she said.

Terry said goodnight then started up the stairs. After the first step, he stopped and took a deep breath, his hand pressing gently on his side.

"You better stay down here," Marion said. "I'll make up a bed on the sofa for you."

"I guess it hurts worse than I thought."

"Swelling is probably making it feel worse. I'll get some ice and that should help."

Marion was tempted to sleep nearby in a chair, but she knew her back would never forgive her. The house was securely locked. Terry and Lily would be safe downstairs without her. Sarge would probably keep watch all night. He had been hurt, too, and he needed to be close to his people.

"Goodnight, you two," Marion said. "We'll sort through all of this tomorrow." At the base of the stairs, she clicked off the kitchen light. "*Goodnight stars*," she whispered. The memory of one of her favorite children's books seemed fitting. Sarge emitted his contented sigh, Marion's sign that all was well with him, and then she went up to bed.

At two a.m. Marion was startled awake by Lily shouting at her door.

"Fire! Marion! The barn's on fire!"

Marion rushed down the stairs and bolted out the back door but stopped at the driveway's edge and stood in a steady rain. Terry and Lily and Sarge stood behind her. In the kitchen, Mildred bleated loudly.

"Lily, call the fire department, now! Then bring that goat out here before she wrecks my house."

"But she'll get wet," Lily complained.

"Do as I said," Marion shouted.

Marion watched the north wall of the barn collapse in reaching flames. "I don't think the rain is going to help," Marion said to Terry. Sarge whined and nudged her leg. "I know boy. I know."

Before long they heard sirens in the distance, then a thunder crack that shook the ground beneath them. Soon firemen aimed their hoses into yellow-blue flames. As a backdrop, lightning lit the sky. Then the rain became a drenching deluge. But all the water in the world was not enough. The barn was lost. In the morning, when the charred remains smoldered their last heat, there was nothing left.

John Muir

The next afternoon, Roger was out behind the house nailing together a lean-to for Mildred, her old pen in the barn nothing but ashes. Marion's neighbor Eugene Marquardt had driven over with a truckload of straw and hay and an offer to do whatever he could do. Other neighbors stopped by with casseroles, which Marion crammed into her freezer.

"Must have been a lightning strike," they buzzed.

Vivian arrived with her own casserole and volunteered to drive Lily to Sheboygan to buy her a few things to wear for the start of school the following week.

"Maybe we'll get a whole new wardrobe," Vivian said, winking at Lily.

While Vivian waited in her car, Marion stuck five dollars into Lily's hand. "After shopping, take your "Auntie Viv" out for ice cream." Marion ran her hand over the girl's head. "And don't worry. Pick out whatever you like," Marion said. "She can afford it."

Marion waved as the two drove off, then wandered back to check on Roger, who was making quick work of his project. The fresh, sharp scent of pine and sawdust contrasted sharply with the smell of smoke that enveloped the farm. While Roger worked, Mildred nibbled on the long grass under the clothesline where she was tethered. There was work to be done, but the incident with Rob and the fire had taken all initiative out of her. What she really wanted was to climb up to her bed and curl up like a baby. But what would that accomplish?

At least their trip to the doctor that morning had given them good news. Terry would be sore for a while, but there was nothing broken. Marion wished she knew what else she could do for him. Though his injuries would heal with time, it was Terry's sadness she could not fix and that bothered her. Roger was likely right when he had said, "The boy's almost a man. He'll figure it out."

Marion wandered along the far side of the house and stooped to deadhead a few marigolds, but even that small task brought her no peace. Around front she found Terry on the porch swing. She asked if she could join him. The sun had started its slow descent into afternoon and an oblique shadow from the big gray willow lay on the gravel near the end of the driveway. Terry and Marion sat on the porch swing and rocked gently.

"I don't belong here," Terry said, his voice breaking the stillness.

Marion felt such an admission deserved time and space, so she rocked gently and watched the willow shadow. She thought it was probably true, what Terry said, but not in the way he thought. He had stood up for Lily. He had fought for her. Such a gentle Galahad. But she knew he blamed himself for letting Rob get away.

She wanted to reach out and draw him to her, tell him he was wrong. He could stay as long as he needed to stay. But she felt there was something else that pulled at him. Another place that needed him.

"Have you ever heard of John Muir?" she asked.

Terry said he hadn't.

"He's a famous naturalist. I was reminded of him when you kids started showing up here. John Muir was born in Scotland but grew up in Wisconsin. He's mostly known for his work in California, Yosemite, the Sierras. But before that, he walked a thousand miles from Indiana to Florida. Can you imagine it? A thousand miles. And he was a writer, too, so he wrote a book about it."

Terry was interested. He peered at her intently. "Do you have that book?" he asked.

"Yes. I'll get it for you later," she said. "What got me thinking about him was not just his descriptions of all the places he passed through, but how he came among strangers who fed him and gave him shelter. There were some who eyed him suspiciously, even wanting to rob him, but most of the people he met along the way were generous folk. That was 1867, after the Civil War."

"How long did it take him?"

"A few months. You would think that when he reached the end of his journey, he would be satisfied and head back home where he could rest. But after he reached the Gulf of Mexico, he took a boat to Cuba. Later, he went out west, where he ended up doing his most important work."

"The longest I've ever walked is about ten miles," Terry said. "Though I guess I've traveled a lot farther than that."

"I sometimes wonder if I've spent too much time on my little farm here," Marion said. "At one time, I wanted to go places and see things. But when my husband died, I no longer saw the point. Staying put felt familiar and safe. Then Bridget came, then Lily, then you. Each of you brought the world to me in your own way."

"I think I probably just brought you a lot of trouble," Terry said.

"Nothing you did caused that young man to go after —." Marion shook her head. She laid her hand on Terry's knee. "None of it was your fault."

Terry nodded and looked off into the distance.

"I wonder what Muir would make of my little crew here," she said. "You think he might approve?"

Terry smiled. "It does seem like he wandered a long way from home," he said.

"That's true," she said. "Very far. And don't you think he was searching for something, too. Maybe he wanted to see what he was capable of. What he was made of. That same kind of strength is in you, too, isn't it?"

Terry shook his head. "What I see in me is desperation."

"You have more than that, Terry. Not everyone who's desperate has enough courage to find a way out."

That night Terry lay in bed paging through *A Thousand-Mile Walk to the Gulf.* Muir had recorded the journey as a diary, chronicling each day's events, describing what he saw, the people he met. Terry's own diary began with a similar intent but urging the words onto the page from where they lay safe and deep within him was not easy.

Terry skimmed a few pages near the end of the book about a place in Florida called "The Cedar Keys." He thought it sounded beautiful.

"I crept away to the edge of the wood, and sat day after day beneath a moss-draped live-oak, watching birds feeding on the shore when the tide was out. Later, as I gathered some strength, I sailed in a little skiff from one key to another."

Life was like that, Terry thought. I'm like that. Since he was fifteen, he'd been moving from one island to another, finding shelter, finding friends, but never really finding home. And each time he left a place, it was harder and harder to take the first step.

He thought about what Marion had said, but it was hard to accept because he had never considered himself courageous. He left his mother's home in fear. He left New York out of fear. And earlier that summer, when he left his father, it was certainly not courageous. Instead, he was afraid of how desperately his father needed him.

And yet, where would he be if Donette had not taken him in? Or Dennis and Sharon? And Marion? The Crazy Train, even. On his own thousand miles, Terry had never been abandoned, which is exactly what he had done to his father. And then it came to him. "He's the one," Terry said out loud. Marion's words echoed in his head. *"Not everyone who's desperate has enough courage to get out."* Maybe I can't fix him, Terry thought, but maybe I'm not supposed to. Maybe all he needs is for me to be there for him, doing whatever I can.

Police Report

SUMMIT ROAD, WISCONSIN 1968

As they sat with their coffee on the front porch, Roger told Marion that Robert Lang, a fugitive from Minneapolis, had been arrested in Illinois.

She said she was relieved to hear it.

"A gas station owner near Lake Geneva had called the police to report a wild looking young man who looked like he'd been in a fight. The young man also smelled like kerosene, he said. Before the man pulled away, the station owner took down the license number and called in the report. It didn't take long for police to find the truck on Hwy 12, headed toward northern Illinois. When the squad car turned on its siren, the truck sped off. They chased him for two miles before Rob lost control and rolled into a ditch. He was thrown from the vehicle."

"My truck," Marion gasped.

"Unfortunately," Roger said, "They say it's a total loss."

"What about Rob?"

"They've got him under police guard in a hospital in McHenry. He's broken up pretty bad, but nothing that won't heal. He confessed to everything. Told them he had driven back to your place, used a crowbar to break one of the windows to his cabin. Once inside, he grabbed his stuff. Then he got the brilliant idea to start the fire to get back at you. He told the officers down there he was sorry that goat wasn't in the barn when he tossed his lighter onto the straw."

"We assumed it was a lightning strike. No one had once thought it was Rob."

"That's not all." Roger handed Marion a small envelope. Marion slid open the envelope's seal. "Mother's ring!" she said pulling out the family heirloom.

"You didn't even know it was missing, did you?"

She clutched the ring in her fist and held it to her heart. He'd been in her room. She felt sick in the pit of her stomach.

"They found it among his personal items. He admitted to stealing it. They had enough on him without prosecuting that offense, so they sent it to our office to return to you."

"How could I have been such a poor judge of character?"

"Don't blame yourself, Marion. No one can anticipate someone like him."

After Roger drove away, Marion took a garden shovel to the end of the driveway. She hacked away at her sign until it lay on the ground in splinters. As of that moment, she was no longer in the egg business.

Accommodations

ELMWOOD PARK, ILLINOIS 1968

Stanley Abbott reminded himself every morning that his son's return meant something. It was one more opportunity for him to be the father he always should have been, and that meant, above all, staying sober. He knew it would take time to get to know his son. They'd been strangers most of their lives. And he knew from their time earlier that summer that talking about baseball games was not the way to communicate with Terry. Terry was a writer, a lover of books, a young man who was generous and kind to others. And though he didn't know how or why, Stanley knew Terry had experienced some great pain. In this, Stanley thought, I understand him.

It also dawned on Stanley that it wasn't necessary to fill every silence with words. After that, things got easier. Unlike earlier that summer when Stanley tried to entertain Terry, he now saw it was just as nice to be alone with him in the evening, reading or watching TV. Terry was a quiet person. After years of struggling to make social small talk, often needing a drink or two to accomplish the company banter, Stanley finally realized he was more like his son, most comfortable saying little.

That didn't mean the two didn't talk. They did. And it surprised Stanley how often Terry would go on and on about something he was interested in, an idea he'd read about, something he'd learned in school. In those moments, Stanley realized how smart and interesting his son was. One thing Terry didn't talk about was the years he had been gone from home, and Stanley knew better than to ask.

When either had something on his mind, he spoke up. At the outset, they both agreed not to keep frustration or anger bottled up. However, Stanley was grateful that there were very few tense moments, and he found that his nearly adult son was easy to get along with.

For a little over a month, Stanley had been working as assistant shift supervisor for a rival company to the one he'd worked for most of his life. So far, the job had not been too demanding. Lenny advised him to keep it all professional. "Do the job and go home. Socializing only means trouble." It was good advice. Besides, Stanley now had a reason to go straight home after work.

Terry was doing well in school. He was able enter his senior year by proving his proficiency on a variety of tests. Even so, in order to graduate that year, he had to add extra courses to his schedule to meet the state requirements. While the extra work seemed excessive at times, Stanley was proud that his son never complained about how much he had to do.

Even though school kept him busy, Terry made time for his dad. It was Terry who insisted that they cook and eat dinner together every night. They worked together on long-neglected projects too. One weekend they repaired a broken window and rehung a loose shutter.

"You didn't know your old man had handyman skills, did you?" Stanley said as Terry watched him reglaze the window.

One Saturday morning, Stanley and Terry had planned to get on the roof to fix the chimney flashing, but it had been raining since seven. Terry sat at the kitchen table writing a summary of Madison's main points in *Federalist Paper No. 48*. Stanley stood at the front window watching the rain, waiting for it to lighten up. The golden leaves that had burned bright in the sun, coloring the living room the day before, were now strewn across the yard, glossy with rain.

By eleven, the sky began to brighten and the weather report on the radio said the skies would clear in about an hour. From the front window, Stanley watched a yellow cab drive past the house. Out on the front porch, he lifted the mailbox cover, took out a soggy *Tribune* and a half dozen envelopes. The cab reappeared. Someone's lost, he thought.

Then cab stopped in front of their house, and a tall, black woman emerged, a plastic rain bonnet tied to her head.

"Does Terry live here?" she asked. "Terry Abbott?"

Stanley tossed the mail inside the house and walked across the lawn toward the woman. When he told her that Terry did live here, she signaled the driver. He popped out of the cab, opened the trunk, and took out a large suitcase, which he handed to Stanley, whose flummoxed face amused the driver.

"She don't pack light, does she?" said the driver, who held out his hand to be paid.

"Oh, here," said the woman, pushing between the two men. She paid the driver, and he got in the cab and drove off.

"You know my son?" Stanley asked, still bewildered.

Her attention was drawn away before she could explain. "There he is."

"Donnie," Terry cried, leaping from the front porch.

He hugged her fiercely. "Donnie," he said, with the relief of one who has restrained a feeling for too long.

"I know, honey. I know," Donette whispered. "I missed you too."

When they finally let go, Stanley was alongside them, still holding Donette's heavy bag.

"This is Donette," Terry said to his father.

"Well, let's get her inside, Terry."

Donette tried to take her bag from Stanley, but he refused. "Go ahead and follow Terry in," he said.

"We're old friends from New York," Donette told Stanley as they walked to the house.

Inside, Donette took off her rain bonnet and laid it on the rug inside the door. "That was some storm," she said. She turned towards

Terry and said, "I came straight from the bus station. I didn't know where else to go. I hope it's all right?"

"I can't believe you're here," Terry said.

"I can't believe it either," she said. "It's nice to meet you, Mr. Abbott," Donette said, holding her hand out to Stanley, who shook it.

"Same here," he said.

"I have so many questions," Terry said, drawing Donette into the living room, gesturing for her to sit.

You have questions, Stanley thought, but he followed his son and his guest and listened while they talked.

"After you left, I just couldn't get back to normal. And then momma died, and it got worse. She was so young—only 52. Got me thinking I might not have much time left either. After the funeral, my aunt Bernice begged me to stay. She didn't want to be alone. I understand that, but Alabama is not my home. When I got back to New York, I took a job at my beauty parlor, answering the phone and making appointments. I liked working there, and everyone was so friendly. But every time you'd call, I realized more and more how much I missed you. Seemed like everyone but me—Sanchez, Maureen—knew I needed to come to you. So here I am, in out of the rain, like the first time I met you."

She patted her hair. "I must look a mess," she said. "Mind if I use your bathroom, Mr. Abbott?"

"Call me Stanley," he said, getting up to show her the way.

After the door clicked shut, Stanley returned to Terry and shrugged his shoulders. "An old friend? She's—. She's almost my age. And she's—."

"She's black, Dad. And she took care of me at a time when I had no one else."

"Well, I didn't mean anything. I just—." Stanley decided to say no more.

He sat back in the chair and tapped his foot.

"Whew. That's better," Donette said, rejoining the two men.

"How long can you stay?" Terry asked.

"I hadn't thought much beyond right now," she said. "Tell the truth, I wasn't sure you were even going to be here."

Terry looked at his father. "She can stay in Linda's room, right Dad?"

Stanley smiled at the woman. "Unless she's already made other arrangements, Terry."

"I haven't yet. But I—."

"No, no. That's fine. We're just two bachelors, though. Not the finest accommodations." Stanley heard himself working the old corporate schmooze. Terry shot him an exasperated look.

"You're more than welcome," Stanley said. "Terry, why don't you show Donette where to put her things, and I'll make us lunch."

"You're very kind, Mr.—. Stanley," Donette said.

Conspiracy

Marion watched Sarge chase after the school bus as he did every morning.

"Come on, boy," Marion called. "She'll be back home before you know it."

Sarge wasn't the only one who felt Lily's absence. When summer dawned, Marion realized she was finally learning to live alone, without Harve. Keeping busy with then hens, the garden, embroidery or sewing on rainy days, an indulgent nap whenever she cared to take one. She had not been unhappy.

Then Bridget changed everything. By the time Terry arrived, Marion had grown used to the daily company and the routine of living with others again, especially Lily, who in nearly all ways, had become her daughter.

A flock of Canada geese squawked overhead. Marion watched them make their way in a vee, wondering at the miracle—how they knew where to go and what to do, all written in their genes. If it were only that easy for people, she thought.

"Come on boy. Let's go." Marion climbed toward the house but stopped when Sarge left her side and started barking.

Marion held her hand over her eyes and read the lettering on a large white van pulling into her driveway. "Leroy's Painting."

"What on earth," she said. Sarge was back at her side, away from the van, which parked near the hen house. A broad-shouldered young man jumped out. He was wearing a white jumpsuit, spattered with paint.

"Marion Goodman?" he asked.

"That's me."

"We're from Leroy's Painting."

"I can see that. What's this all about?"

"We've been hired by Mr. Armistead to paint your house."

Marion was speechless and stepped aside as they got to work.

That man, she thought as she dialed Roger's number, her heart swelling with emotion.

"I just couldn't let it stay half done," Roger said, "a constant reminder of him."

Later, Marion had to admit she liked the new color. She suspected Lily had a hand in the conspiracy. The soft yellow was a perfect match for the hen house.

October Moon

Summit Road 1968

Early in the morning on the third Saturday in October, a caravan of trucks and wagons full of lumber and other supplies pulled into Marion's driveway. Her neighbors, friends, and former students had come to rebuild her barn. The design featured a lower profile than her old barn and would be built over the existing concrete floor that had survived the inferno.

"Surprised?" Vivian asked.

"Shocked," Marion said.

"We tried so hard to keep it a secret."

"Was this your idea, or Roger's?"

"I'm not telling," Vivian said with a wink.

The idea had actually come from Terry. He and Lily had taken Sarge out on the meadow path the morning before they drove Terry to the bus station. "I don't know if it is possible," Terry said, "but in older times, neighbors came together to build a barn for someone. They called it a barn raising." Lily had given Terry a hug and told him he was a genius. That Sunday, Lily mentioned it to Roger, and Roger said he would call Vivian and they would take it from there.

The timing of the new barn was perfect. Lily and Marion had been worried about Mildred, since they learned from the vet that she was having twins.

With most of her neighbors on hand to help, the men got to work outdoors, and the women invaded Marion's kitchen, where Vivian took control. The women made a midday meal of hamburgers and fried chicken, cole slaw and potato salad. They filled large coffee urns and set out dozens of cookies. Marion was shooed away. She stole a cookie and headed outdoors, where she found Roger, who was nursing a sprained ankle.

"Guess my ladder days are over," he said.

"You got that right, old man," she said, laughing.

He lowered his chin and looked into her eyes in a way that made her knees weak. He wiped a cookie crumb from the corner of her mouth. "Who are you calling old?"

Marion was speechless, her throat dry. Rising in her was a desire she had not felt for so long she wondered how such a thing could still take hold of her. "You go on," she said, her freckled cheeks warming.

Mid-afternoon, Marion took Sarge with her into the meadow, where she planned to read for a while to keep her anxious mind occupied. She sat on the bench and opened the book. When she realized she'd tried three times to read one paragraph, she shut the book and laid it on the bench. A flutter of small white butterflies rose into view. They were pretty, but evidence that there could be cabbage worms in her garden. She sighed. Keeping ahead of garden pests was an increasingly unsatisfying chore, she thought. Sarge used his nose to try to get Marion to move.

"All right, boy," she said. "Let's go take a look at the progress."

When they emerged from the meadow, Sarge bounded toward the men working on the barn. Marion followed him to where a young man in his thirties had come down off a ladder. The man petted the dog. "What do you think, Mrs. Goodman?" the man asked.

"It's a miracle," she said.

"Well, we, that is, my dad and I—. He's up there, framing the roof." Marion squinted to see him.

"We all wanted to help."

"I'm sorry," she said. "I don't remember your name."

"Jim. Jimmy Lorenz. I wasn't your best student, but I loved 'spin the globe day,'" he said. "You taught us a lot about the world."

"I'd forgotten all that. It is nice of you to remember."

"You have a nice dog," he said.

"Nice and pesky, right boy?"

"Not at all," Jim said.

"Thank you, Jim," she said, "for coming here today."

Marion shaded her eyes and watched Jim climb the ladder, behind him the moon, a waxing crescent. It was possible to make out shadows, the dish-like craters. Only days ago, the three Apollo 7 astronauts had splashed down in the Atlantic Ocean after being in space for nearly eleven days. The newspaper had reported the current distance to the moon was about 227,900 miles. It was astonishing, she thought, that people could propel themselves so close to the heavens and return to earth to tell their stories. The world would never again be defined by one small globe, she thought.

Marion found Lily on the back porch keeping an eye on Mildred, who was tethered nearby. Lily had her notebook in her hand.

"I've got more names for the babies," Lily said.

Marion climbed the steps. They sat out of the way of the activity in the kitchen, but close enough to hear the chatter, the occasional loud cackle of the women inside.

"They're having a great time, aren't they?" Marion said.

Lily nodded. "But it's crazy. I almost got squished between two ladies."

Lily flipped the cover on her spiral notebook. The names on her list so far were Betty and Veronica, Gilligan and Mary Ann, Paul and Ringo, and Wilma and Betty.

"What about Romulus and Remus," Marion asked.

Lily looked at her, perplexed.

"Never mind. I'm sure you'll come up with the perfect names all on your own."

Mildred had been safe in the lean to, but with a new barn, they could move her little shed inside it. When the kids came, they would be warm and cozy.

"Are you ready for this, Lily? Three goats instead of one is a lot more responsibility."

"I'm ready."

"You could raise the kids and sell them."

Lily shook her head.

"That money would go a long way to pay for college," Marion said.

"I've never thought about college," Lily said.

With the evening meal eaten and all the dishes dried and put away, the last of the work crew began heading home at 8:00 p.m. Marion could not believe that the shell of the barn had been completed in one day. The next day many of the workers would shingle the roof, set the doors and windows, and paint the exterior.

When everyone had left, Vivian and Lily sat in the kitchen with hot tea. Roger sat with Marion on the back porch, the dog between them, the moon bright in the now black sky.

"Are you pleased?" Roger said.

She smiled and took his hand. "I suppose you'll tell me you had nothing to do with arranging it?"

"Honestly, I wish I had thought of it."

"I don't quite feel deserving, though," she said.

"Those kids and their parents owe you a lot. It's not just your runaways that you've had an impact on."

Talk about herself made Marion uncomfortable, as lovely as it was to hear.

"Don't you know how much you're loved?" he said. He squeezed her hand and looked into Marion's eyes. He could not say the words that echoed in his head.

"I'd best be getting home," he said. "I'll check on you in a few days."

"You'd better," she said and kissed him on the cheek.

When Marion came into the kitchen, Vivian noticed the odd expression on her sister's face. Marion got a dog biscuit from a jar on the counter and gave it to Sarge, who took it to his favorite place on the rug by the back door.

"You feeling all right, Marion?" Vivian asked.

"Never better, Viv. Never better."

Dear Marion

ELMWOOD PARK, ILLINOIS

November 19, 1968

Dear Marion (Lily, too),

I hope you're both well. I meant to write sooner, but I've been really busy trying to keep up with schoolwork.

I'll bet you have a baby goat by now, Lily. You'll have to write and tell me all about it. I hope you're enjoying school and that you have good teachers.

I've been lucky there. It was a lot easier to fit in here than I thought. I've made a couple of friends and my teachers are great. I don't have much time for anything other than school, but I will graduate in spring.

I turned eighteen last week. I thought it would make me feel older, but it didn't. I think I've always felt older.

My dad is doing pretty well. I wasn't sure how things would be between us, but it's getting easier all the time. He's proud of me. That's a nice feeling.

The biggest news I have is that my friend from New York, Donette,

282

I'm sure I told you about her. If not, I should have. Anyway, she's living with us. I'm really happy she's here.

My dad says we're a little family, which I think is kind of amazing. He was alone for most of his life and now he's got me and a new "mom." Ha ha. But seriously, she kind of is. She was for me those years I lived with her in New York, and she takes care of my dad now too. Not that he needs to be taken care of. I don't mean it like that. She's just a happy presence. She jokes with him. She gives him a hug when she sees he needs one.

He still gets into moods sometimes. My sister Linda says it's a special kind of melancholy that soldiers get. Depression. Linda says it doesn't matter how long ago they were in the war, some men never get over that experience. Oh, yeah, Linda is studying to be a psychologist, so she is learning all about things like that. She tells me she might need an extra year in college to learn what's wrong with me.

She visited for my birthday and brought her little girl. She is barely walking, so watching her run is pretty funny.

I haven't stopped writing, in case you were wondering, but I have given up trying to write stories for a while. My English teacher had us read "Walden." Of course, I really liked it. And I still have the Muir you gave me. They've inspired me to write about life around me instead of fiction or fantasy.

And I walk a lot, just to see what there is to see. I'm not by a pond or staring up at mountains, but cities are landscapes too. I'm trying to really see beyond the ordinary and look deeply at things.

That day on the porch, you said I must have seen a lot of beautiful places, but a lot of the time I'd walk miles on a highway and only see my shoes. I missed so much.

I'd like to come back to Wisconsin someday. I barely had time to really see the place you live. But being there will never leave me. You will never leave me. You gave me more than a couple of books. You gave me a way home. I won't ever forget that.

If you see Roger, tell him hello. He's a good guy.

I guess I'd better close this letter. It's getting late, and I've got school tomorrow. I hope you have a terrific Thanksgiving.

Sincerely yours,

Terry

Epilogue

The Long Road

SUMMIT ROAD 1978

After finishing the lunch dishes, Marion joined Roger on the front porch and settled into the wicker chair next to him. Sarge curled up by Roger's feet. A portable radio sat on the table between them.

"Who's winning?" Marion asked.

"Brewers are up 3-0 in the second," Roger said.

They listened without speaking through the next inning when Marion noticed Roger had fallen asleep. Marion closed her eyes. The sun had retreated to the edge of the porch's painted floor, and Marion's new white Keds rested in cool shade. She easily drifted off herself, lulled by the calls of balls and strikes.

A while later Sarge lifted his head at the sound of tires on gravel. Marion woke and shaded her eyes with her hand. Roger snored on unaware. She did not recognize the car, a green station wagon with wood paneled sides. "Who is it, boy?" Marion whispered. The driver had pulled all the way up the driveway, near the barn.

The first one out of the car was a young boy in blue jeans and a red striped shirt.

"Stay here, Mikey. Don't run off," a woman called as she got out of the front seat.

The woman wore blue jeans and a gauzy top, the yoke embroidered in colorful flowers. Her wavy blonde hair hung past her shoulders. She

287

took off her sunglasses as she approached Marion.

"Can I help you?" Marion said.

"You don't remember me?" the woman said.

Marion cocked her head, looked closely at the woman's face. "Bridget?"

The woman smiled and reached out to Marion, who drew her into a warm embrace.

"My goodness, it's Bridget." Marion held her at arm's length now. "After all this time."

"This is my son," Bridget said. "Say hello to Mrs. Goodman, Mikey."

"Hello," the boy said, but his focus was on the dog.

"He's friendly," Marion said. "Go ahead and pet him." Marion held onto Bridget's hand. "My goodness, it's wonderful to see you."

Bridget stepped up onto the back porch and ten years fell away. She looked behind her at the garden, still neat and prosperous. The furniture on the porch had not changed, the two white rockers, a small table between them, clay flowerpots filled with herbs. As for Marion, she looked only slightly older. Short silver hair, a few more wrinkles, but as full of life as ever. Bridget and Marion went inside.

Roger appeared. He'd woken and seen a small boy chasing Sarge in the yard.

"Bridget, this is my husband, Roger," Marion said.

"So, you're the one," Roger said, in a playful way.

Bridget smiled, though not sure what he meant.

"He can be ornery, so don't mind him," Marion said.

Roger winked conspiratorially. "The young man belongs to you I take it," Roger said.

"He's not bothering the dog too much, is he?" Bridget said.

"Sarge? No. He's loving the attention."

"That's for sure," Marion said. "Bridget, can I get you something? Coffee? Iced tea? Lemonade for the boy?"

Bridget said any of that would be fine and offered to help. She went to the refrigerator. Magnets held photographs of people she didn't recognize. A dark-haired young man in a cap and gown, a round faced woman in a nurse's cap, a photo of Marion and Roger with a short, grey-haired woman, their arms linked, a giant cactus in the background.

"Did a boy named Terry ever come here?" Bridget asked.

"That's him right there," Roger said, pointing to Terry's college graduation picture on the refrigerator.

"He was with us only a short time, but he's become very dear to us over the years," Marion said.

"He's so grown up. I didn't recognize him. Though it was a long time ago that I knew him. I remember he was quiet. And sweet. I was sorry when he left us. I always hoped I would run in to him again. So, he's doing well?"

"Very well. He teaches American literature and composition at a community college," Marion said. "And now he has a girlfriend," she added. "A woman friend, I should say."

"This is our Lily," Roger said pointing to the woman in the nurses cap. "She came to us that same summer. She saw your notes on the wall."

"Yeah. I probably shouldn't have done that. Sorry," Bridget said.

"Well, that's okay. I think it was meant to be. Lily needed us. And—," Roger said, slipping his arm around his wife's waist, "we needed her, too. Didn't we?"

"Yes," Marion said. "It's as if those two—Terry and Lily—are our children. We're so proud of them. Lily's an RN, and this past Christmas she got engaged to a young man who works as an agricultural insurance agent. And Lily and Terry are great friends."

With their glasses filled, Marion led them to the front porch. Mikey was reluctant to leave Sarge, but he sat on a step to eat a cookie and gulp lemonade. As soon as he was finished, he returned to the dog who waited for him.

Mikey threw a stick and told Sarge to fetch it, but Sarge just sat by Mikey's side, looking up at him.

"I'm afraid that old dog has given up games," Marion said to Mikey. "But you can walk around with him. He'll follow you to the end of the earth."

"Come on boy," Mikey said, "Let's go explore."

"Don't wander too far," his mother said before sitting on the porch swing.

"You're obviously doing well, too," Marion said. "You have no idea how many times I have thought about you over the years."

Bridget pulled her legs up to her side and put a small pillow in her lap. "It wasn't great when I left here," she said. "I felt so guilty, taking advantage of you. I wandered the rest of that summer. There were others I met along the way, not all of them as nice as you, of course. You'd think a night in jail would be the worst thing, but at least a jail cell is warm and dry and they feed you. When they sent me home, I decided not to run anymore."

"What changed?" Marion said.

"My parents were so glad to see me, so glad I was alive, I thought maybe home was no longer a threat. They treated me well. But then things started to slide, started to go back to how they had been. So, I stood up to my dad and told him how it would be. He realized I wasn't a kid anymore, I think. Whatever it was, he let me be."

Marion said she was happy to hear it. "I often wondered whether or not you would find your way home."

"You saw something in me," Bridget said.

"Saw what?" Marion said.

"Capability, for one thing. On the road, if it came to it, I learned to do anything to protect myself. After my time with you, I started to believe in myself. That's why I wanted to see you again. To thank you. More than that, I wanted you to see who I am now."

Roger looked at his wife with pride.

"I still have your mason jar," Bridget said.

Marion looked puzzled.

"You sent me away with food and a jar of pickles. I keep small stones and trinkets in that jar now, things I picked up when I was on the road. There's a black stone in there that I took from your garden. Whenever I feel like life's thrown me something I can't handle, I take out that stone and think about where I have been. That jar keeps me balanced."

Mikey came up on the porch, Sarge at his side. "I saw a snake," Mikey said, "a real snake."

"Were you afraid?" his mother asked.

"Nope. It was just a little one." With that declaration, the boy was off again.

Bridget looked at her son with pride. "He's not afraid of much," she said. "Like his father."

"Where is he, dear?" Marion asked.

Bridget explained that her husband had been killed in the last months of the Vietnam War. "When those uniforms came to the door, I thought I would crumble. But I didn't. I had a two-and-a half-year-old toddler who needed me."

"Mikey seems like a fine boy," Roger said.

"What is it you do, Bridget?"

"I teach middle school. Seventh grade."

Marion wondered if she had something to do with that decision.

"It might surprise you to know I'm good at it," Bridget said.

"Not a surprise at all."

Bridget described her classroom, from the desks and bulletin boards to one of her more interesting students. Marion said she knew that type. "Don't give up on a single one," Marion told her. "Everyone grows up and amounts to something."

When it was time for Bridget to leave, she and Marion faced each other at the car, not ready to say goodbye.

"I never forgot you, Marion. Whenever I wanted to give up, I'd close my eyes and find my way back to you. I've tried so hard to become someone you'd be proud of."

"My goodness," Marion said, choking back a sob, "You make it sound like I was your mother."

"You were much more." Bridget wiped the corner of her eye.

Mikey stuck his head out the car window. "It was nice to meet'cha, boy," he said. Sarge was standing next to Marion. His tail wagged.

"Keep in touch, Bridget," Roger said. "And visit any time. We'll always be happy to see you."

Bridget gave Marion one more hug, then got into the car. When the station wagon was no longer in sight, Marion turned to Roger and hugged him fiercely. He wrapped his arms around her and felt her body shake.

"I know," he said. "I know."

Inside, Roger stretched out on the couch and Sarge curled at his feet. Marion draped an afghan over Roger. He squeezed her hand before she went into the kitchen.

She stood at the screen door looking out across the yard. A light breeze carried the smell of midsummer flowers. Her shoulders rose and fell in a satisfied sigh. The garden had begun its riotous bounty. Pole beans, tomatoes, and cucumbers had started to form. Weeds had also begun to multiply, and she would need to take care of them. But not today.

Marion watched as cottony clouds floated against the infinite blue sky, so bright it almost hurt to look at it. Some people say they feel small when they place themselves in the scope of the universe. But in that moment Marion felt immense. It was a feeling she couldn't quite articulate—more than happiness, more than contentment. It was as if all she had ever known had merged to remind her that life was a marvelous thing and how lucky she was.

Acknowledgements

Readers often ask me where I get my ideas. The germ of this story came in a dream. Not all the characters—not Rob, not Donette—but Marion and Bridget came to me as vividly in that dream as any real people I have ever known. And the premise was nearly fully formed.

As a teen, I knew a boy like Terry. He read a lot of books and worried about where life would take him. He was one of hundreds of thousands of young people adrift philsophically in the era of the Vietnam War. I thought of the boy I knew in romantic terms, a lone hero, hitchkiking his way across the country in 1970. He was interesting, a bit dangerous, and every bit a poet. A friend tells me that Marion is me. It's true her instinct to care is something I share. But Marion is probably a lot stronger than I am, and she learned before I did to mend wobbly fences.

However, as the story progressed over the past four years, the characters, their situations, and the events in this novel came to me on their own. The world in SUMMIT ROAD is entirely fictional.

A second novel has a lot to live up to. It is so easy to come up with an idea. It is even easy to purge those first few chapters from the creative space within. But the real work of cutting, shaping, and rethinking every line is the true job of writing. And that takes time. Bringing this story to readers took more time than I hoped it would. But SUMMIT ROAD would not be what it is without that time or the influence of many readers and critics along the way.

My editor Signe Jorgenson was my first reader, and she assured me I had an interesting and compelling story. Jeff Elzinga's careful reading of an early draft provided honest and much needed feedback and often just the right word when I struggled to find it myself. Lisa Vihos and I formed a private novel club: she read mine and I read hers. We helped each other find the voices of our characters as well as those bits that didn't strike the right chord.

I am grateful to novelist and poet Carrie LaSeur, whose critical questions forced me to look even closer. Thank you also to Jessica VanDerven who begged to read an early galley and reminded me of what I'd long been told: readers are anxious for this book.

I will never forget the week I spent as a writer in residence at WRITE ON, DOOR COUNTY. Some of the scenes in this novel were drafted in Norbert Blei's converted chicken coop/writing studio, a sublime space for thinking and writing on the grounds at Write On.

I want to thank my friend Peggy Weiner Smith for her careful proofreading, but I'm primarily indebted to her for her first-hand knowledge of New York City and surrounding locales. She made sure I got things right.

Peggy wasn't the only former English teacher who helped. I knew I could count on my online colleagues as well. Thank you to *The Talkies* for helping me sort out a small, but important bit of dialogue. In particular, I am grateful to Dawn Sahouani for sharing her knowledge of chickens and goats.

A special thank you goes to my friend Janis Jarosch, who provided the perfect word at the perfect time, and to Eric Plahna, for his careful eye on the sky.

I owe even more to the strong women in my life—my mother and grandmothers, who were my Marions, my Donettes. And my sisters, loving women who have always believed in me.

To my family, thank you always for your love.

Reading Group Discussion Questions

1. Does Marion do the right thing when she takes Bridget into her home? Explain.

2. If Marion had turned Bridget away, what would the effect have been for the other characters? In other words, what might the trajectory of life have been for them if Marion had not been compassionate?

3. Terry and Lily are obvious victims of abuse. In what ways do other characters suffer poor treatment from those supposed to love and care for them?

4. Who is the hero of the story? Why did you choose him or her?

5. Would this novel make a good movie? If so, who would you cast in the main roles? Which parts would you leave out if you had to?

6. There are numerous animals in the story. How does their presence add to the novel's themes, plot, or suspense?

7. Vivian tells her sister, "You married the man you deserved, instead of the man you fell in love with." What does she mean?

8. Who is your favorite peripheral or secondary character and why?

9. Donette tells Terry "You were never meant for this life. No one is." Why do you think Donette stays in sex work for as long as she does?

10. Is Mandy justified in stealing Rob's car and money? Why or why not?

11. Discuss the effectiveness of the setting, from the historical time (1968) to the geographical places.

12. Make a case for the character who best exemplifies the qualities of a good parent.

13. Which character do you empathize with most?

14. Which character is most like you?

15. Even as a child, Terry finds escape in books. In what other ways do books have an impact on his life? Is the author's view of the value of books realistic for most people?

16. How effective are the title and cover in representing the book's events and themes? Do these elements suggest more than one meaning?

17. Did you reread or mark any passages? If so, which ones and why do they stand out to you?

18. Do you wish the novel had ended differently? If so, what outcome were you hoping for?

19. Is this a novel you would read again? What would you hope to get from a second reading?

20. Who should read this book? Why?

About the author

Dawn Hogue is a Wisconsin writer who lives near Lake Michigan with her husband and two Cavalier King Charles Spaniels. She taught high school English for 25 years and later tutored gifted students in an online writing course through Johns Hopkins University. Her poetry appears in various literary publications and anthologies. In addition to writing, she enjoys reading, knitting, and quilting. SUMMIT ROAD is her second novel. Learn more at dawnhogue.com

Also from Dawn Hogue

A HOLLOW BONE is a multi-generational family saga set in Sheboygan Wisconsin from the mid 1920's to the late 1970's. It is a rich chronicle of one woman's family, their hopes and dreams, and the sharp frailty that makes them human. When forty-year-old Angelina Miranda is told she has stage-four breast cancer, she realizes that everything she has done in her life has not been enough. It has not been nearly enough. And it's not just that. She realizes that it has all been wrong, too. So, with only months to live, Angelina knows she must set things right with her daughter, Sophie, something she regrets she never did with her father. It's her relationship with her father—complicated by her mother's tragic accident—that propels teenage Angelina on a reckless course that shapes her life and robs her of the love she craves.

PAINTING SOUTH PIER is a collection of poems inspired by Sheboygan, Wisconsin's South Pier neighborhood through each of the four seasons. Hogue looks deeply at all aspects of nature: sky, wind, river, lake, and of course, the interactions of neighbors with the power and beauty of it all.

Available at watersedgepress.com

Made in USA - Kendallville, IN
72644_9780999219492
01.25.2022 1428